Flash Point

Newman Fire Dept Series

Rae Fields

Developmental and Line Editing: Jessica Snyder, HEA Author Services

Copyediting and Proofreading: Marie Edits, Mia Downing, and Julie Kramer

Cover design: Kari March

www.raefields.com

ISBN-13: 978-1-961803-04-6 (ebook)

ISBN-13: 978-1-961803-10-7 (print)

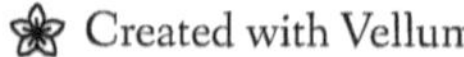 Created with Vellum

Chapter One

*T**horen***

Hangovers sucked ass. And this particular hangover could suck big brass donkey balls. That I could open both eyes and stand at the vanity, unassisted, while my heartbeat pulsed in my head gave me some hope that I'd make it downstairs before roll call and pass-down.

Just the thought of debriefing with the crew coming off-shift had my stomach roiling. A splash of cold water helped wash away more of the cobwebs and cleared some of the dregs of a long night out with friends.

I'd meant to leave the bar before midnight. Had every intention to do so. But then my buddy had come in looking all beat down, and I made the conscious decision to violate my own no-drinking-after-midnight-before-a-shift rule. A couple hours, and rounds of Jameson later, he was folded into a Lyft when we finally took pity on the bar owner and left.

Or maybe we'd been kicked out at closing. Call it what you will.

Not wanting to risk over-sleeping, I made the dumbass

call to get dropped off at the station to sleep it off in my bunk, quite possibly the worst decision I'd ever made. Now, a mere three hours later, I had a dilemma. I couldn't call in sick, seeing as how I was already at the station, and I didn't know if I'd live through this bastard of a hangover.

Running a hand through my hair, I winced at my pale reflection in the mirror. With any luck, it would be a typical slow Sunday. I'd just go down, struggle through roll call, check off the truck, then head back upstairs and sleep it off for a while. Easy-peasy.

I was easing down the stairs when my cell phone buzzed in my hand. My mom's name flashed across the screen.

Fucking great.

I hadn't heard from her in at least a year. Only one reason she'd be calling me out of the blue. The only reason she'd ever called me in the past. My brother.

I couldn't deal with news about that asshole and his antics. And right now, I for damn sure couldn't handle a conversation like the last one I'd had with my mom.

Hitting *ignore* on the call, I grabbed the clipboard to begin morning inspection. Twenty minutes was all I had to get through. Twenty short minutes and I could sink into a recliner for a nap.

I clambered into the engine, cranked her up, and checked the gauges, engaged the pump, climbed out and wiped at the cold sweat on my brow. Then I opened the exterior compartments, checking all the equipment, and made my visual inspection of the truck. I was bent over checking tire pressure when a massive wave of nausea rolled over me.

Shit. I should've gone home. This wasn't cool. Neither was the number of shots I'd done. How many shots *did* I do?

Bracing a hand against the truck to steady myself, I swallowed the bile that rose as the world tilted around me.

The wave passed, and I rounded the truck to continue my inspection only to spot a white Ford pickup with the Newman Fire Department logo rounding the building.

Fuuuuuck.

This was bad. This was so bad.

Head down. Don't call attention to yourself, dumbass.

Interim Chief Richards parked his truck and walked directly to me.

Oh. Shit.

I was so fucked.

A retired chief from another department, Chief Dick, as we called him, was known for his penchant for PR. The man loved shaking hands and kissing babies. He also was a stickler for following the rules. As merely an interim chief, he'd come in and changed our operating procedures and protocols, a move that left a bad taste among the crews. Especially when he started taking on disciplinary actions with a vengeance.

My best chance at keeping my job was to avoid him as much as I could and then hide in the bathroom. I opened the closest compartment above the tire and ducked behind the door.

"Morning, Watkins. Is Captain Collins around?" The high-pitched whine of his voice echoed through the bay, bouncing off the wall and through my head, the effect going straight to my churning guts. I dropped to a crouch, breathing deeply through my nose, fighting for control.

"Morning, sir," I said to the tire. "The captain is in the day room." I straightened and made a show of ticking off the boxes on my checklist. All I had to do was get through the next minute. Just get him out of my space and make it to my bunk, where blissful sleep could make everything better.

The door from the gear room opened, and Captain Mac Collins walked out, cup of coffee in hand.

Shit.

"Morning, Chief," Capt said around the ever-present toothpick he chewed on. I spun and rounded the front of the engine, crossing to the other side, away from the two officers, either of whom could fire me on the spot.

Jesus, I'd kick my own ass if I made it through this without getting caught.

"Morning, Captain. I just wanted to stop by this morning and bring you gentlemen some breakfast. The foundation had an early morning meeting, and Mrs. Velda made me promise to deliver the leftovers."

Mrs. Velda was our local philanthropist who loved public safety. As the chairwoman of a foundation helping first responders in all manner of need, she organized annual events and fundraisers, like her pet project, a calendar of local public safety personnel.

"Y'all met on a Sunday morning?" Skepticism laced Captain Collins's words. Capt never had tolerated the BS politics of the fire service.

"Apparently they couldn't find any other time."

The officers chatted, and I took my sweet time checking every nook and cranny of the engine until I couldn't stall anymore. I willed myself to hold it together for just a few more minutes. If I could get this done, I could sneak out the front of the bay, and go pass out.

I snuck in behind them to finish the last section, just as the chief pulled back the aluminum foil. A waft of smoky, tart odor assaulted my fragile senses. My poor stomach couldn't handle it. I clapped a hand over my mouth and made a mad dash for the nearest bathroom.

The clipboard clattered to the floor just before the contents of my stomach erupted in a violent spray of liquor-infused nastiness. I prayed that the vile sauerkraut and sausage breakfast concoction was enough to cover the scent of my late-night mistakes.

I splashed cold water on my face, rinsed and spit to the sound of tones dropping. Fuck, this just wasn't my day.

* * *

"I should fire your ass right now!" Captain Collins boomed through his small office as I tried not to cower on the other side of his desk. No doubt the rest of the crew heard him shouting.

On the best days, Captain Collins was a gruff son of a bitch. On the worst, we all steered clear of him. He had an air about him that warned off any bullshit. Working for him meant doing the job, doing it well, and there'd be no issues.

I'd seen him frustrated plenty of times. But I'd never seen him this mad, face so red that the vein in his forehead protruded. Never had him yell at *me* for being the world's biggest dumbass.

Nausea rolled through my system again, this time for a different reason. "Sir, please, don't fire me." I deserved every ounce of the current ass-chewing, but hoped he wouldn't send me packing. What the hell would I do if I got fired?

I should've been smarter.

I shouldn't have come here after the bar.

I shouldn't have put my job in jeopardy.

I shouldn't have had that first drink. Or the second. Or all the ones that followed.

After all the of bullshit I'd grown up with, all the times I'd bailed my little brother out of his dumbass situations... Now, I found myself equally low, making piss-poor decisions, just like he did. Threatening the only real thing I cared about.

My job.

"Do you know how bad that could've been?" The low rumble of his voice scraped over the remains of my pride. "Do you know how many lives you could've put in danger?"

He stalked around his office, looking for all the world like he'd like to punch me right in the face. I hung my head and took it like a champ.

"What the fuck is wrong with you? You don't have your shit together. You show up half-drunk, unable to perform your duties. What the fuck, Watkins?" He paused and passed a hand over his face, relaxing his shoulders like he was forcibly trying to collect himself. "I'm so fucking disappointed in you."

I flinched, wishing he'd hit me instead of muttering those quiet devastating words.

"I'm sorry, sir," I mumbled, blinking against the sting at the back of my eyes.

Disappointing Captain Collins had to be the lowest of lows. I'd looked up to him since the day I'd started as a brand-new rookie, fresh out of training academy. I'd come to this department to start a new life for myself. And a decade later, one stupid decision might have ruined it all.

Silence, heavy as lead and thick with tension, fell. Capt did some deep breathing, and I envisioned my career swirling down the toilet like the remains of the previous night.

He dropped to his desk chair, still silent, still watching

me, and began flipping a pen between his fingers. The weight of his stare stifling as I waited for my punishment.

The pen clattered to the desk, and he rose, bracing his extra-large frame on the desktop. "I can't even stand to look at you anymore."

The low rasp in his voice made the words harsh. Or maybe it was just the disappointment in his tone. Capt was a fair man. If he was pissed it was for a reason. And it sucked being the reason.

"You're suspended for two shifts. Go home. You're relieved from duty." He leaned towards me and lowered his voice. "I'd advise you to handle your shit before you come back."

I swallowed my pride and said the only thing I could say. "Yes, sir."

"Now, get the fuck out of my station."

Chapter Two

Kylie

The trek up Rabun Bald in the north Georgia mountains was a short, but steep, beauty.

The trail climbed through rhododendron tunnels that, on a clear day, would've been punctuated by sweeping views of the valley below. This morning, the view was obscured by clouds, the trail made even more enchanting by a blanket of snow. Wet patches where water ran off the mountain had frozen over, leaving little ice slicks in places. Like tiny surprise ninjas, waiting to sweep the feet out from under an unsuspecting hiker.

I paused in an opening to catch my breath after a skid that nearly sent me tumbling over the edge into a deep ravine, the icy air burning my lungs with every inhale. A normal person, a smarter, more rational person, would turn around and call it a loss. Maybe go home and sit fireside and pop open a couple of post-hike beers.

Checking my GPS tracker, I realized I only had a half mile left to reach the summit, and the payoff from reaching the fire tower on the top of the mountain was supposed to be a spectacular view. I was hoping for a break in the clouds, just long enough to have a peek. Just a little push and I would be there. And given my mental state, I needed to see, and experience, something beautiful. To feel the exhilaration of knowing I made it to the top. I needed to prove to myself I could do this.

I needed to feel like the old me.

The snow fell harder now that I was higher in elevation, which naturally made sense. It'd probably be a total whiteout when I reached the summit.

I slipped the hose of my hydration bladder out of the clip on my chest. The frigid bite valve burned my chapped lips as I sucked on the hose once, twice. Nothing. The water had frozen inside the tube.

"Shit."

Once I made it to the fire tower on top of the mountain, I'd find a spot to rest, set up my camp stove and make a cup of hot tea.

One hour and a half mile later, I left the semi-shelter of the Georgia pines and stepped into the shallow field that surrounded the stone tower. A two-inch layer of snow and ice covered the ground. I'd slipped enough that every muscle in my body sang in protest from being endlessly clenched. Why was I doing this to myself? I should've turned around. But I was sooo close, too close to quit. And since this mountain was so far from home, and I'd had to get a hotel room to even attempt it and didn't know when I'd be able to get up this way again, I simply *had* to finish.

Hiking had become my refuge after my diagnosis. A way to escape and sort through my emotions. To prove to myself that I was still me underneath this layer of skin. Hiking hadn't changed the outcome, just the way I felt about myself. So it was imperative that I not quit. That I not give in and accept defeat or wallow in misery.

I'd finished this challenge strong, despite the odds.

At the summit, the stone fire tower stood like a sentry in the swirling whiteout conditions. I climbed the stairs to the platform and turned in a slow circle, squinting against the icy wind and stinging snow. There was no freaking way I could make hot tea in this mess. A quick glance at my phone also showed zero cell service. Coverage had been spotty on the way in.

Choosing to ignore the defeat that seemed to be my shadow, I set up my tripod and did my usual summit success photo, and did a little butt wiggle in snowy triumph, before slipping and sliding back down the trail.

At the base of the mountain, I found at least four inches of snow on the hood of my Jeep Cherokee and the road from the trailhead a solid blanket of white.

Normally, four inches wouldn't be such a horrible thing. However, in Georgia, snow tended to turn to ice, and without the proper road treatments, roads could get very slick, very fast.

Pushing for the summit had been foolish. As I turned out of the trailhead parking area, onto the narrow main road, the Cherokee slid sideways. My heart pitched into my throat as the vehicle skid, despite me standing on the brake. I managed to wrangle it to a stop just shy of a massive ditch.

In the stillness of the aftermath, my breath poofed into the chilled car. I pried my fingers from the steering wheel, stretching one hand at a time, before resecuring my grip. Like that could stop me from sliding clean down the hill before me.

What the fuck was I going to do?

Why in the fuck didn't I turn around and get off the mountain sooner?

And why hadn't I gotten four-wheel drive when I'd bought this vehicle?

"It's not like you can do anything about it now." My voice sounded oddly loud in the stillness of the moment. I could be the only person for miles. There were houses around, but I hadn't seen a single person out, or passed any cars.

I had no choice. I had to keep going, had to get out of the road.

I eased down the steep section another mile or so, using the steering wheel to control my skid as I went, doing my best to stay in the center of the road. Every muscle in my body clenched, like I could control the outcome by sheer will. My heart pounded. One wrong move could be disastrous.

With a few more skids and slides, I reached the bottom of the hill and paused, shaking out my tired arms. This mountain road might be a rollercoaster, and fun to ride on a good day, but covered in ice and snow, it was treacherous. And up ahead I faced another incline, not as bad as I'd already come down, but enough to present a challenge without the proper equipment.

Stupid salesperson convincing me that I didn't need four-wheel drive. Being stranded served me right for not sticking to my guns on that one.

The people who lived in these parts probably got a good laugh at unsuspecting visitors like me. How'd they build houses up on these hills, anyway? And who wanted to live on a stupid winding curvy steep road anyway?

I noted the lack of service bars on my cell phone. Getting back to town would be tricky, but I had no choice.

It was stay here and try not to freeze overnight or keep pushing forward.

I took a deep breath and tried to relax my shoulders. My entire body ached from being tense for so long, and I had such a long way to go. I couldn't give up now.

Halfway up the next hill, I hit an icy patch. My tires lost traction, the vehicle coming to a stop before beginning a slow backward slide, the rear tires of my Cherokee inching ever closer to the shoulder. I reversed back down the hill to have another go, staying clear of the icy ruts caused by people smarter than me. People who had all-wheel or four-wheel drive.

The second attempt also failed, and this time my backward slide landed with a jolt as my tires connected with something solid. The road? Something along the side?

I studied the road in front of me. Maybe if I could get a little more momentum to start and turn off my traction control, I'd get up the incline and around the corner.

I climbed out of the warm cocoon of my car to assess my situation. Tires seemed to be in good shape and the road didn't seem to be impassable. But as I stepped onto the pavement, my foot slid.

Beneath the snowy tire tracks, a thin layer of icy slush covered the road. If I could just get some traction...I scrubbed at an icy spot with the toe of my boot and reached pavement. In the matter of a few minutes, I cleared as much as I could and got back behind the wheel.

Please let this work.

I hit the gas. The car lurched slightly, and the tires spun again, sending me sliding farther backward... and into a ditch.

The snowy road before me swam as tears threatened. I'd made the situation worse, and now I was completely stuck. I banged my hand on the steering wheel, my frustrated scream absorbed by the snow-blanketed windows.

Shit on a stick.

The wintery mix still fell, my dash thermometer reading temps in the teens, not counting the wind chill. And I was in a ditch on a mountain.

My hands and arms shook uncontrollably. The more I tried to contain the tremors, the worse they got, spreading through my body as adrenaline letdown hit me full force.

With no other choice, I waited, breathing deeply through chattering teeth, riding out the shudders.

I needed a plan, a hot meal, and a warm shower, not necessarily in that order. Maybe if I could just see some hope...

Climbing out of the car, I surveyed the area. I was basically in someone's front yard. The house only took a minute to jog to, but when I peeked in the windows, it was empty. Back at my Jeep, I checked the damage, finding none other than the slick ground beneath my tires. No doubt the owners would be pissed that I'd wrecked their ditch.

The wind picked up, pelting my face. I needed a plan immediately, because there was no way I was getting out of here.

I opened the back hatch and pulled out my gear box. I'd planned on camping at least once during this trip, so I had shelter and sleeping supplies, food, and even a small lantern. This wasn't a life-or-death situation. It would just be an uncomfortably cold night with temps in the single digits, but I had enough stuff to keep me alive, if not warm.

Dropping the rear seats forward, I piled up my sleeping bag and prepped a little cocoon for myself in the cargo area. Better to do it in remaining daylight hours, plus the activity helped shed the remaining jitters.

This was fine. I was fine, everything would be okay. I'd wanted an adventure. I'd just roll with it and make the best of this shitty situation.

I grabbed my food bag and jumped back into the front seat. Hopefully a passerby would stop to help. Best case scenario, I'd be rescued. Worst case, I camped out in my Cherokee.

My phone rang as I closed the door. I squeezed my eyes shut at the name on the display.

Of course, I'd have reception right now. Of all times. And she would call and check in on me when I was barely holding it together.

My best friend, Leah Miller, had my itinerary and would worry because I hadn't checked in per our safety protocol. The only reason she didn't completely freak out over my solo hiking was because I promised I'd always call when I got off the trail and was safely at my car. Given the circumstances, I'd completely forgotten.

"Hey, girl," I answered, squeezing my eyes shut. I refused to be defeated in this situation, even if my voice gave me away.

"Hey yourself. What's happened? You didn't check in."

I hated the way she could be so calm and yet sound so worried at the same time.

"Yeah, I'm sorry about that." I looked out the window, trying to find my calm center to keep me from losing my shit. "The hike was amazing. It's snowing here and the trail was magical."

"I'm sensing a but..."

I closed my eyes and swallowed, not wanting to admit my epic failure. "But the roads got icy, and now my car is stuck."

"Where are you?" Her voice went high with fear.

In the background, I could hear her boyfriend, Mike. As a former police officer and general badass, Mike would be extremely displeased about my situation. He'd have a Man Opinion and I'd probably hate it.

I should've turned around as soon as the snow picked up. I shouldn't have set out on the hike.

If I'd listened to my gut, I would be sitting in a coffee shop with a Bailey's Irish Cream laced latte rather than trying to figure out how comfortable I could get in the back of my Jeep. Instead, I was stuck having to rely on someone else to save my ass.

I absolutely hated looking like such a fool.

She must've flipped to speakerphone because Mike's deep voice came on the line. "Hey, Kylie. Tell me what's going on and where you are."

That was Mike. Efficient and all business.

"Um—" I glanced back up the road. Even my tire tracks were now covered. "I guess I'm about a mile from the trailhead on the main road to Rabun Bald. My car is ass-end in a ditch. The stupid thing is, it's not even a real ditch. It's just enough that without four-wheel drive, I can't get out." I didn't tell him I'd never make it over the mountain, even if I got myself unstuck.

"Okay, stay on the line with Leah. Let me make some calls." Mike was in full protector mode, barking orders that would normally get under my skin.

"Mike, wait. You don't have to do that. I'm sure someone will be by soon." The last thing I wanted was to be the reason someone else suffered these treacherous conditions.

"Just standby, let me see what I can do." Mike had all sorts of weirdly convenient connections, and despite my arguments, if he could help me out of this situation, I'd gladly do as he asked.

Leah told me how her classes at our yoga studio had gone, deliberately helping me focus on anything other than my current situation. Then Mike came back on the line. "Thoren is up at his cabin. He's on his way to you now."

Fucking great.

Fucking Thoren. Way to make a bad day even worse.

I swallowed a groan. Right now, this beggar couldn't be a chooser. But damn, spending the night in a frigid car might be better than having *that* asshole come save me. I'd never hear the end of it.

And the worst part was, I couldn't let on to Leah or Mike without them finding out that Thoren and I had accidentally slept together.

A one-time thing that needed to be kept secret from our friends, from everyone...because never let it be said that Kylie Monroe had a one-night fling and caught a case of the feels.

He'd started dating another girl almost immediately after, and I was mad as hell that I was replaced so quickly. To be fair, I'd been the one to walk away, to make sure I didn't get hurt first. But he could've at least pined a little. He could've fought a little harder if I was truly someone he wanted.

Instead, Thoren had let me treat him like the rest of my lovers. Love 'em and leave 'em. Leaving behind a slew of one-night stands, with zero strings. Just the way I liked it.

I usually made sure to pick partners I'd never see again. Thoren had been a mistake.

"Great," I said weakly. "Thanks for saving the day, Mike." I tried for genuine appreciation.

Before we hung up to save my phone battery, Leah

made me promise to text every so often and call as soon as Thoren got to me.

In the meantime, I pulled my overnight bag out from under my gear explosion, and made sure I had what I needed, gritting my teeth the entire time. As much as I appreciated Thoren rescuing me, I still didn't want to face him. No doubt, he'd have some smartass comment to make, and I was not in the mental state to sass him back.

I didn't want him to see me this weak.

It was near dark when a set of headlights flashed around the corner, blinding as they passed over me. I shivered from cold in the cramped space of my front seat. Even pulling on every layer I had with me hadn't been enough to combat the frigid temperature that seemed to just keep dropping. I'd run my car to the point that if I didn't conserve gas, I'd be having to ask for help with that too.

And the last thing I wanted was to be even more beholden to the one man who'd managed to get under my skin.

Once upon a time, I'd have given anything to have this type of scenario. Being rescued by a super-hot firefighter? Yes, please. And I would've found a way to make sure he knew I appreciated him. Probably by sleeping with him.

But that was before everything changed.

Before my life was turned upside down and inside out. Back in the day when I knew who I was and used every tool I had to get what I wanted. Then, I could lure any man I wanted with the crook of a finger.

Now, I doubted I could even garner a second look.

A former beauty queen—albeit one who hated the scene and all the stereotype surrounding it—who'd had her day and was realizing she was no longer the prettiest in the room. That, in fact, if the world saw the truth about her, they'd back away and send her pitying glances.

It had happened just the night before, when my cap slid from my head as I'd bent to gather my bags at the hotel. I'd made a grab for it, and tugged it back on, but not before the desk clerk had gotten a good look at the great big bald patches shining like spotlights through my thinning hair.

The mix of horror and concern that had flittered across the girl's face cut like a knife.

Before my world changed, I would've been bold and made some smartass comment, would've owned my situation. But my boldness had vanished, dwindled away with every strand of hair lost, and all I could do was slap my hand over the keycard waiting on the counter, tuck tail, and run.

Alopecia areata had done a number on me—stolen my hair, my confidence, my identity as a woman. And a woman in the throes of losing her hair was, unfortunately, something people stared at.

It'd taken a good long while to talk myself down after that exchange. To recommit to the hike and remember that it served a greater purpose than just putting in the miles.

The hike had served as a reminder that I was otherwise healthy and strong, regardless of what was happening on the outside of my body, and hopefully that would resonate as it had with past hikes and fill that empty spot inside of me.

I tugged my wool beanie lower over my ears as a familiar truck rolled to a slow stop in front of my Cherokee. The passenger side window rolled down and the most beautiful, most frustratingly handsome man peered at me, a stupendous scowl on his face.

If looks could kill...

I opened my door and stood to face the music and beg a

ride from the one man that hated me. Well, probably not the only one. But definitely the one man that, once upon a time, might've been someone who'd fight for me. Not anymore, though. I'd killed that opportunity with one very good night of bad decisions.

"Hi." I offered him a timid smile.

He'd obviously been off-duty for a while because he sported a sexy scruff of beard on his normally clean-shaved jaw. The look was delicious on him, made all the better because I could imagine exactly how that scruff might feel on my body.

"Are you stuck?" His deep voice was a welcome familiarity in an otherwise terrifying scenario. However, the pissy way he delivered the words struck a nerve. Good looks or no, I couldn't deal with attitude.

"Nah, I just like sitting in the frigid cold and calling people to drive for hours to meet me so I can show them how badly I drive on snow." I rolled my eyes, propping a boot in the open door, my hip jutting out in what I hoped was an impertinent stance. "Yes, I'm stuck."

This was our usual song and dance. Snarky attitudes full of piss and vinegar. I had to admit I had a love-hate relationship with him. Or maybe it was hate-love. Either way, he was my favorite person to pester.

He snatched his ball cap off and scrubbed the back of his head, resettled the hat, then ran the same hand through his light beard. His very attractive beard. In that moment, he looked like someone I knew, but was seeing for the first time.

"Let me get turned around, and I'll see if we can get you out of the ditch." He rolled the window up and drove away before I got a chance to tell him not to bother.

Well.

This was great.

He obviously was under the impression that we were getting out of here with two vehicles. I didn't know much about rescuing people. Or icy roads. But I knew there was no way in hell my car was getting over the mountain if this little bit of a hill had me at a standstill.

Thoren pulled his truck to a stop in the middle of the road and climbed out, walking his sexy lumberjack-looking self to the toolbox. I let myself stare at the way his jeans molded to the perfect roundness of his perfect butt. The way his waist tapered in, magnifying the flare of his lats and shoulders as he reached into the toolbox on the back of his truck. I'd had my hands and lips all over his warm skin. The memory of our one night had fueled many a fantasy.

I shook my head. That ass was mouthwatering.

And not for me.

"T-bird," I called, deliberately using the nickname I knew he hated. Seeing him get flustered brought me such joy. "Don't bother. I can tell you right now it's no use."

He turned with a massive strap in hand, expression set to level ten serious. "We can get you out."

"It's no use," I tried again. "Even if you get me out of this ditch, I can't make it over the mountain unless you're going to tow me the entire way."

He went down on a knee in the snow, leaning under the front end of my car. "You'll be fine, just put it in four-wheel drive. It's slick in places, but I got through well enough."

Yeah. If only I'd been patient enough to hold out for four-wheel drive when I'd bought my SUV.

He pushed to stand, dusting the snow off his knee, then his hands.

"You wouldn't be here if it was that easy. I don't have four-wheel drive," I sniped, hating the weakness of not being able to take care of myself, and covering it with more sass.

"Why in the hell not?"

"Look, I don't need your judgment right now, Mr. Hero Macho Man. Can you just give me a ride back to my hotel? I need your help. Not your attitude."

Silence stretched between us while he glared at my SUV, jaw clenching and brow furrowed. Pissed off and totally hot. "Let's at least get you out of the road and moved to a safer place, then we'll figure the rest out."

It became apparent quickly that not only were we not making it back into town, we might not even make it off the mountain at all.

In the time it took us to pull my car out of the ditch and secure it in a flat spot off the road, the temps had dropped even farther, and the slush on the road began refreezing. As Thoren's truck slipped and slid, and the tires spun, I wondered if we'd have to spend the night in his truck after all.

I'd well and truly fucked us both, and I'd never hear the end of it.

"It's worse on the eastern side. At least it was earlier. If we can get to the main road, we should be able to make it to my cabin." Thoren spoke to the headlights.

Should be.

Great.

"I'm really sorry," I offered. Thank God for the darkness of the cab hiding the flush on my face.

"For what?"

I stared at his profile. The line of his jaw was a stark line, the muscle working there as he kept his eyes glued to the road, hands fisted on the steering wheel. He really had gone out of his way to help me today.

"For causing so much trouble. For dragging you out here."

He blew out a breath as if he were letting the bullshit between us go, as if my apology meant something.

It was then I noticed the smell. The stench of day-old alcohol.

"Have you been drinking?" I demanded.

His fists bunched tight again.

"Oh my God!" I pitched forward, immediately irate, and turned to face him. "You idiot. Stop this truck right now."

Chapter Three

Thoren

Kylie Monroe, the most beautiful woman in the world, raged in the seat next to me. I sat quietly and suffered her yelling. This was normal for her. Spewing off at the mouth, ranting, and being over the top. It was one of the things I liked best about her. Even when her ire was directed at me.

There was just something about the fire in her that I found irresistible.

We'd circled each other too many times to count since our best friends, Mike and Leah, had started dating. But it seemed our paths were never on the same trajectory, and we'd only cross paths for a moment. Like that time she'd walked up to me in the bar, in front of my then-girlfriend and boldly zipped up my jeans. In general, we'd both respected each other's space in relationships.

But it seemed like we just kept dancing backwards into each other.

Until that one mind-blowing night when we'd both let our guards down.

I hadn't expected that she'd get under my skin, that I'd want more than one night. But she made it clear it was a one-and-done thing, making me promise to keep our hookup a secret from our friends.

Since then, our relationship had been...antagonistic.

If it weren't for Mike and Leah, maybe I would've tried again. But in case something went wrong, I never made my move.

And now, here we were, both apparently single, alone together for the foreseeable future. And there was no way I would start something with her. Not that she wanted to. She'd made that clear—she never wanted a repeat of that night.

"I'm serious, Thoren. You pull this truck over right now. I'm not going to let you drive drunk on icy roads. What in the hell were you thinking?" She raged. And I let her because I deserved it. Not that I'd ever admit to it.

"I'm not drunk." I growled. "Pipe down."

Hungover after a pity-party for one, yes. But not currently drunk. A situation I would remedy as soon as we got to the cabin. If I could get us there.

An image of the two of us cuddled in the back seat of my truck flashed in my head.

Cuddling for body heat wouldn't be a bad way to spend the night.

I needed a drink if I was seriously considering spending the night out in this frigid weather.

"Why do you reek if you aren't drunk?" She made finger quotations around the last two words. "I'm serious. Pull this fucking truck over right now. I'm not dying because you're a dumbass."

Her words ticked me off, but I pulled over anyway.

Better to let her drive than to listen to her bitching the whole way.

The truth was, I wasn't currently drunk. But that didn't mean I hadn't been hitting the bottle pretty hard ever since I'd been suspended.

So what if I made the ill-advised choice to go to the station instead of going home?

So what if I'd nearly barfed on my Captain?

That didn't mean I was a drunk.

That didn't mean I couldn't handle myself around alcohol. It just meant I said yes too often when the urge hit, and I didn't stop after the first few rounds.

But the fact that she could smell it on me was embarrassing. I probably should've showered in the days since I'd been at the cabin.

I eased the truck to a stop.

"Settle down. I'm not drunk. I just need a shower."

"I don't care. I'm driving." Before I could stop her, she popped her door open and launched herself out of the truck, slipping on an icy patch and landing flat on her ass with a screech.

I winced. Damn, that had to hurt.

"Shit, Kylie! Hold on, I'm coming."

I eased my way out of the truck and around to her to find her slipping up a small ditch on all fours.

I'd pulled the truck too close to the edge. Maybe it wasn't a bad thing for her to drive. Maybe I needed a few more hours to sleep the past few days off. Maybe I shouldn't have downed that last drink before leaving.

Leave it to me to rescue a woman, and instead of being the hero, directly put her in more danger. I helped her up and she limped away from me, muttering under her breath as she walked off the fall.

Any other time, I'd dish it back to her. That was the game we played.

Now though? Shame rose hard and hot, burning off any residual buzz I might have had.

I could've really hurt her. Hurt us both. Though of the two of us, she was the one who mattered.

She returned to me, bracing herself on the side of the truck, and looked me dead in the eyes, as if she could see to my soul. I flinched at what she might see. At the way her teeth ground together, and the way her brows drew tight.

"Thoren, I'm driving." Her tone held no room for discussion. We both knew I didn't need to be driving.

Heat crept up my neck as a wave of humiliation washed over me, adding to the growing pile of self-recrimination. She was right, we were safest if she drove. I'd never admit it aloud though.

To save face, I countered with, "You ever driven on ice?"

"Other than today? No, but you can coach me along the way." Her answer was swift and sure. Almost as if she trusted that I could do this. I couldn't be trusted to do it myself, but I could coach her on how to get us safely to the cabin?

Gritting my teeth, I gave her a slight nod before turning away to avoid the look in her eye.

I'd been avoiding the way people looked at me for days.

Even my own reflection in the mirror was a judgmental bastard.

Kylie settled in the driver's seat and adjusted it to match her short frame as I watched her movements from the corner of my eye. From the damn passenger side.

After she'd buckled her seatbelt and adjusted the

mirror, she finally looked over at me. "You put us in four-wheel drive, right?"

"No, I didn't. You jumped out the door before I could. You're lucky you didn't slide off the damn mountain." I wouldn't admit it was my fault that she'd been so close to the ditch in the first place. Just because I knew I was in the wrong didn't mean I needed to tell her.

"Just tell me what to do so I don't rip the transmission out of your truck, you jerk." Her voice was like a knife, cutting and harsh. I'd never been around Kylie when she was truly angry. Her hands gripped the steering wheel, but her eyes roamed all over the dash. The firm set of her jaw clenched when my gaze lingered too long on her.

Note to self—don't look at Kylie.

I coached her through engaging the four-wheel drive and she cautiously rolled forward.

The headlights cut a swath of light across the road. The snowfall picked up, racing at the headlights, making the world feel distorted. Like we were in a vortex of blinding whiteness.

"I've never seen it snow this hard, much less driven in it." She focused on the road ahead, tension lacing every word.

Riding shotgun, not being in control of the truck, rankled. "Slow down a little before taking the next curve, there's a downhill on the other side of it."

The corners of her eyes pinched in concentration, and she sat straighter in the seat.

"You know, sitting up on the steering wheel like that isn't going to help you see any better," I groused.

"Shut up and turn the radio down. I can't think."

Oh great. Now it would be doubly hard to drown out

the bullshit in my head. I couldn't wait to get back to the cabin and drown out everything. Again.

"What the hell were you doing out here," I asked her, "especially in a two-wheel drive vehicle anyway? Didn't you pay attention and know to expect snow? Hell, they've been talking about it for days."

That little muscle in her jaw pulsed. I could almost hear her teeth grinding.

"Is that why you are up here? Were you hoping to get snowed in at your cabin?" she clipped.

Oh, no. We weren't going there.

This was about her stupid choices. We'd not be discussing mine. Silence reigned. She drove, and I glowered.

"I don't listen to the news," came her pinched reply. "I checked the weather app. I knew to expect snow, but not this much."

I sighed and shook my head. "Those apps don't do you much good up in elevation. You're a good fifteen miles from town and a good three to four thousand feet higher in elevation than where they gave that forecast for. A lot can change with every thousand feet of elevation."

The leather covering the steering wheel creaked as she released it, stretched her fingers then gripped it again. The drone of the engine and the crunch of the tires over the snowy road filled the otherwise silent cab.

She wiggled in her seat, repositioning that frustratingly toned body of hers, still leaning forward, almost sitting on the steering wheel. Ridiculous.

"Sit back. If you crash us, you're going to get a face full of airbag."

She shifted back an inch. Still ridiculous. Too bad she couldn't call forth some of her normal confidence. Too bad she was in the driver's seat in the first place.

I chose not to think about it.

We approached a curve too fast and I grabbed the oh-shit handle. "Slow down, dammit. Do you have a death wish?" She was going to slide us off the damn mountain.

She eased up a little, but the back end started sliding as we headed for an intersection. Flashes of us sliding and crashing blazed through my mind in a series of mini horror clips. I gripped the oh-shit handle harder. "Don't hit the brake! Turn into the skid."

We miraculously skidded to a halt just past a stop sign.

Kylie popped the truck into park and sat back, her arms dropping to her sides as she expelled a deep breath.

She turned her body to face me, as though she wanted my full attention. I risked meeting her eyes. The light in hers flashed, first with anger, then with something else.

"Thoren," she said with an eerie calm, "at the risk of getting myself kicked out of this truck, I'm gonna need you to just sit there and navigate." She swallowed thickly, and her chin wobbled. "I'm doing the best I can. It's been a crappy few hours and believe me when I say, I realize exactly how much of a pain in the ass it's been for you to come out here. I don't need your attitude or your judgment right now."

I tore my gaze away from hers, propping my elbow on the window ledge and staring out into the dark night. I wiped a hand over my face.

She was right. I was being a dick.

Fuck, I'd have to swallow my pride. Again.

"You're right." The words cut into the last shred of my dignity. "I'm sorry."

Regardless of what she'd done, my situation wasn't her fault. She shouldn't be receiving my anger. It was time to suck it up and trust that she could handle getting us to the cabin.

I reached over and placed my hand over hers, giving it a squeeze. "You're doing fine. I'm just not used to being a passenger in this kind of situation. I'll just sit over here and try to be quiet."

She looked down at our hands and sniffed.

Oh god. Oh, no. "Don't you dare start crying on me."

If you'd told me yesterday this woman was capable of tears, I would've called you a damn liar. Yet, here we sat, in the middle of a mountain road in a snowstorm, and I might as well have been witnessing hell freeze over. Because a tear slid down her cheek and ripped my heart right out of my chest.

Kylie Monroe should never have tears on her face. She was meant for smiling, for happiness and laughter.

Before I could move to wipe that offensive tear away, she turned her hand over in mine and clasped me like a lifeline. Or maybe that was my hand squeezing our palms together.

She swiped her forearm across her face, and offered a weak, "Truce?"

Anything. I'd do anything to make her stop crying.

It took two tries to get sound to work its way out of my throat.

"Yeah. Truce."

She made no other sound. She just squeezed my hand and wiped her face again, then released me and faced the road once more, squaring her shoulders as she blew out a breath.

"You got this," I said quietly. As if she needed encouragement from me.

She didn't need anything other than directions from me. And I was a fool sitting here thinking maybe I'd like it if she did want more.

"Yeah," she said, her voice stronger now. "I got this."

Chapter Four

*K*ylie

Pulling up at Thoren's mountainside cabin, after navigating those harrowing icy mountain roads, was a godsend. Immediately relieved, I finally allowed my body to relax. My back and shoulders ached from being tensed for so long. No doubt my clenched butt had left a permanent pinch mark in the seat. My only saving grace was that the snow had ended, and visibility had improved along the way. Still, it had taken forever.

Lit up by the truck lights, his cute little cabin sat nestled under a blanket of fresh snow.

"Looks like we may have lost power." Thoren's voice broke through the stillness of the truck cab. "Leave the lights on, and I'll go get the house opened up."

He'd been mostly silent after I'd lost my shit and cried on him.

I hadn't meant to. In fact, I was mortified that my emotions had leaked out of my eyes like that. I don't know what happened. One minute I was red-hot angry, the next, the weight of his condescension had been too much.

Usually I could verbally spar with him, but tonight...I just didn't have it in me.

Thoren made his way to the cabin door, his feet slipping and sliding, but his body remained steady and strong. He looked so dang confident and sure of himself. I allowed myself to relax against the seat, and appreciate the moment of stillness, drinking in the view of this man that I harbored a secret crush on.

I hated that I noticed how good his ass looked in jeans. I hated that despite him hurting my feelings, I still had the hots for him. I hated that I was so ridiculous. I just hated life at the moment.

Being stuck with him sucked, and everything was stupid.

I ran a hand over my soaked beanie and shivered in the cooling vehicle, wishing I had one of my wigs.

If things were different, this adventure would have been the perfect time for us to try a do-over from our one-night stand. If only this had happened six months ago. Or even three months ago.

I tugged the wool cap firmly down over my ears.

No, now wasn't the time to start anything.

There was no way he'd find anything remotely attractive about me in my current state. I could hardly stand to look at myself. It was hard to feel attractive and self-confident when you could barely look in the mirror.

Thoren came out of the cabin with a lantern in hand, his deliciously thick thighs eating the ground with sure steps. I waited to see if he'd bust it on the ice, but no, he had to be all capable and shit.

I killed the truck lights and got out. "What'd you do, magically shovel the walkway?" I called to him.

"No, just stay to the side. The sidewalk is iced underneath the snow, but the grassy part is fine."

That explained his sure-footedness, though I couldn't tell what was sidewalk and what was grass.

He grabbed my bag from the back seat, then led the way to the door. The blanket of snow cloaked the night in silence. The usual night sounds had vanished. There was no background noise of forest critters, just the occasional groan and creak of tree limbs bent under the weight of snow and ice. I paused and soaked in the ambiance. "Wow."

I felt him halt, as if he'd paused to soak in the view as well.

"Yeah, it's a great place," he replied softly, almost as if this was the first time he'd noticed it. If he'd been a different man, or maybe if I'd been a different woman, this moment could've been almost romantic.

"It's so peaceful," I breathed, unable to contain my awe.

Thoren grunted a response. "Come on in before you freeze." And we were back to his bear-like attitude. Yay.

He led us into the cabin, setting the lantern on a small table by a wall of windows, toeing off his boots just inside the door. The soft glow of lantern light illuminated the warm colors inside. Wooden walls and floors, and dark furniture were contrasted by Southwestern printed rugs and pillows.

The place felt like a hug.

It would've been perfect, except for the empty liquor bottles and food containers littering the coffee table. It looked like Thoren had been on a binge before he'd come to help me. No wonder he reeked.

"Um, sorry the place is a wreck." He stepped in front of me, cutting off my study of the room. I shifted my focus to his biceps as he scraped a hand through his hair before shoving his hands into his pockets. "I wasn't expecting company."

Something was wrong about this situation but even still, I cringed at the implication of his words. "I'm sorry, I don't mean to be a burden."

In the time I'd known him, Thoren had never been a heavy drinker. Unless he'd been good at keeping it hidden. And though sometimes he'd been awkward or shy, he hadn't been this closed off and surly.

"Bathroom is that way." He motioned with his chin. "Why don't you get out of those wet clothes, and I'll get us a fire going."

Now that he'd mentioned it, the cold seemed to seep through my damp layers of clothing, and I shivered.

"You need something dry to put on?"

Of course I'd have to accept his help, again. "Um, yeah." I plucked at my shirt. "I put on everything I had after my hike. I could probably use a shower too." This constant neediness was getting fucking old.

I'd been on my own and handling my shit for as long as I could remember. It didn't feel right having to rely on him to direct me into taking care of myself. I needed to get my shit together.

After leading me through the small cabin, he pushed open the only door at the edge of the room and walked into a bedroom. "No power means no water for a shower. I've got some bottled water though, you could at least freshen up."

He placed the lantern on a tall dresser and rummaged around in the drawers then tossed items to the bed. The very large, very comfortable-looking bed piled high with a fluffy comforter. In direct contrast to the mayhem in the other room, the bed didn't look to have been slept in, and everything in this room was pristine. Like he'd kept his partying restricted to the couch alone.

"I'll leave the light with you. I can use my phone flashlight to get the fire started," he explained and abruptly left. The sounds of him moving through the cabin echoed off the walls. With the total lack of background noise from the loss of power, the silence was almost...loud in a weird, unsettling way. There was no way to hide, no masking my movement.

I grabbed the dry clothes and lantern, and pushed a door open to discover a lush bathroom. The room was almost as large as the bedroom with a double walk-in shower on one side and a tub for two in front of a large window. Across from the tub, a double vanity stretched along the wall. As a woman who appreciated a good long soak with a good book, the tub called to me.

I set the lantern on the vanity and began peeling off my wet layers, draping them over any available surface. I dug through the drawers to find a rag and towel and suffered through a quick pit bath.

My knit hat had come off with my shirt. The cold air of the cabin on my scalp sent a shiver through me. Once upon a time, I wouldn't have noticed the cold so sharply. It wouldn't have penetrated my system the way it did now. I would've just felt a slight chill from having a wet head. Now though...now things were different.

And I hated how different they were.

Once clean, I pulled on Thoren's clothes, feeling oddly sensitized by having his personal items on my skin.

Gathering my courage, something I had to do more often than not nowadays, I faced the mirror. The t-shirt hung on me, which wasn't surprising. Thoren needed a muscles-R-us size to fit all those pecs and biceps into. I tugged on the hem of the shirt, trying to conceal my extremely cold nipples.

My cheeks were still red from my frigid wipe down, and I had circles under my eyes. That was also expected considering the stressful day.

I forced my eyes up to my hair. My super thin, no longer red, hair with pale patches of scalp that stood out, magnified by the lantern light.

I passed a palm over the sparse hair that remained, its softness and texture so different than what I'd once known. All my life, my hair had been the attribute I'd been most proud of. I'd had a head full of thick, beautifully manageable hair that I'd been able to style however I wanted. From the time I was a little girl, my mother had primped it, teasing it into gorgeous creations that had helped us win pageants for several years. Then later in high school, she'd primped me through proms and homecoming court.

Ripping my gaze away from my reflection, I tamped down the despair for what I'd once had as I tugged the damp hat back on.

Once upon a time, I would've reveled in this situation—stranded in a cabin with the sexy lumberjack-looking firefighter.

Now, I was mortified. No way was I letting Thoren see me this way.

He was used to Ballsy Kylie. Ballsy Kylie would say and do whatever the hell she felt like because she didn't care what people thought. That girl had been silent for a while.

But I'd put her mask on to get through the night.

Slipping out of the bathroom and back into the main room of the cabin, I found Thoren sitting on the edge of a chair with his elbows on his knees and his head in his hands in the classic Unhappy Man pose as he stared at the fire crackling in the fireplace. Guilt and something like rejection, or maybe it was remorse, washed over me. I didn't want to be a burden to him. But still, it was just a few hours, not the end of the world.

"Why do you look so dejected?"

He jumped at the sound of my voice. The dim light from the fire hid his expression, but I could read his body language well enough.

I set the lantern on the small table between the couch and chair, curling a leg under me as I settled into the couch. We needed to clear this air between us.

"Thoren, is my staying here that big a deal? I promise, I'll pull my weight."

I glanced around at the now-clean room. He must've made a mad dash through the place. The table had been cleared of trash and the liquor bottles were nowhere in sight.

He sighed heavily and sat back. Under other circumstances, he'd have been a delicious snack, slouched in his chair, thick legs splayed open, arms draped lazily on the chair's arms. It'd be so easy to straddle him, grind down–

"No, it's no problem for you to be here." His voice was low and raspy, and he seemed even more subdued than on the ride over.

My face flamed at the direction my thoughts had taken, again. *Calm down, you horny heifer.*

Instead of crawling into his lap, I studied him as he gazed into the fire, the dancing light flickering over his face. His coloring was off, even in the low light. The bags under his eyes were stark, and his hair stood on end as though he'd just tugged his hat off and gone about his business.

In my fantasy alternate scenario, it might look like bedhead. Like fingers had been run through his hair. I pressed my legs together at the thought of it being my fingers running through his hair, while his big body pressed mine into the couch, or maybe while I snuck over there onto his lap.

I cleared my throat in effort to clear my mind. Having a mostly bald, horny party crasher was probably not on his agenda.

"So, do you want to talk about what was going on before you played hero for me today?" I instantly regretted the words and the attitude that laced them. It wasn't my intent to sound like such a bitch, to be so insensitive.

Note to self: lower the defenses and think before speaking.

His eyes snapped to mine. "Nothing was going on."

I shot him a disbelieving look. He couldn't really expect me to believe that, could he? "This place looked like a frat party for one when we got here."

Sensitive, Kylie. You wanted to be sensitive.

I gentled my voice. "Come on, T-bird. What's going on?"

Maybe using the nickname I teased him with would lighten the mood, or at the very least get him fired up. I wasn't used to him being so melancholy. "Look, we already called a truce. We can do this. We can be friendly. And friends help each other."

The fire sputtered and dimmed, and Thoren left his chair to kneel at the hearth. I took the opportunity to appreciate the way his Henley stretched tight over his wide shoulders, following the taper to his trim waist. He leaned forward, putting a log on the fire, and the t-shirt rose with his movements, giving me a hint of skin. I ignored the temptation to go over and stroke his flesh.

He sat with an arm draped over a knee, watching the

fire, stoking it until the flames were high and bright again. He took his time, quiet and pensive. Sensing that maybe he was close to opening up, I stayed silent.

"I don't know what's going on." He spoke to the fire as if it were easier to avoid looking at me while we had this conversation.

Something about his tone struck a chord. Reached that space I normally kept private.

This wasn't the upbeat Thoren I'd always known. His tone suggested a man fighting some inner demons. Come to think of it, he'd been surly for a while. This version of him was making me sad. But maybe I was seeing the real Thoren. Lord knew I hid behind a façade, especially lately.

Maybe there was more to him than I realized.

I waited, giving him space to continue his thoughts. Even if I didn't like the situation or want to be stuck with him, I could see the man was hurting. And I found myself wanting to comfort him.

Eventually, exhaustion settled over me and I shifted to lay my head on the arm of the couch, my eyes closing of their own accord while I waited him out.

Sometime later, the couch shifted at my hip, and warm fingers slid up my hairline.

"You need to get this wet hat off," he murmured.

"Don't..." I squeaked, reaching up to still his hand, but it was too late.

He had my hat off before I could stop him. Instinctively, I covered my head with my arm, but not before my secret had been revealed.

He froze in shock, eyes riveted to my scalp.

"Don't be an asshole." I snatched the hat from his hand and tugged it back on. "It's not nice to stare."

My attitude snapped him out of his trance.

"Kylie, what the hell?"

I couldn't stand the way his gaze roamed over my head. The curious and concerned way he stared. The pity that morphed his face. Having someone watch me like he did now had been my worst fear all along.

I pushed him away and scrambled off the couch, escaping to the kitchen. "What? You've never seen a balding woman before?"

So what if "bald" wasn't exactly the correct term. I'd been thinking of actually shaving what little hair I had out of spite anyway.

On the small counter was a case of bottled water. I stabbed a finger through the plastic wrap and wrenched a hole into it, struggling to get a bottle free.

Warmth spread across my back, emanating from his body to mine as he stepped close. "Kylie."

My name whispered in that tender tone did things to my heart. Tears pricked my eyes, which pissed me off.

I spun and faced him, glaring at his audacity, shoving a finger into his chest. "Don't do that. Don't feel sorry for me."

The tenderness etched on his face made it worse. Then, he reached for my face, brushing the back of a finger across my cheek.

The softness was too much. It pushed me right over the edge of tough strong woman into the messiness of all the emotion I'd locked away for months and months.

An uncontrollable sob ripped from me and before I knew what happened, he'd tugged me into his arms, wrapping me in a warm embrace.

Curling in, I buried my face in his strong chest and allowed all the anger, the embarrassment, the self-loathing, I'd kept bottled up to wash over me. I sobbed in his stupid arm like he alone could make it right.

Eventually, I realized that my fists clenched his t-shirt, holding him close. He'd tugged my hat off and his big hand was smoothing my head. Caressing the patches like it didn't matter that they were different, that I was different.

"It's okay," he murmured against my temple, pressing a kiss there then laying his cheek against my head. I unclenched my hands and snaked my arms around his waist. His tightened around me, and I allowed myself to be comforted for the first time in forever.

"Talk to me," he whispered.

I swallowed thickly against the emotion that threatened to erupt again. Accepting my situation had been the hardest part. It was still hard.

I wanted to burrow into the comfort of his arms and stay there forever.

With a small squeeze, I released him and pulled away, swiping the last of my weak moment from my cheeks. Man, how quickly the tide had changed. I'd gone from digging for his secrets to him digging for mine.

"Come on," I said.

He followed me back to the couch where I waited for him to sit. Could I do this? Could I open up to him? We'd never been close, not even after our hookup. Maybe that's why it felt like I could confide in him.

Plus, we'd go home and go back to our love-hate relationship. No one would ever know.

But for one night, it would feel so good to be open and honest and vulnerable with someone. I hadn't even told Leah about my diagnosis yet.

He dropped to the couch, then patted the seat next to him before draping his arm along the back of the cushion. I tucked myself into the curve of his arm, curling my legs under me and tossing a blanket over our laps.

The dim light from the fire lent a quiet intimacy to the moment. The darkness a safe place to voice secrets and shame. It didn't hurt that he'd snuggled me close.

"I started losing my hair a couple of months ago," I started.

Thoren's hand covered mine, stopping me from picking at the blanket.

"Are you sick?" His guttural voice had my gaze shooting up to find his eyes swimming with concern.

Aside from Leah, how long had it been since I'd been shown such compassion? My heart thumped in my chest, and I struggled to understand why.

"I'm not dying, if that's what you mean. I'm not going through treatments or anything you'd normally associate with hair-loss."

I turned my hand over beneath his, linking our fingers. "I have a condition called alopecia areata. It started with a few patches where my hair just...fell out. Then the patches grew larger and more popped up. I've tried a number of things, been to all kinds of doctors, but so far, nothing has stopped it."

"What caused it?" His thumb smoothed across my hand, the gesture comforting.

"Not sure. It's an autoimmune thing, where the cells attack the hair follicles, but they don't really know what triggers it. There's a lot of research being done. A couple of treatments to try. But no real cure right now."

He eyed my scalp, then met my gaze. "May I?"

I closed my eyes and dropped my chin, humiliated, vulnerable at this open study of my greatest flaw.

But this was my new reality. I'd have to accept it.

At my nod, Thoren's hand gripped mine tighter. I felt

the softest brush of his other hand as he ran his fingers over my head.

"I thought about just shaving it all off. I mean, half of it's gone already. Maybe I wouldn't feel like such a freak," I admitted to my lap, unable to make myself look up and face his scrutiny.

"Does it hurt?" he asked softly.

"No, it's just embarrassing."

"What's embarrassing about it?"

I gave a huff of laughter. "That's easy for you to ask. You aren't on the receiving end of the stares and pitiful looks. I feel ugly. And weird." I swallowed thickly. "I don't even recognize myself."

He cupped my cheek and forced me to look at him. "Kylie, whether you have hair or not doesn't change the person you are on the inside. You are still a beautiful woman. A kind, caring, sometimes pain in the ass, gorgeous woman. Your looks don't define your beauty."

His words were beautiful and in direct opposition to everything I'd ever known to be true.

With my dad being a renowned plastic surgeon who catered to the rich and famous, and my mom running the luxury beauty spa attached to his center, I'd been featured in many of their advertisements during college. I was the face of their brand, and my looks, along with my sisters', helped sell their services.

Only along the way, things had changed, and instead of making me feel good about myself, they'd started dropping hints at cosmetic procedures to "enhance my natural beauty."

The slightest bit of cellulite had my mom suggesting liposuction. When I hit my twenties and wasn't a D-cup, they'd hinted strongly at implants. No matter that I'd won contests judged solely on my beauty, I was never pretty by their standards and never enough for them.

Their compliments became criticism.

I'd rebelled.

Left the shelter of their posh lifestyle, taken the money I'd saved up, and struck out to start my own life, eventually investing everything I had saved into starting the yoga studio I co-owned with Leah. Our shared mission was to help our clients find inner beauty and strength.

Thoren's words were everything I'd once wanted to hear, filling the empty space within me that seemed to constantly be looking for acceptance beyond my physical appearance. That he could so easily understand what I needed to hear scared me.

"That's sweet of you to say. And even though it's not right it's still a fact that people will stare at someone who is...different."

I pushed off the couch and stretched, needing to put some distance between us. And put an end to this conversation.

"So, is it okay if I use the bathroom?" I had to get away from him. This sweet version of Thoren was lethal to my heart. I'd gladly take the embarrassment of him knowing about my bodily functions over him knowing the truth of how broken I was on the inside.

He regarded me as if he knew I was running scared but relented. "Yeah, just don't flush if you don't have to. The well pump is out until we get power."

Setting my pride aside, I escaped him and his stupidly handsome face, and his understanding eyes, and his ridiculously sexy body. Now was not the time to start anything with anyone. I needed to focus on myself and determine how my life would look going forward. And how to get through the next day or so.

Chapter Five

Thoren

Kylie essentially ran from the room, away from me, retreating like she was ashamed of opening up about her condition.

As the door closed behind her, I sat forward and braced my elbows on my knees, burying my fingers in my hair, in what seemed to be my favorite position lately. Seemed like shit was always pushing me right up to the limits of what I could handle.

Kylie putting herself at risk and getting stuck in a snowstorm was stupid to say the least, and I was pissed off that she'd taken such a chance.

But I was also grateful I'd been around to help her. I was also mighty embarrassed she'd caught me at such a low point. Essentially stripped of my pride, forced to sit in the passenger's seat and instruct her on how to drive in the winter storm, like some unreliable drunk. Instead of me being the one to save her, she'd called me out—rightfully so—then saved us both.

Any other time, this stranded situation would be something I'd jump all over, because I'd had the hots for Kylie since day one. She was beautiful, smart, sassy, and bold as hell.

Everything about her was perfect, even her imperfections.

But discovering her condition and seeing her breakdown opened my eyes. Maybe there was more to her than I originally thought. The Kylie in my mind wouldn't give two shits if someone stared. But the reality was, she'd cried on me because she hurt.

And her tears burned my soul. Absolutely gutted me.

She was so much more than her outward beauty, and it ripped me up to think that's all she thought of herself. Someone somewhere had done a number on her. But maybe I could help with that.

I could make sure she knew how wonderful she was.

Except she had exactly zero reasons to believe a word I said, not after I'd shown up smelling like day-old alcohol, even if I'd driven through a snowstorm to rescue her. I was supposed to be a professional hero, not some unreliable chump.

All my life, I'd been the responsible one, keeping tabs on my brother, handling situations for my mom, only to have it blow up in my face. How many times had my brother fucked me over? How many times had my mother blamed me for the trouble he found? I'd tried to escape those feelings of failure by starting my career in a place that wasn't tainted by him. And here I was again. Failing.

What a fucking idiot.

"So, do you have any food in this place or is there just liquor?" Kylie called.

I'd been so caught up in my own head that I'd missed

her going into the kitchen. Now, she stood at the counter, opening cabinets, inspecting the contents.

"Honestly, I'm not sure what's in there. I made a grocery run on my way up, but just for some basics," I said sheepishly, squatting before the fire again. Weren't we a pair? Stuck in a cabin trying to hide from each other.

She hummed while she searched, and the sounds of things hitting the counter piqued my interest.

My appetite, missing for days now, roared to life with a vengeance. As I rose with a long stretch, my body roared back to life also.

Days spent lying around weren't my usual gig, and my muscles were strung tight as a result.

"Do we have a way to heat food?" She had a couple of cans set out on the counter. Instead of dwelling on the ugly conversations we'd had, she was moving forward. Her resiliency fascinated me.

"Yes, the range is gas."

"Excellent. Come find a can opener and we are in business."

A half hour later, we'd polished off bowls of canned chili in front of the fire and were tucked under blankets. It was late if Kylie's continuous yawns were any indicator of time.

"We need to decide on sleeping arrangements." She spoke from behind her hand.

"You can take the bed and I'll sleep on the couch," I offered. Hell, I'd been sleeping on the couch anyway.

"That's not going to work, T-bird. Have you been in that room? It's colder than a witch's tit in there."

"Okay, I'll take the cold room and you can sleep in here by the fire."

"Suit yourself, but I think you're crazy when we can both sleep in here."

My full-body reaction at the implication of sleeping anywhere near Kylie had me dragging a pillow over my lap. Now was not the time to get ideas about how we could keep each other warm.

That I was having a physical reaction to her presence at all had me all kinds of off-kilter, trying not to remember one particular drunken night of pleasure.

"I'm good," I croaked as I stood. "I'm gonna head to bed." Time to get away from her before I did something even more stupid. Like push her up against the wall or bend her over the counter. See if my memories of that night lived up to reality.

The bedroom was fucking freezing.

"It's not too late to change your mind," Kylie called as I stood frozen in the doorway.

No way was I spending the night in here. After grabbing a pillow from the bed and all the blankets, I went back to find Kylie curled into a corner of the couch, her tired eyes watching me closely.

I stood helplessly, waiting on her to give me direction, as if I couldn't think for myself. And maybe the truth was I couldn't.

In these past few days, I couldn't think for myself. Couldn't take care of myself. Couldn't seem to function.

I'd hit a low spot and there wasn't a handy ladder around to pull myself out.

Kylie sat up, as if she understood my indecision. "You brought stuff for a pallet. Great idea."

She moved furniture out of the way so we could be close to the fire, and together we made a cozy nest of blankets and couch cushions.

We'd been settled for a few minutes, and I was actively trying to ignore her gorgeous body radiating heat next to mine, when she snuggled closer, pressing close, with a whispered apology. "I'm still cold."

Desire flashed over me in an instant.

My arms hovered over her shoulders. Should I put my hands on her? Was it crossing a line to touch her when we were alone and vulnerable? I shifted to put my arm around her and felt hers snake across my waist.

"Sorry, I don't know what to do with my hands," she said, effectively stealing my breath.

If this were any other time, I'd be making my move on her. Offering to show her all the ways I found her beautiful, trying to help soothe her internal struggles over losing her hair. Showing her exactly where I wanted her hands.

Instead, I shook off the urge to turn and press her into the blankets and took comfort in having her close to me. In rubbing my hand down her back in effort to warm her.

The night embraced our intimacy.

"Tell me about the bottles." Her voice broke the silence.

"What do you mean?" I hedged.

She shifted closer, our legs brushing with the slight movement. It was sheer torture being this close to her and not acting on it.

"Do you have a drinking problem, Thoren?" Her words skittered across my skin, sharp as knives slicing into me.

The hard-on I'd been sporting since she walked into the room shriveled and withered away.

My intent when I'd arrived here had been to just get away and take a break from the bullshit in my life. To escape the disappointment of getting myself suspended. If that meant I'd spent days drinking any liquor I could find, so be it.

But did that mean I had a problem?

"No, I was just blowing off some steam after a rough couple of days."

She came up on an elbow, looking down at me. Her gaze burned over me as if she could see all my secrets. "You want to talk about it?"

Everything I'd been trying to avoid came crashing back. The tough calls, the suspension. Ignoring my mother. Even being such an irresponsible jerk when I helped Kylie.

I slammed my eyes shut. I was a fucking mess. Who was I kidding?

She lowered back to my side and tucked herself in again. "It's okay," she said. "We don't have to talk about it."

"I got suspended at work." I clamped my damn loose jaw shut, grinding my teeth so hard it hurt.

She stiffened next to me. "What happened?"

Every fiber of my being revolted at the words I needed to say. I crossed my arms over my chest and focused on the way the firelight danced across the ceiling.

"I slept off a night of drinking at the station, only I didn't sober up in time for shift."

We lay there for a long time, listening to the fire crackle and pop. Eventually, she relaxed into me, her breath becoming slow and steady. I took a measure of comfort in the fact that she hadn't jumped all over me, splashing her opinion around like some kind of cure-all.

Instead, she let me sit with my own admission and hold her. An anchor in the storm.

After a long minute, she slid an arm across me, squeezing my waist. "We'll figure these problems out together, T-bird. We're a mess right now, but we can get through this."

* * *

Just before dawn, I slipped out of the makeshift bed and stoked the fire, then set about making a pot of coffee on the outdoor gas grill. I'd lain awake for a long time thinking about the day, unsure of what I felt and what any of it meant.

The back door opened, and Kylie's toboggan-head peeped out. "There you are," she said softly, her voice still raspy from sleep.

At least one of us had rested well.

Shoving my hands into my pockets, I jerked my head to the grill. "Just making us some coffee."

"On that thing?"

"Yeah."

"Why not just do it inside? It's freezing out here."

"Because this is my camp pot. Used to be my grandpa's, and he always made his coffee on the camp stove outside when he was camping, and this sort of feels like that. I've made it this way before. Trust me, it'll be amazing."

"Okay, if you say so." She rubbed her hands together as if she were cold, then wandered to the deck rail, peering out over my mountaintop view.

The snow had left a blanket of white across the valley, and tree branches bowed under the weight. The morning had a peaceful silence to it, as if all of nature's creatures were tucked up someplace warm and couldn't be bothered to greet the day.

The sun barely crested the horizon, hidden by the distant mountain range, offering up pink hues in a cloudless sky.

A lone bird began to chatter, singing its morning call,

and it was soon answered by another and another until we were surrounded by birdsong.

"It's beautiful here," Kylie whispered.

I studied her in profile, the curve of her chin, the softness of her cold-reddened cheek. The way her clouded exhale hung on the air. The softness of her lips. Her eyes as she took in the world around her.

Kylie's orbit had pulled at me from the first day we'd met. I was drawn to her lighthearted laughter, her sassy attitude that never failed to piss me off and made me want to kiss her at the same time. Longing to be a part of this woman's world thrummed through me.

But in my current state, I wasn't worthy of her. She had enough on her plate, dealing with this condition she had and the emotions and stress that came with it.

For just a moment, I longed to wrap my arms around her. To chase away that haunted, subdued light in her eyes. To kiss the brightness back into her spirit.

The coffee percolator did its thing, distracting me. I shoved down all those feelings.

Now wasn't the time figure out feelings. Right now, we had to figure out how long we'd be stuck in this cabin, and we needed to handle the chores of keeping ourselves warm and fed.

And if my hands shook as I drank my coffee, well, I'd ignore that, too.

"Why don't we take a walk and see how things look at the main road?" Maybe some exercise would help me burn through this pent-up energy.

An hour later, we'd bundled up and checked the conditions outside the cabin by taking a short hike to find the road covered in snow with an under-layer of ice.

"Do snowplows come through here?" Kylie asked.

"At some point. This small county can't afford a whole bunch of equipment. They have enough to do the main road through town and some of the more travelled roads, but that's about it. We're pretty rural here, so they don't usually get to us." The only visible tracks were four-wheelers probably owned by locals. "If we're lucky, one of the neighbors has a plow they can put on their four-wheeler."

She kicked at a small snowdrift. "It must've snowed again after we got in last night. I don't remember it being this deep."

"No kidding. This has to be some kind of record snow-fall. I've never seen this much in these parts."

With the cap pulled low on her forehead and her arms wrapped around her, I couldn't tell if she was cold or nervous. "How long do you think we'll be here?"

"I have no idea. Could be a day, maybe two."

Wide eyes met mine. "What are we going to do? You think we'll be okay?"

I wanted to hold her again. Comfort her. But without the intimacy of darkness, it felt awkward. "Yeah, we'll be fine. We've got plenty of wood to keep the fire going, and we can make do with what food we've got." I checked the weather app on my phone. "Looks like temps should be rising tomorrow, and this will begin to melt. We might get out of here late tomorrow afternoon, or the next day."

Kylie whipped out her phone and sent a text. Our eyes met as she slipped it back into her pocket. "Just letting Leah know I'm okay, but that I won't be able to cover my classes."

I slipped my hands into my pockets, rocking back on my heels. "It's pretty impressive."

Her head tilted adorably to the side. "What is? Me sending a text?"

I smirked, turning away. There was a waterfall a short hike around the bend. Maybe that'd take her mind off being stuck with me. "No."

Her boots crunched in the snow behind me, catching up. "Uh, T-bird, you're being all weird."

I studied the snow-laden branches of the trees along the road. "You and Leah, opening a yoga studio. A successful one, from the appearance of it. How'd you get into it anyway?"

"Yoga? I started as a way to meet people in college, then stayed for the stress relief. Leah and I met, and eventually went and got our teaching certificates together, and taught classes on campus. Then after college, we went our separate ways for a bit before she settled in Newman, and we started Blue Lotus. The rest is history."

"Y'all have been friends a while then?"

She nodded. "Yeah. Like every friendship, we've had times where we've been closer than others." Lines formed at her brow. "But yeah. She's my bestie, and I couldn't imagine running the studio without her."

"It's impressive. Being a small business owner takes guts and smarts."

The corners of her mouth tipped up. She looked so beautiful and vibrant with the snowy backdrop.

"What about you? How long have you been with the fire department?"

My shoulders hitched up. "A decade now. I can't believe it's been that long. I met Nate and Mike during orientation, and we've been friends ever since." And I'd nearly pissed it away like an idiot. I thought about how she'd called and checked in with Leah.

I doubted Capt wanted to hear from me.

We turned to head back to the cabin. Kylie scooped up

a mound of snow as we walked, packing it into a ball. "How long are you out?" she asked.

"I got two shifts off without pay, so I have to be back Wednesday."

"So what's that, like a week off?"

"Yeah, we work twenty-four-hour shifts with forty-eight off, so...that makes it a full week off."

I shoved my cold hands into my pockets and focused on the snowy ground, replaying the events of that meeting with Captain Collins. Lost in thought, I hadn't even noticed she'd fallen behind until a snowball hit me square in the back, knocking me off kilter.

I spun and found Kylie packing another snowball. "Oh, you want to play? Two can play that game." I reached down for my own ammunition, smiling at her squeal as she dodged my snowball.

Her next one hit me in the side of the head, and her laughter followed, taunting me.

"It's on, Monroe."

We played like kids for a few minutes, chasing and throwing and laughing. She finally bolted for the house, yelling "Home base!" as she crashed through the front door.

My last snowball splatted against the doorframe a second behind her. After peeling off our wet outer layers, I rebuilt the fire while she scrounged up some cheese sandwiches.

"Oh my gosh, that was fun." Kylie balled up her napkin and pitched it at me.

"You've got an arm on you. I'm pretty sure I'll have a black eye," I teased.

"Serves you right for shoving that handful down my pants. That was cheating, by the way."

I grinned at her. "You know the saying—if you ain't cheating, you ain't trying."

She rolled her eyes, and I couldn't help but laugh.

"Is that a checkers set?" Kylie asked, eyeing a corner shelf stacked full of books and games. Organizing the place was one of the projects I'd not gotten to.

"I have no idea."

"You don't know if you have checkers?" It was good to hear the sass leaking back into her tone.

"All the furniture came with the cabin, and I haven't done much exploring. I have no idea what we might find."

"You just bought the thing with everything included? Dang, moneybags!"

Wood popped in the fireplace as the fire caught. I'd need to split more soon if we kept blazing through it at this pace. I shoved another log in and picked up the poker, positioning them for good airflow. "I didn't buy it. I inherited it from my grandpa."

"Oh, I'm sorry."

"Thanks. I haven't been up here in years. Haven't really explored much of the inside other than to make sure things are in working order. It's a cool place though. Reminds me of the summers spent with Grandpa as a kid."

"Aww, baby T-bird and his pawpaw," she teased. "That's so sweet. Well, we can explore while we're stuck here."

She stood to throw away our trash and I couldn't help but watch. Her leggings showcased her toned legs, lean from years of teaching yoga. And she had no problems with showing her body. The only part she seemed shy about was her hair.

We'd agreed to not discuss that one tonight.

But that didn't mean I didn't want her. That I didn't

wonder if we should try again. I shook my head at the thought. She'd probably kick my ass if I suggested that we ride out the storm naked.

"So, tell me more about your grandpa." Kylie drew my attention, trailing a hand across a stack of books on a shelf.

"Well, there's not much to tell. Every summer, we'd come and spend a week with him and Grandma. Those memories are etched on my soul. My grandpa was the best."

"Sounds like you miss him." Her voice curled around me like a hug.

"Yeah, I do." The sudden tug on my heartstrings made me uncomfortable. Dwelling on the good memories too often led to the bad. "My dad left when we were little, and we didn't really have another man in our lives. Mom never got over it. My grandpa did as much as he could with us. He would take me and my brother fishing and teach us manly things." I tried for a joke to ease the tightness in my chest.

"I'm sorry, Thoren," she said softly. "I had no idea about your dad. But I'm glad your grandpa was there for you."

I fell silent, lost in memories of happier times.

Kylie snagged a book off the shelf, releasing a cloud of dust. "Well, I thought I might read a little. But I think we should run over this with a rag first."

"We?"

"Yeah, unass that chair. We've got some exploring and cleaning to do."

We spent a few hours cleaning and organizing until she saw a dead bug and declared cleaning time to be over. The constant physical movement and instant change from dusty to neat, jumbled to tidy, made me feel weirdly accomplished. By the time she called it quits over a spider, the cabin had transitioned from bachelor pad to home. Or at least home-*ier*.

Now, as the sun set outside and the temperature started to drop again, the fire crackled in the hearth. Kylie snuggled under a blanket on the couch, across from where I sat in the easy chair.

I stared at the flames and idly picked at a thread in the outside seam of my pants leg. "I think I might have a problem." Fuck. I didn't mean to say that.

She lifted her head from where she'd been watching the fire, shifting her gaze to me. "What kind of problem?"

I avoided her gaze. Couldn't even stand to know she was watching me.

"Maybe...a drinking problem," I told the thread in my pants. I couldn't handle how she might react.

There was a rustle of the blanket, and she stepped in front of me, cutting off my safety net. I kept my gaze firmly down. Her hand rose, cupping my jaw.

I closed my eyes at the touch.

Gentle pressure of her hand had me meeting her eyes.

Then she was climbing into my lap. "This feels like a hard conversation. It helped me get through the tough part when you held me as I faced my secrets—maybe it will help you too." Her arms slid around my shoulders, her hand at the back of my head, pressing my face to her neck.

I resisted only for a heartbeat before returning the embrace. Maybe she was right. This connection between us eased something inside me.

"How can I help?" she whispered to the top of my head.

"I don't know."

She squeezed me tighter. Then released me and settled into my lap, curled up against my chest as if it were the most natural thing in the world.

I shifted, wrapping my arms around her. It was strange and wonderful to be held this way, even if it was only payback. And even though I didn't want to talk, I couldn't find it in me to push her away.

"Talk through this with me, T-bird." That stupid nickname. She used it anytime things got too serious, or when she was trying to pick a fight. And somehow it worked both ways, to settle me down and spin me up.

I shuddered at her acceptance. At this overwhelming feeling that even after my dark confession, she didn't shy away from me. Didn't start offering me immediate advice of things I needed to do. She accepted me for me.

"Let's start at the beginning," she said. "What makes you think you have a problem?"

"I don't know. I suppose it's not so much that I have to drink every day, though lately I have been. It's not that I wake up in the morning craving it. It's more like, once I start, I can't keep it to a reasonable few drinks. I let myself get wasted. Trashed to the point that I pass out."

I waited for her to have some snappy comeback, or words of wisdom, or reproach. Hell, she could even yell at me like Capt had done.

Instead, she tightened her hold on me. I relaxed into the moment, into her.

"I don't know much about how to help. But I do know that the hardest part is admitting the truth to yourself, Thoren. So take a measure of peace that you are on the right track to finding a solution to this problem."

Leaning my head against the chair, I closed my eyes and let her words sink in. Maybe she was right. Maybe I needed to give myself a break. I sat in the moment, in the truth, with a warm woman in my arms, finally feeling like maybe I wasn't a total fuckup. After some time, I drifted off to the crackle of the fire, feeling lighter than I had in days.

Chapter Six

*K**ylie*

Spending a weekend stranded in a mountain cabin with a hot lumberjack-looking firefighter and *not* jumping his bones at the first opportunity was evidence of how far off my game I was. My former self would've never believed it possible.

But two nights had passed, and though I'd wanted to jump Thoren—the chemistry between us was just as off the charts as I remembered—instead, I'd slept peacefully snuggled next to him. I gave myself props for fighting the urge to shove my hands into his pants.

That changed the second morning, when I woke up with the sun and felt his erection against my backside and his hand sliding up from my waist to caress my breast. My body's involuntary reaction was to arch into the caress.

A low rumble rose from Thoren's chest, and he pressed his thick length harder against me.

The hand at my breast tightened, cupping me, his thumb passing over my nipple. A shot of lust ran straight through my body, lighting up every nerve along the way before pooling between my legs.

It had been so long since I'd felt anything other than shame at my body, it was as if I was awakening to his touch. And I wanted more.

His hand relaxed and gave a long, slow stroke down my belly, his fingers leaving a trail of tingling nerves, each one begging for a second pass, before settling at the apex of my thighs. One slight movement and he'd be cupping me.

I shifted my legs slightly, arching my back again, encouraging him to continue. I wanted this. I wanted him to explore me and slide his fingers into me. Use me for pleasure until we were both wrung out.

Realization that I was taking advantage of the man in his sleep doused my arousal instantly, and my whole body went rigid.

He tensed behind me, his breath a sharp inhale. With a sudden jerk, he snatched himself away from me.

I rolled over to find him wiping a hand down his face.

"Kylie, I'm so sorry. I was asleep, I didn't realize…"

Tugging the covers up to my shoulders, I tucked them under my chin. "Um, I don't think you were alone in that little scene. Don't beat yourself up."

His head snapped toward me, gaze roaming my face, lingering on my lips before finding my eyes. "I shouldn't have taken advantage of the situation. I'm sorry."

I held his gaze for a minute, the sincerity in his eyes curling into that place deep in my heart no one ever touched.

"Me too," I whispered, unsure if I was sorry for taking advantage of him, or him of me, or that it hadn't gone any further.

Thoren rolled out of the pallet and knelt in front of the

fire. I took a moment to appreciate the flex of muscle under his shirt as he stoked the fire.

His fear of his possible drinking problem lay heavy between us. I didn't know what to tell him. I'd never dealt with a situation like that before, but if I had to guess, right now he didn't need my judgment. He just needed me to support him, be there for him.

Maybe once we got back to normal life, I'd have the chance to study up on the best programs. I'd even go with him to meetings if he needed me to.

Our late-night secrets had forged a bond between us.

I'd do my best to not harm that trust.

We fell into morning chores, me making up the pallet, him sorting the fire. When we crossed paths in the kitchen, he avoided my eyes, like he was embarrassed or uncomfortable. I needed to set him at ease, so I intentionally kept my tone light. "What do you want to do today?"

Thoren turned to the window. "It looks like it's snowed again overnight."

"You're kidding. This is some kind of record, isn't it?" I moved to stand beside him at the window.

"Pretty sure it is. If I've got any battery left, I'll check the weather app in a minute."

I smacked my hand to my forehead. "I've got my portable charger in my backpack. I don't know why I didn't think of that earlier. I'll grab that, then maybe we can go do something fun. Maybe we can go down the hill and see if the roads to town have been cleared."

Thoren shook his head. "I doubt it. We're usually last to get treated, and after the drive up, I don't want to risk crashing into a tree."

"Well, do you have a sled here? Cause we're gonna need to do something to pass the time."

Thoren found an old sled in the back of a shed, and we found the perfect hill and acted like little kids for a while. I called uncle after the second round because the hill was super steep. Then we took a walk on snow-covered trails to a not quite frozen waterfall on a nearby property. The spray frozen and shimmering along the edges of the falls as the water rushed through the center. Magical.

On the way back, we passed a neighbor who'd tried and failed to get to town. By the time evening rolled around, we'd laughed ourselves silly, seen some beautiful sights, and I was tired and sore.

"Oh my god. Every muscle in my body hurts right now." I flopped onto the couch after stripping off my outer layers. "But I'm so glad we decided to hang here and not risk going to town."

Thoren chuckled from the kitchen. The clatter of pans followed by the smell of food filled the little cabin.

"I want to see those videos you took," I said, snagging his phone from my charger.

"I didn't get many before my phone died, but I got the one where you fell off and rolled down the hill."

I groaned at the reminder of exactly why my body hurt so bad. Like he was with everything else, Thoren was an expert sledder.

After watching the replay of our fun day, I opened his music app. "Mind if I turn on some tunes?"

"Sure, go ahead." He looked so at home in the little kitchen, a towel slung over his shoulder.

I scrolled through his playlist. "A person's playlist says a lot about them."

He didn't respond, just kept up with stirring whatever he had on the stove.

"I just made that up. I do find it fascinating that you

have an entire playlist of classic diva songs. I mean, Mariah Carey, Whitney Houston, all the good stuff."

I tapped play, and Fantasy by Mariah Carey blasted from the speakers. Suddenly, my soreness and exhaustion were forgotten. "Come on, T-bird, this is my favorite. You can't just be still and listen. This song requires dancing."

I grabbed his hand and spun him away from his meal prep, forcing him through some moves, until he finally let loose and joined me, shaking his tail feathers like a champ. Two more epic songs later and he was the one collapsing into the chair, watching me with an amused expression while I serenaded him with Hero, overexaggerating my movements and the lyrics, until the meaning of them sank in.

This man saved lives every day. He'd rescued me, and probably countless others. No telling who was celebrating an extra birthday because of him.

As the second verse started, his expression changed again. His smile fell away as he stopped singing and just held eye contact with me.

I grabbed his hand and pulled him up, tugging him into a dance because I needed to give him a hug.

"Don't roll your eyes at me, just go with it," I ordered.

"I didn't roll my eyes," he huffed, but fit his arm snugly around my back and held my hand firmly in his. In that moment, we were anchors for each other in our drifting boats.

I curled our hands in between us and pressed close to him, swaying slowly. As the song ended, I leaned back, capturing his intense brown gaze. Leaning up on tiptoe, I pressed a soft kiss at the corner of his lips.

"Thanks for being my hero, Thoren."

Heat flashed in his eyes, and for a moment, it looked as

if he might return the kiss. I ducked away and turned off the song, tossing him his phone.

"I'm going to go see if my other clothes are dry, then I'll clean up from dinner," I said. As much as I'd wanted him to kiss me at one time, now I didn't think I could handle a pity kiss from him. Not when I wanted so much more. I was vulnerable and needy in my current state, and he wasn't in much better shape. It was best if we made it through this escapade with our hearts intact.

* * *

Thoren

Kylie hustled out of the room. Running away from me, the emotional moment, and almost-kiss before I even knew what happened.

All I could do was stare after her helplessly, wanting to go after her and pull her back into my arms. One slow dance wasn't enough.

In her rush, she didn't close the bedroom door all the way. That small opening taunted me with glimpses of her. The smooth expanse of her leg as she slipped off her leggings, replacing them with my sweats, was pure torture. My hands itched to slide over her sculpted thighs, touch that softness, then test it with my lips. Then her shirt was up and off, and I caught a flash of her stomach before she turned away.

Raging desire demanded I go into that room, rip those clothes off her, and bury myself in her.

But I was kind of enjoying this truce between us. I didn't want to jeopardize it by adding sex to the mix, no matter how badly I wanted her.

Kylie—with her effervescent personality, her outrageous

mouth, and that gorgeous body—called to me. She always had, probably always would. She was the forbidden fruit just beyond my grasp.

The bedroom door swung open, and I turned away before she could catch me being a peeping tom.

No matter how much my head kept me realistic, the body wanted what it wanted. And my body wanted hers.

Earlier, I'd woken up with the most painful erection I'd ever had, my body begging to be buried in hers. It'd taken every ounce of will power I had to not roll over her and slide into her silky warmth.

"Fuck." I scraped a hand through my hair at that mental image.

God knew we both had too much emotional baggage between us, but damn.

I escaped the hold that open door held over me and moved to the kitchen window. Bracing my palms on the counter by the sink, I hung my head and tried deep breathing. Anything to change the direction of my thoughts and chase away that teasing glimpse of her bare skin.

I recalled how we'd spent the day, trying to get my body under control. Kylie laughing, making me laugh, the singing, the dancing.

A rustle of fabric was my only warning before Kylie brushed against my elbow. Her dainty hand ran up my arm, leaving a trail of tingling nerves.

"You okay, T-bird?" Her voice was as soft as the snow falling outside. A gentle dusting over my troubled soul. What was wrong with me?

Unable to resist, I turned, folding her into my arms and burying my nose in her neck, which did nothing to curb my desire. When had we slipped into this quiet acceptance of each other? It felt...right.

"I'm okay," I lied, hating myself for it. Knowing I should push her away, yet unable to let her go.

Whatever lie I was living in this moment was worth it though, because Kylie wrapped her arms around me, running her hands down my back. Just holding me.

"You need to talk about it?" she whispered into my neck, her breath a soft brush against my skin.

I pulled back to see her face, tracing her cheek with the back of a finger, finding her skin soft. Inviting.

Her lips parted, drawing my attention, and once there, I couldn't drag my gaze away. I wanted to know what those lips tasted like.

"I'm so wrong for wanting you right now." I shifted my focus to meet her eyes. "But I do."

With gentle pressure to the back of my neck, she pulled me closer, skimming her lips against my cheek before whispering in my ear. "You're under my skin too."

Withdrawing, she hovered her lips close to mine, sharing my breath but not closing that last remaining space between us. "We should do this, just once more. Just to see if we really were as good together as I remember."

Desire slammed through me, had me tightening my hold on her and my dick growing impossibly harder.

I made to close the distance between us, to see if those lips tasted anything like I imagined, but she leaned away from me.

"You remember the rules. No kissing."

That stopped me cold. She'd drawn that line the last time we'd given in to the heat between us, but to be honest, then it'd been more about getting inside of her as quickly as possible. A frenzied, explosive, one-night-stand. But now, when we had the time and space to linger, I had trouble making sense of the words. "What did you say?"

"You heard me. No kissing."

"Why?" I might die. Just up and have a heart attack, right here in this moment. She was telling me she wanted sex and that was all my brain could process. Except I couldn't have all of her. I didn't like it. Not one bit. I wanted every inch of her. I wanted a sober memory to carry with me. The taste of her lips, her skin, what she looked like when I was buried inside her. How she sounded when she fell apart in my arms.

"I can't have you falling for me." Her tone was teasing, but an ounce of something more lingered there. This wasn't about feelings or emotions. This was about satisfying a physical need. Even still, a fission of doubt skittered through my mind.

"That's the most ridiculous thing I've ever heard. I'm not going to fall for you because of a kiss."

"That's just the way it is. Haven't you seen the movie Pretty Woman? We can fuck, but kissing is too personal."

Her mouth bending around that four-letter word did things to me. Crazy things. Blow my mind things.

Her hand drifted across my chest, brushing down my stomach, grazing lower across my aching dick. "I know you want me, T-bird. Trust me, the feeling is mutual. We've been dancing around each other long enough. Let's just get it out of our system. One more time, while we have the chance. Like before, Mike and Leah never have to know."

My thoughts scattered as she gripped my dick through my pants, squeezing, setting my blood on fire. Though her idea of keeping secrets rankled, I wouldn't turn down the chance to have her again. "I'm in."

With all the skill of a teenage boy, I fumbled her shirt off and pushed her pants down her legs. Trailing my fingers up her legs to her delicious ass, I lifted her to the counter.

Her naked body glowed in the firelight. Her breasts fit my hands perfectly. I cupped one, rubbing my thumb over the budded tip, drawing a gasp from her.

I might die not ever knowing what her lips tasted like. But at least I would have this. And there were other, equally delicious ways I could taste her.

"No kissing at all? Or just not on the mouth? 'Cause I really want to kiss these pretty tits."

"No kissing, of any kind." The breathless reply made me think she wanted my mouth on her.

Spreading her legs wide, I dipped my knees, and ran my nose along the side of her breast.

"Are you sure?" I blew a soft breath across her chest.

"Yes."

Well damn. No kissing it was. But she didn't say I couldn't tease. I'd just have to get creative. Opening my mouth over her nipple, as if I were going to draw it into my mouth and feast on it, I hovered there, letting my breath heat her skin. Then I blew out, watching the tip harden in the cool air.

"I can stand it if you can," I teased.

Chapter Seven

*K**ylie*

Thoren's breath left a hot trail across my skin. I instantly regretted my stupid rule, but I'd had it in place for as long as I could remember, latching on to it like a lifeline. I'd become obsessed with *Pretty Woman* after a crippling heartbreak during my college years.

Spread out like a buffet on his kitchen counter, I questioned if the gorgeous Vivian Ward was wrong in the movie.

It was no secret to anyone that I was sex positive. Sex was a physical release meant to be enjoyed by two, or even more, willing partners. I loved sex. I just didn't like the emotional crap that sometimes came with it.

But somehow with Thoren, things felt different.

Maybe it was that we'd been frenemies, basking in the sexual tension that sparked between us. Maybe it was that we'd had a fling once before, and our bodies recognized each other. Maybe it was that we'd shared some pretty intense secrets and I'd shown him my biggest vulnerabilities, which he'd treated with care. Whatever it was, as his body teased mine, this didn't feel the same as my normal hookups.

Indecision washed over me. I *wanted* this time to be different than all the other hookups I'd had. I wanted him. If we did this, I'd probably lose a little piece of myself anyway.

He'd been amazing over the last few days. I hadn't been focused on my changing looks, or any of the other worries that had popped up since I started losing my hair, because things between us had been so easy and so right. I felt closer to him than anyone. No one else looked at me like he did.

He stood and leaned over me, hovering there as his hot gaze set my blood on fire. "What's wrong? You just got all tense, and not in the good way."

I gave myself a mental slap. What in the hell was wrong with me? I shoved my pesky feelings aside. I wanted him and he was ready and willing. Simple as that.

I tugged the hem of his shirt, eager to get my hands on those abs of his. "Nothing. Are we doing this?" God, I sounded so freaking needy.

Thoren's hand landed on mine, stopping me from lifting his shirt.

"Kylie..."

A cell phone ringtone pierced the moment like a bucket of ice water, causing us both to jump. Thoren's gaze skittered across the counter, a deep crease forming between his brows as he looked at the name on the screen.

"I've got to take this," he said without looking at me.

All my self-doubt roared back to life when he turned away and lifted the phone to his ear without hesitation.

"Hey, Capt." He withdrew, leaving me cold, naked...forgotten.

The desire I'd been feeling moments before withered and died, replaced by burning hot anger and scorching embarrassment.

Who took a phone call in the middle of sexy times?

A fucking idiot, that's who.

Snatching my clothes up, I made a show of getting dressed before stalking past the asshat on my way to the bathroom. It didn't matter if he had his back to me and couldn't see my indignation. Hopefully, he could feel the death glare I shot at him.

I scrubbed my hands and face, glaring at the mirror.

"Idiot," I muttered to my nearly bald reflection.

No one left Kylie Monroe hanging, naked on the counter. He'd had his chance, and he'd fucked it up.

I stomped back to the front room, pulled my covers out of the pile of blankets we'd been using for a pallet and curled into a ball on the couch, facing the back cushions.

The cold air of the room skittered across my naked scalp. Blindly, I reached for the hat I'd left on the back of the couch and tugged it on, covering the ugliness of my hair like I was putting lipstick on a pig. It might look cute, but it was still just a pig.

Hot tears burned the backs of my eyes.

I didn't hold his interest because he couldn't stand to look at me.

It was a mistake to start something with him. I should've known better. Shouldn't have put myself out there. No one could stand to take me seriously as a woman because I didn't look like a woman, didn't feel like a woman.

I felt like a speckled Easter egg. With a spotty dye job that didn't take all over.

No wonder he didn't find me attractive.

"Kylie." Thoren's voice broke my internal berating.

I would not let him see me upset. I would not let him see these stupid fucking tears that threatened. I pinched my eyes shut and tugged the blanket closer around my shoulders.

"That was my captain. I am cleared to come back to work next shift."

I spoke slowly so my voice wouldn't tremble. "That's good."

"So, you're going to sleep? We're not gonna…"

I huffed an incredulous laugh. "No, Thoren. We're not gonna do anything. That was a colossal mistake that we thankfully avoided," I snapped.

Sounds came from the fireplace, and warmth began to spread from the stoked fire while I lay seething in silence.

"You don't want to sleep down here where it's warmer?" he asked quietly.

Stupid soft voice. Stupid imagined longing.

"I think it's best if we have a little space," I told the blanket.

"Oh."

He grew quiet for so long I thought he might be asleep. I chanced turning over, needing to get my face to the warmth of the fire.

He lay on his back, arms behind his head, staring at the ceiling.

When I settled, his eyes were on me.

"I'm sorry about earlier," he whispered.

My heart clenched the tiniest bit. "What are you sorry about?"

He looked back at the ceiling. "I'm sorry we started down that road and I'm also sorry that we got interrupted." He turned his head towards me. "Mostly, I'm sorry I upset you."

More stupid tears filled my eyes. I blinked and flopped to my back.

With a huge sigh, I let some of the hurt go. "It's probably for the best. It would've been awkward to go home and have to face each other around everyone anyway."

The fire crackled. Outside, branches popped, and the gentle rain of melting ice spattered on the roof.

"I'm not so worried about what they think," he said quietly.

Well, color me surprised. "You used to be. You were the one who agreed that we couldn't let anyone know."

"Things change. Besides, that was your rule we were following." He paused, and the weight of his words registered. He'd kept our night together a secret because I'd wanted it. My anger started to deflate as I considered how things might've been different if we'd not made that agreement.

"Are you still mad? Will you come down here to sleep?"

"Why?" I asked dubiously.

"Because I got used to your snoring for the last two nights. It's too quiet in here with you way over there."

I flipped the blankets down, letting my hands plop at my sides.

"Seriously?"

He chuckled. "Yes. Since you're obviously over being mad, come snuggle with me." And then, "Please?"

It was the please that got me.

Grumbling, I sat up and gathered my blankets, making sure he heard me huffing. I settled myself back on the pallet we'd slept on for the last two nights.

This time I left some space between us.

Thoren tugged me closer, turning me so my back snugged against his front, tucking an arm around my waist.

I lay stiffly for a moment, then finally gave up and relaxed into him.

He tightened his arm around me. "The roads should be clear tomorrow. We can go home."

I wasn't sure if the sudden moroseness that washed over me was from the letdown of my anger, the missed opportunity to hook up with him again, or the knowledge that things would never be the same. I'd go back to the studio, back to my empty apartment, back to sleeping alone.

One thing was for sure.

We'd no longer be dancing around each other because I'd left the dance floor.

* * *

True to Thoren's prediction, the temps had risen quickly, and the sun shone bright in the sky the next day. It was enough that the roads thawed, and we were able to go home.

We spent the morning in stilted silence, cleaning the cabin and closing it down. After we finished, Thoren dropped me off at my Jeep, then followed me to the nearest gas station.

"Look after yourself, Kylie." He'd cupped my cheek tenderly, his voice a low gravely sound as his gaze roamed my face as if memorizing me.

It'd felt like a goodbye, and I couldn't for the life of me figure out why it hurt so bad.

I'd cried all the way home.

In fact, I'd cried more in the last few days than I probably had in the last ten years. I was ready to get back to normal life and leave all the emotional shit behind.

By the time I got home, I was exhausted, but unable to sit still. Everything in my apartment looked different. Like I had new eyes. The before Thoren eyes, and the after.

My apartment, just off the square in downtown

Newman, was part of a revitalization project. They'd converted all the old buildings over the years, and mine had been a factory, a store, and eventually ended up a quaint set of smallish apartments.

The units were accessed through a wrought iron gate that secured a private alley, which also functioned as a courtyard. Strategically placed flower beds lined the red brick building, and a fire pit surrounded by Adirondack chairs sat in the center of the old, bricked road. The outside world could see in, but only the residents could access our little patio.

It'd been a great place to hang out and have beers or morning coffee, until the pizza shop had opened down the block. After that, the voices of rowdy teenagers pierced the peacefulness of the space.

I dropped my hiking gear inside my front door and looked around at the mess I'd left before my trip. Helping Thoren clean the cabin was more work than I'd done to take care of my own shit lately.

My cell phone rang.

"Hey girl," I said to Leah.

"Did you make it home okay?"

"Yes. Had no trouble at all. The roads were clear once we got out of the mountains." I didn't mention my waterworks all the way home. "Listen, thanks for sending Thoren to come get me," I added grudgingly. No matter what had or had not come of the weekend, he'd saved my ass.

"Sure. I couldn't bear the thought of you spending the night in your car. I was so worried. You guys didn't kill each other, did you?"

"No. Actually, we had a good time together." At least we had until I'd gotten naked.

"You did?" Her voice was incredulous. I heard her

boyfriend's low voice in the background, asking who she was talking to.

Mike and Leah's whirlwind romance had started pretty much the moment big, bad Mike had laid eyes on my sweet friend. They'd been inseparable since then.

"Kylie says she and Thoren didn't kill each other. They actually had fun together." Leah's voice was muffled, as if she'd dropped the phone away from her mouth.

"That's what Thoren said, too," came Mike's reply.

"You talked to him?" I blurted. Then my dumbass mouth kept talking despite my brain sending warning signals to stop. "What did he say?"

If he'd told them I'd gotten naked for him on his kitchen counter, I was going to literally kick his ass.

"Here, let me just...okay, Kylie, I put you on speaker. What did Thoren say, honey?" Leah asked Mike.

"Just that y'all didn't kill each other. And that he had a good time playing in the snow. Which I'm grateful for, because he's had a shit few weeks and needed something good in his life. So thanks for taking care of him, Kylie."

Oh.

Well.

That took the wind from my sails.

"Sure thing," I croaked. I didn't want to ask, but I couldn't let it go. "Um, what kind of shitty stuff has happened?"

"Not my story to tell, but I've been worried about him for a while."

Suddenly, those tender looks and touches from Thoren made me feel like a giant asshole for getting so irrationally mad about him halting the possible sexy times we might've had.

"You know, it would be awesome if you and Thoren

actually started liking each other." Leah floored me with the words. "I'd love it if you two could work things out."

She had no idea. And what a shame things would never work out with us.

I finished the call with Leah, promising we'd talk more in between classes the next day.

The urge to call Thoren was strong. Instead, I focused on cleaning my space. Maybe a tidy apartment would help ease the chaos in my head.

Once I'd organized and put away my hiking gear, I tackled the laundry, then the dishes. The whole time, I replayed every interaction Thoren and I had, from packing snowballs to throw at him...to feeling lonely at the prospect of sleeping alone.

By the time I got the last of the dishes put away, I gave up the fight and went in search of my phone.

I stared at his contact info on the screen. It'd only been a few hours since I'd last seen him. It was ridiculous to miss him, to want to talk to him. Why was I like this?

Then the phone rang in my hand, and I nearly dropped it. His name flashed across the screen in some kind of karmic irony.

"Hello?"

"Hey, it's me, Thoren." He sounded nervous, hesitant.

I smirked. The big goofball. "I know, I saw your name when it popped up."

"And you still answered?" He sounded incredulous. Did he think I was that big of an asshole? He continued, "I was prepared to leave you a message."

No way was I going to admit I was about to call him, but since he'd beaten me to it, I'd enjoy the moment. "What's up? Did you make it home okay?" I deliberately kept my tone light.

"What happened between the cabin and home? Did someone body snatch you?"

And suddenly things between us were right again. The push and pull of our teasing set me at ease.

"Don't be an ass," I quipped.

"It's just that you were mad as hell at me, and I'm not trusting this one-eighty."

I rolled my eyes. "Never mind. Did you get home okay?"

"I did."

Mike's words flittered in the back of my mind and had me asking, "You okay, T-bird?"

He grunted, but I couldn't tell if it was in amusement or something else when he answered. "Yeah. It's too quiet at my house."

The images of all the empty bottles in the cabin flashed in my head.

God, I was such an asshole. He must be struggling if he was calling me.

"You don't have any booze at your house, do you?" I asked tentatively.

He cleared his throat. "No, I uh, just threw it all out."

An awkward silence fell between us, then he said, "I just wanted to let someone know. Since you're the only one who knows about my little maybe-problem...anyway. So I thought maybe it would be okay to call. Unless you're still mad about the thing that didn't happen." The longing in his voice tugged at my heart.

Oh God.

He was killing me.

Making me his confidant, making himself my safe space, then rejecting me, and now making me feel like the world's most inconsiderate person because he sounded like he needed a friend.

Swallowing my pride, I admitted, "I'll get over it. I just need a little space to lick my wounds."

"I'm really sorry, Kylie. I didn't mean to hurt your feelings, and I had a long think on the drive back. I realize how it seemed to you. And I'm so damn sorry you got mixed up in my baggage and got hurt because of it."

He sounded sincere. Still, I wasn't going to put myself out there, even if I missed being with him. "It's okay. Let's forget it ever happened and just move forward."

The other end of the line was silent. It took courage for him to take the steps he'd taken. I could imagine that he was feeling awkward, maybe a little unsure. And if we were going to move forward as friends, I needed to be supportive. "Thanks for letting me know about the steps you took. I'm glad you're taking care of yourself, and I'll be here if you need me."

We said our goodbyes, and exhaustion from the snowed-in escapade, the long drive home, and the emotional turmoil dropped over me like a curtain. I curled into a ball on my couch and passed out.

Chapter Eight

T*horen*

My first shift back after my suspension was humbling.

Captain Collins called me into his office first thing and issued me a terse *"Sit"* in his deep gravel voice.

Once I'd settled into the chair across from his desk he began, "I'm not fucking around when I tell you, you are one of the best on my shift. You pull a dumbass stunt like that again, and I'll take you to the lake house and beat some sense into you. If you've got a drinking problem, I'll be the first to help you. If you're just being a dumbass, you better get smart. Real quick. This job is too dangerous for you to be putting the lives of my crew on the line."

I nodded stupidly. Somehow, Capt always reduced me to a scolded teenager. "Yes, sir. It won't happen again," I'd vowed and left his office with my tail tucked between my legs.

I'd spent the entire shift reassuring the guys that I was okay. I'd learned my lesson. The worst had been facing Nate.

His hurt expression and his puppy dog eyes. His muttered, "Why didn't you come to me for help?" just about did me in. By the time dinner rolled around, I'd had enough, and I snuck off to my bunk room to hide from their well-meaning, but judgmental, treatment.

They all treated me like a drunk, when maybe I'd only been a dumbass.

Though truthfully, I couldn't blame them. If anything had happened, if I'd been the cause of one of my brothers, or a civilian, getting hurt, I wouldn't have been able to live with myself.

Their reactions had been exactly what I'd feared, which was why I'd avoided my phone all weekend, until Capt had called me back in to work.

Only Kylie had offered me no judgement.

Only Kylie had just... sat with me, offering me support without condemnation.

The days I'd spent with her had been such a far cry from my normal. We'd laughed and played like kids. And the last day would've been amazing if I hadn't lost my shit when I got that phone call and fucked everything up by rejecting her. Hurting her feelings.

I missed her.

I had a Kylie-size hole in my life that hadn't been there before I'd picked her up off that snowy road.

Longing to pick up the phone, just to hear her voice, I rolled over in my bunk. My eyes didn't even close all the way before tones dropped and I was back up, sprinting out the door.

* * *

"Good job this morning, guys." Captain Collins clapped me on the shoulder as I threw my nasty bunker gear into the industrial washing machine. We were stripping down, getting ready to head home after a night spent battling a structure fire. The crew currently on duty would finish on-scene cleanup, and then come back to the station to clean our gear and get the engine back in service.

"Hey, Capt, did you ever hear anything from the fire inspector?" Nate asked, stripping his pants off and standing in his sock feet and underwear.

"They may have finally gotten a lead from some evidence they found on scene. Seems they found the accelerant."

"What'd they find?"

"Doesn't seem like much, but they found a liquor bottle with some fingerprints and possibly some DNA."

I was a couple days behind on the news.

"Is that from the suspected arson case?" I asked Capt, using air quotes.

"Yeah. And we had another structure fire while you were out of town." The way he phrased my suspension gave me a shred of my dignity back.

"Damn, what's that? One per week for the last month?"

"Seems like every shift now."

Nate and Big Mo talked over each other from the washroom.

"Plus this one." A frown lined Capt's craggy face. "It's a dangerous time when some jackass is out there playing games with people's lives. So far, it's been empty structures. I'm afraid they're ratcheting up though, and a citizen is going to get hurt. It's just a matter of time till we catch this asshole."

"Yeah, he'll fuck up sooner or later," Nate chimed in, positive as ever.

We hustled out to our cars and said our goodbyes. Mo was headed to do his part-time job of landscaping. Nate was headed home to Jordan, and they'd be leaving for a camping trip within days.

Everyone had someone or somewhere to go it seemed.

Captain Collins stood at the back of the bay as I walked to my truck. "Good to have you back, Thoren. I'm here if you need me."

It was as close to warm-and-fuzzy as the man ever got.

"Thanks, Capt. See you later."

I was still running on an adrenaline high from being in a burning building. It always seemed to take me longer to calm down than it did the other guys, and I needed to find a way to work it off.

I had a pile of wood I could go home and chop. That had seemed to take the edge off before I started turning to the bottle more frequently.

I slowed for a red light on my way home, talking myself out of stopping to restock my beer cooler, when I realized I was at the intersection where Kylie and Leah's yoga studio sat. A quick glance at the parking lot, and I spotted Mike's Fire Marshal SUV.

It wasn't unusual for him to stop by the studio, but on the off chance something was wrong...I flipped my blinker on and pulled in beside his running car and jogged up the front walk.

The studio, Blue Lotus Yoga, was a renovated old house Kylie and Leah had made over into a yoga studio. I'd been there before when we'd done a photo shoot for the annual public safety calendar photo shoot.

I shoved the front door open and almost tripped over Mike and Leah in a steamy embrace.

"Uh, hey, guys." Ugh, awkward. "Sorry to interrupt."

Mike and I had been friends for a long while and I was happy he'd found Leah, but I didn't need to see them in a full-on clench.

"Hey, Thoren," Leah said, her cheeks flushed bright red.

With her hair piled into a messy bun and her flowy yoga style, she was a direct contrast to the buttoned-up cop next to her. No matter what title he held, he'd always be a cop in my eyes.

"What's up, man?" Mike offered me a handshake. "Heard y'all had one helluva structure fire last night. I was just on my way over to check it out." As fire marshal, Mike worked a regular day shift, rather than a twenty-four-hour shift.

"Yeah, the house was gone before we got to it."

Mike's radio crackled at his shoulder, and he grimaced. "Sorry, babe. I gotta go."

"Can you drop this off by Kylie's later?" She motioned to a bag on the tall wooden front desk.

"I can, but it'll be a while. You might as well take it between classes."

Her face fell. "But that's hours from now, and I hate for her to have to wait for this medicine."

The front door opened and three ladies filed in, skirting around us to check in at the iPad on the front desk.

Mike answered his lapel radio and gave Leah a sympathetic look. "I'm sorry, babe. Gotta take this call." In addition to his fire-marshal title, Mike had also become the new chief fire inspector. He was going to have his hands full for a bit at the scene I'd just left.

"I can do it." The words were out of my mouth before I knew what I'd committed to. But if it came to helping Kylie, it would give me an excuse to see her again. I didn't want to think too much about why, I just knew I wanted to.

Leah's eyes lit up. Mike leaned over and gave her a peck on the cheek and hustled out the door with a "see you later."

"Really, Thoren? You don't mind?" she asked, already reaching for the bag.

"Sure, it's no problem. Uh, exactly what am I delivering?"

Leah shoved the bag into my hand and stepped over to assist one of the ladies waiting. "I had to send Kylie's stubborn butt home yesterday. She started feeling poorly during a class. She was pale and shaky by the time I finally convinced her to let me finish her classes so she could go home and rest. I gathered up some oils and stuff to take over to her, but my other teacher also called in."

Concern shot through me. Kylie was sick? "I'll go check on her."

"Thanks, Thoren. So much. But be warned, she's not the nicest of patients. Oh, and here's the key to her apartment and the code is 4321."

Back in my truck, I glanced inside the bag and winced at the homeopathic remedies Leah'd packed for Kylie. They probably weren't going to do anything for her. I'd check things out myself and then make a run to the store.

I let myself in through the gate using the ridiculously easy code, and noticed the courtyard needed some attention. The shrubs were overgrown, and a light was out. It wasn't safe. There were too many places for someone to hide. Her landlord needed to fix this, and if he wouldn't, I would. I considered just taking on the task as I tapped gently on Kylie's door.

After three tries, I used the key from Leah and unlocked the front door, tapping again as I entered. I didn't want to scare Kylie by barging in.

"Go away, Leah. I don't want your crappy herbs," Kylie grouched from the next room. This statement brought on a fit of coughing. From the doorway, I could hear the wheeze and rattle in her chest. How'd she get this bad so quickly? A niggle of guilt rolled through me. Maybe we shouldn't have played in the snow so much if the result was her getting sick.

I crossed the room, dropping the bag of herbs Kylie would not be taking on the table. "Not Leah, but I do have her herbs. Sounds like you need something a little stronger though." I'd bundle her if I had to carry her in protest to see a doctor.

The blanket covered mound on the couch moaned again. "Noooo, you can't be here."

Sinking to a knee at her head, I tugged the edge of the blanket back. "Hello to you too."

She looked pitiful, her face pale and drawn. I placed the back of my fingers gently against her brow, frowning at the heat radiating from her.

"You're burning up. When's the last time you took anything for fever?"

"I don't know. I ran out of aspirin a while ago. What day is it?" The more she talked, the raspier her voice got.

"It's Tuesday morning." I ran a comforting hand over her hair. "When's the last time you drank anything?"

"It hurts to drink. Everything hurts."

I tsked. "Poor thing."

Assuring her I'd return immediately, I went to rummage through my truck. I usually carried some basic meds in my work bag in case I needed it on duty. I found what I was looking for and went back to her apartment.

Kneeling by her head, I held a glass of water in one hand and a cocktail of Leah's vitamins and my fever-reducing pain meds in the other. "Take these," I ordered.

With a pathetic groan, she lifted to an elbow, swallowing the meds with the glass tipped at an awkward angle. I'd need to remember straws.

After making sure she was resting comfortably, I made a mad dash through the nearest drugstore, returning with bags laden with all kinds of things a sick person might need, only to find her restless again.

It'd been a long time since I'd taken care of a sick person besides a patient. I made sure patients had air going in and out and blood going round and round, or helped stabilized broken bones, until someone from a medic squad got to the scene.

But actually taking care of someone who was running a fever and feeling generally miserable...not so much.

This was a different scenario, and I was way out of my comfort zone.

I tried to recall what my grandma would've done before she got sick. I figured Kylie probably hadn't eaten and would need some soup or something. While she slept, I poked through her kitchen until I found some, and opened a can, and set it to low on the stove.

She probably hadn't had much to drink either, so I refilled her water glass and put a straw in it.

I'd grabbed a forehead thermometer, so I took her temperature. It read 102 degrees. No wonder she felt so bad. Even with meds, her fever was high.

From the blanket, Kylie's phone rang. I dug around until I unearthed it and saw a missed call from Leah.

My ringtone shrilled in the quiet apartment. I silenced it quickly, to keep from disturbing Kylie further.

"Hey, Leah."

"Hey, how's our girl?"

Our girl.

I liked that. *My girl* sounded better.

I stepped to the kitchen so I could talk to Leah without disturbing Kylie. Keeping my voice low, I answered, "She's running a fever right now. I gave her some medicine before I went to the store. But it's still too high."

"I can't leave right now, but I could look in on her on my way home?"

Leah still had at least another few hours of yoga to teach, then she'd be going home to Mike.

My gaze flittered to Kylie. She looked so pitiful bundled under her blanket. I couldn't leave her.

"Nah, I'll stick around. I don't want to leave her here alone." Plus, if I stuck around for her, I could trust that the job was done.

Leah promised to check in again, and we said our goodbyes.

Kylie moaned in her sleep. Instinctively, I hurried over and bent to check on her, running a knuckle over the bags under her eyes, over the soft curve of her cheek. Seeing her this way broke my heart.

I missed my lively, sassy woman that joked and teased and made inappropriate comments.

Her brow furrowed, maybe from a dream, and I quieted her. "Shh, sweetheart. I'm not going anywhere."

As if she could hear me, her brow relaxed, and she snuggled deeper under the covers.

And that decided it.

I was sticking around for the long haul. Besides, I was off for the next two days. I could make time for her.

Chapter Nine

Kylie

"Come on sweetheart, wake up and take this medicine."

A deep, masculine voice, which sounded nothing like my mother's, pulled me from the recurring nightmare of my mother berating me for my choice of yoga gear.

No, it was more like my mother to tell me to get up and get dressed. "A little lipstick will perk you right up," she'd say.

A straw hit my lips and a warm hand cupped my cheek, prompting me to open my mouth.

"There you go. Take a sip. Now swallow it all down for me."

The tender voice sounded oddly like Thoren's when he was in sweet mode. But that didn't make any sense. I'd told him to get out when he'd come by.

Or at least I thought I had.

I pried open my gritty eyes to find Thoren's face right in front of mine. He was on his knees beside the couch, looking like he hadn't slept in days.

"Well, hello, sunshine." His eyes crinkled with a smile, an odd mixture of concern and relief crossing his features. "How are you feeling?"

"Like total shit. What are you doing here?" I reached up to wipe the drool from my mouth. Ugh, how embarrassing.

Not only had he rejected the idea of having sex with me, now he was seeing me at my absolute worst. A pretty patient, I was not.

A slow grin spread across his face. "I'm playing hero. And doctor. And let me tell you, you are one testy woman when you don't feel good."

I rejected the idea of him helping me. "Uh-uh. No way. I already got naked for you, and you walked away. I'm not playing doctor-patient with you."

A low chuckle rumbled through him.

"Sweetheart, you're in no condition to play games right now. You've been out like a light for over twenty-four hours." He pressed his hand to my forehead. "Feels like the fever may have finally broken."

I swatted his hand away and pushed to sit up, allowing myself a moment for the dizziness to pass.

"Seriously, why are you here?" I couldn't wrap my brain around the thought of him being in my apartment, much less him taking care of me. I looked down at my rumpled clothing, damp with perspiration. The same clothes I'd been wearing for who knew how long.

"Leah asked me to stop by on my way home from work. I found you curled into a miserable little ball and couldn't leave you here to suffer by yourself."

"How magnanimous of you." I couldn't stand being pitiful. And I really hated that he was seeing me at my worst. But still, my heart flipped over, going belly-up at the thought of him caring enough to stay with me, to take care of me.

Swallowing my emotions, because those bitches never did anyone any good, I passed a hand over my patchy hair.

Thoren eased away, moving gracefully into the chair beside the couch.

"Well, I'm up now. You don't have to stick around." Even as I said the words, a tiny little piece of me admitted that I really didn't want him to leave, and yet, asking him to stick around felt like too much.

"Are you kidding? I'm just getting to the good part of my book." He held up my Kindle. "I can't leave now."

"Um, that's my Kindle."

"I know. I found the most fascinating book. I didn't know you had a penchant for multiple partners."

"You're reading a reverse harem?"

"If that's one girl and multiple guys, yes. The knotting is particularly interesting. I'm kind of liking this whole omega-verse thing, too."

My face heated, although I didn't know why. I had nothing to be ashamed of. "My reading preferences are private. I don't share my TBR with just anyone." Which was one of the reasons I preferred an e-reader over a book.

He pretended not to hear me. "I also liked the ones with the blue aliens. I like that whole fated-mates trope. Next up is the one with the dog named Marshmallow. You've got such a wide library to choose from."

My jaw dropped open even as my face grew hotter. "Who are you?"

"What? Why are you looking at me like that?" Confusion spread across his face.

I closed my mouth and shook my head, a bad move that left me instantly dizzy.

Oblivious to my discomfort, he continued, "There's nothing wrong with a guy reading and enjoying a good romance. Although, the size of some of these dicks could give a guy a complex."

He had nothing to worry about.

And I had no business thinking about his dick. In my mind, he'd already made it clear that he didn't want me.

My anger flared with that little reminder. "Well, you can go now. I'm up. I'm feeling better."

Thoren sat forward, resting his elbows on his knees, pinning me with a look. "No, you don't. You're just embarrassed."

Hell, yes, I was. But I wouldn't admit it to him.

"Tell you what," he started in a reasonable tone that suggested I was acting like a child, "you go take a shower, and we'll see how you feel after that. I'm not comfortable leaving you here alone, until I know you aren't going to collapse again."

Even though I hated the thought that he was right, a shower did sound amazing. I flipped the covers back. Only then did I realize I was wearing the shirt I'd stolen from Thoren's cabin. Shit. Dragging the last of my dignity with me, I stumbled off the couch, hoping he hadn't noticed.

Of all the t-shirts in my closet, why did I have to pick this one to curl up in?

Because you wanted to feel close to someone.

I shoved that little voice in my head into a box and slammed the lid. With frustration fueling me on, I sashayed to the bathroom and stood under a hot shower, trying to get my bearings.

Thoren was here, apparently of his own free will, taking care of me when I was in a bad way.

That thought whirled around in my head while I

finished my shower. What was I supposed to make of that? Honestly, it frightened me a little.

I dressed and went back out to find him lounging in my chair, still reading my Kindle. The blanket on the couch had been replaced with a clean one. The table had been cleared of the cups and medicine. As I glanced around my apartment, it looked like he'd done quite a bit of tidying. All the dishes were clean, my shoes were all neatly placed on a rack by the door. The sheers covering my window were pulled back, letting in the waning sunlight.

Thoren had been busy while he'd been here. This random act of kindness confused me. Unsettled me. I thought he didn't want anything to do with me. I'd made my mind up on the long drive home. Our paths would cross as minimally as possible.

"You cleaned my apartment too?"

Not looking up from his book, he gave me a nod. "I was bored. It didn't take long and I needed something to do. Plus, you cleaned the cabin. Seemed the least I could do."

His easy acceptance of the situation, the way he looked at home in my apartment—like it was no big deal for him to be here doing random chores and taking care of me—sent me into an anxious spiral.

When Kylie Monroe had a problem, she solved it. Although it had been nice to let him take over when I hadn't been able to lift my head.

I didn't have the energy to stay mad any longer. The remains of my indignation drained away, pushed out by a wave of exhaustion so staggering, I barely made it back to the couch.

Thoren lowered my Kindle, watching me crash and burn from a simple shower. As my head hit the pillow he leaned forward, running his hand tenderly over my hair.

"Why don't you go lay down in the bed? You'll rest better."

Because if I went to bed, I'd be alone. And suddenly, I didn't want to be alone. My heart couldn't take the rejection if I asked him and he turned me down.

"The couch is where sick people sleep. It has magic healing properties." I closed my eyes, enjoying his touch on my scalp. "Why do you do that?" I asked blearily, needing to know more about why he was here, and why this connection to him felt so good, even when I didn't want it to.

"What?"

"Rub my non-existent hair like that?"

After a beat, he answered, "I like how it feels."

"It looks gross," I muttered.

"No, it doesn't," he said softly. "It's not good or bad, it's just different. I like how soft it is."

I squeezed my eyes shut against the tears that threatened. I'd been brought to tears more since he'd picked me up off that mountain than I had in years.

Clearing my throat, I tried to make my voice firm. "You don't have to stick around. I'm fine now."

"Yeah, you really look like you're fine," he huffed, amusement in his voice. Another brush of his hand over my hair, and then he said softly, "Go back to sleep, sweetheart. We'll argue later."

Visions of Thoren cleaning my apartment danced through my head, and his smile was the last thing that played through my mind as I drifted off.

* * *

"Wake up, sleepyhead."

Thoren's big hand on my shoulder jostled me.

"Wha?"

"Let's go. You can be mad later."

I opened my eyes to find him rising, slipping the strap of my duffle bag over his shoulder.

"I don't wanna move," I groaned, snuggling deeper into my blanket.

"I know you don't, but I can't do another night in that uncomfortable chair, and I'm not leaving you here alone. So perk up little trooper, you're coming home with me."

Thoren's declaration had me pushing the cover away and cracking one eye at him. "I'm not going anywhere. And my chair isn't uncomfortable."

"Oh yes, it is, and yes, you are. Come on, I've already got everything packed."

"No." I closed my eye and flipped the blanket back, this time covering my head.

The front door opened and closed, the sudden silence making me sit up and instantly miss him. Funny how things had changed so quickly. In however many days since he'd been nursing me, he'd taken over my space so thoroughly that it seemed more than empty without him.

Like he'd displaced all the particles, and they didn't know what to do in his absence.

The door reopened and his energy burst through the room again, all the little particles falling back into place.

Good God, I was sick. Delusional.

The next thing I knew, a pair of arms slid under and around me and I was being lifted, blanket and all. Tangled up in a blanket burrito, trapped against a warm chest, and unable to move.

"Put me down!" I struggled in his arms.

He grunted as my knee connected with a firm body

part. "Quit wiggling before I drop you. And don't knee me in the gut again."

Somehow, he managed to get the door locked and me tossed into the car with a terse, "Stay put."

"I'm not a dog. Or a child," I retorted, my voice sounding a whole lot weaker than I would've liked it to.

"Then quit acting like one."

Then he slammed the door.

Apparently, I was going home with Thoren.

* * *

Thoren

What in the actual fuck was I doing? Hauling Kylie around, demanding she come home with me?

All I knew was one minute my mind had been racing, working over possible scenarios of leaving Kylie alone, sick, still running a fever. The next, I'd remembered my scheduled floating holiday for the next shift, and I'd gotten up and packed her bags, determined to sleep in my own bed for a night.

I blamed my lack of sleep and general discomfort.

I'd moved her to her bedroom, but she'd whimpered in her sleep and woken up multiple times. She claimed the couch was where sick people recovered. I just figured her bed must not be comfortable. But when I'd finally broken down to lie in it while she slept, it had felt all wrong without her being there next to me.

So, I was taking her to my place.

Where she'd probably still claim the couch, but at least I had a sectional, and we could both be comfortable.

Kylie dozed on the short drive to my house, or

pretended to at least, only rousing as I turned into the long gravel drive.

"Wow, this place is gorgeous," she said, her voice filled with awe. "I had no idea you had such nice digs."

My house sat on a rolling hill of cleared land, enclosed by a wooden fence that lined the long road frontage. The house itself was a small two-bedroom cottage I'd refinished myself. It wasn't much, but it was mine.

Kylie climbed down out of the truck wide-eyed, taking everything in. "What's that?"

I glanced over to see her looking behind my house. "That's where my side business happens."

"It looks like giant stacks of wood."

I chuckled at her. "That's because it is. I have a firewood delivery business that I run when I'm not at the fire station. There's more to me than what you think you know, sunshine."

"Is that how you get all your manly muscles?"

I grinned at her. "It's one way."

"One?"

"I can't tell you the other," I said, shooting her a wink, trying to make her uncomfortable. Maybe if I nudged her just a little, we'd get back to the flirty playful space we'd been in before that interrupted scene in the mountains.

The reminder of her being naked in my hands had my dick going hard in an instant.

And I didn't need to be thinking this way because I couldn't go there with her.

We got inside and settled, and Kylie passed out on the couch while I showered and ate a sandwich. Then, I lay down on the other side of the sectional, our heads nearly touching, and let sleep claim me as well.

After a good rest, we fell into a pattern for the next few days. Watching movies, napping, me plying Kylie with medicine every now and then, and endless hours of conversation. After so much time off, even though I enjoyed it, I was getting restless as hell. At least at my house, I could keep busy with my side business while she napped. If she hadn't been improving, I would have taken her to the doctor, but I was pretty sure she'd had the flu and had let the virus run its course.

The more she let me care for her, the more I wanted to. Little things, like making sure she stayed hydrated, making her some soup. Watching endless reruns of her favorite shows. After a couple of days, her color was better, the fever gone. Even if she wasn't at full speed yet, I had no other excuses to force her to stay longer.

The night before I was scheduled to go back to work, we lay on the couch. Somehow, we'd transitioned into snuggling every evening, arms around each other, legs entwined. It was innocent and sexy and left me hard as a rock every night.

Now it was time to move back into the real world, and I didn't want to lose the intimacy we'd found. I was afraid that once she was out of sight, she'd make up things in her head about me, us. So I broached the subject that had driven us apart.

"So, about what happened at the cabin."

Kylie groaned. "Can't we just forget about that? I like this comfortable thing we have going right now. I don't want to get pissed or hurt all over again."

"That's exactly the reason we need to talk about it." I took her hand, my chest heavy, knowing I'd caused her pain. "I didn't mean to make you feel rejected or to hurt you. I shouldn't have started it in the first place."

I glanced at her plush lips, wishing I could taste them.

Just once. But she'd said no kissing. And from the moment she'd laid the rule down, that's all I'd wanted to do.

If only I could go back and re-do that whole scenario. But if I did, would she have rejected me when we got back to our regular lives? Probably. She did put her foot down after the night-that-didn't-happen and demand that we keep it a secret.

She linked our fingers and laid her head on my shoulder. "I guess I may have overreacted a bit."

"You? Overreact?"

She shoved her elbow into my side. "I still hate that I got naked for you, and you could walk away. What does that say about me?"

She had no idea how beautiful she was, how much I wanted her. But I had to do the right thing and keep things neutral. "I had to take that call. I don't want to lose my job. Plus, it's like I said. I was in a bad headspace. Takes a strong man to walk away from you. Or an idiot. I'm guilty of the latter."

She tilted her head up, her glistening eyes finding mine. I hated being the source of the hurt that lingered in her gaze.

"Thanks for taking such good care of me, T-bird. First for saving my ass in the freezing cold, and now while I've been sick."

Her gaze floated down to my lips. On any other woman, the look would have been an invitation, but on Kylie...

Instinctively, I leaned toward her, noticing her sharp inhale, the way she stopped breathing. She might've said that kissing was off the table, but her body language indicated otherwise.

I paused, enjoying the tension radiating between us.

The more she denied it, the more I wanted to prove her wrong.

A heartbeat passed, then two.

I broke first. It was either devour her mouth or retreat. So I closed the distance between us and kissed her on the nose. Then, like a total pussy, I retreated, leaning back and cuddling her closer to me.

"T-bird, I've been thinking."

"Uh-oh, that's always dangerous."

She fiddled with the blanket. Again.

"Stop fidgeting," I said. "What's on your mind?"

"What would you think if I just shaved off the rest of my hair?"

I gave her my full attention, but she wouldn't look at me. I ran my fingers through the thin hair, letting the silk drift over my fingers. "You'd look like a total badass babe with a buzzcut."

Her eyes met mine. The insecurity and doubt reflected in her gaze broke my heart.

"You don't need my validation, Kylie." I traced the gentle slope of her cheek with the back of my finger, wanting to make all of this better for her. "Or anyone else's for that matter. You are beautiful inside and out, regardless of what clothes, or makeup, or hairstyle you wear. If you want to do it, do it. Fuck what everyone else thinks."

She ducked her head, then dropped her forehead to my shoulder.

"Will you help me shave off the rest?"

I froze, a hot ball of emotion settling in my chest. It must've been incredibly hard for her to ask. Touched that she would trust me with something so personal, I pulled her into a hug and pressed a kiss just above her ear. "I'd be honored."

I grabbed my clippers and set up a station in the kitchen. My diva playlist, as Kylie called it, cranked up over the Bluetooth surround sound, Whitney Houston declaring she was every woman. Kylie glided in with, finally, a spark of her old self shining through.

She perched in the chair before me, flinging her head as if she still had her long locks, and was tossing them over her shoulder. "Make me fabulous, T-bird. And try not to nick me in the process."

I swallowed hard against the trust she was showing me. "You got it, babe."

I made quick work, pausing to show off my dance moves when it looked like she might start crying, then led her to the bathroom mirror. I stood silent sentinel while she hesitantly faced her reflection, ready to step in and offer my support if she needed it.

She glanced into the mirror, and then away.

"You like it?" I asked, my voice gruff with emotion. Seeing her be so vulnerable and so strong pierced me right in the heart.

She faced the mirror again, surer this time, leaning in to check out the sides, then met my eyes in the reflection. "It's pretty badass."

If I hadn't been paying attention, I would've missed the tiny tremble of her chin. "You're damn right it is."

She turned and stepped into me, wrapping her arms around my waist. "Thanks, Thoren."

Emotion, a confusing mixture of sadness and pride and longing, clogged my throat. I didn't know what to say to her to make this any easier. Instead, I pressed a kiss to her temple. "I'll let you pick the movie tonight."

She was so fucking sweet. This spitfire woman, who was struggling with seeing herself as the rest of the world saw her, hiding her tender side under a smart mouth and sharp tongue. But I'd seen behind that mask of sassitude, and I liked what I saw.

She grabbed snacks and made us a nest while I cleaned up and started the movie. I climbed into the pile of blankets, draping my arm around her shoulders when she leaned into me.

"Will you drop me off at my apartment on your way in tomorrow?" Kylie asked quietly as the intro began.

Something sort of like dread rolled through me. "I will." I pressed a fist to the hollow feeling that settled at my chest.

She picked at the blanket. Her tell. She didn't want to go home any more than I wanted her to go. "It's going to be weird being by myself after you've been stuck up my butt for a week straight. I appreciate everything you've done for me."

"You won't even notice. I'm just glad you are feeling better. You can get back to work and hopefully, things will go back to normal," I lied. Things would never be normal again. I also hated knowing she'd be better off without me.

She shifted, her arms snaking across my torso. "Yeah, I guess."

As the movie started, she grew quiet, and my mind raced. What was I going to do without her? The past week, I'd had her to focus on. Before that, before the suspension, I'd let myself get out of control. I could admit now, that though I wasn't an alcoholic by the traditional definition, it felt like a slippery slope.

What would happen without her there to focus on? Would I slink back into my old ways of tipping a bottle when I felt like it? I hadn't even thought about taking a sip when I had her beside me constantly. I'd have to find something to distract me. But could I find something to distract me from thinking of her?

Chapter Ten

Thoren

My station was the newest in town, and the city had spared no expense. Extra-large, oversized black leather recliners sat in a row, facing the big screen TV hanging on the opposite wall. We had the nicest engine, the newest SUV, a tricked-out gym, a mini-pool table. We even had monogramed pillow covers. It was all over the top, but after a long day, those recliners were heaven.

Captain Collins flopped into the seat next to me with a groan. "Good job on that detail today."

We'd had a busy day full of out-of-the-ordinary tasks. We'd hung the flag on the main road, just down from the court square. The huge flag took two ladder trucks to display and was only brought out for the most special occasions, like soldier homecomings or funerals. This display had been for the funeral of a retired police officer who'd passed away at the age of eighty-five.

"Sure, Capt. I thought the wind might get us for a while. But we got lucky." I leaned my chair back and stretched out. "I don't know about you, but I'm fucking beat."

"Don't say that. You know what happens."

In my decade of experience, anytime someone complained of being tired, it meant we'd run calls all night. "I know. I hope I didn't just jinx our night."

It was my second shift back to work after the week I'd spent taking care of Kylie. While I hadn't had so much as a drop to drink, I'd come damn close to tipping the bottle out of sheer boredom. Instead, I'd picked up a pocketknife and some wood and began whittling, something my grandpa had taught me. The act took me back to a simpler time in life.

I grabbed a nearby newspaper and spread it over my lap. Then I pulled my knife and latest creation out of my pocket and began the mindful task of creating something from nothing.

"You have a problem with Nate today?" Capt's question came out of the blue.

"No, why?" Why would he ask me that? Had I done something to piss Nate off?

He kicked the foot part out on the recliner and threw an arm up behind his head, a casual position I figured was staged for a heavy conversation. Capt didn't do small talk. Didn't talk much at all. He was the kind of guy who if he spoke, you listened.

"Just noticed you taking over something he should've done."

We all chipped in and did the job; that was the nature of the fire service. If I sometimes stepped in, there wasn't anything behind it. It was just how I rolled.

"Me and Nate are good. I don't even know what you're referring to."

I turned the block of wood and started on the next

section. My mind whirled over what could've happened that caught the captain's notice.

He remained silent, flipping the channels to his favorite show that seemed to play on repeat on every cable channel we had.

"Just making sure all my guys are taking care of each other is all. Everyone has to pull their own weight around here. Don't want anyone to think they have to do everything. If Nate is too up his ass with his new lady friend and starts shirking his duties, I need to know. Slack in the little things, you'll slack when it counts."

"We're good. Nate's fine, I'm fine." Unless you counted being obsessed with a certain yoga teacher.

I replayed the day in my head, finally realizing I'd made sure the hoses got rolled correctly, something Nate would do as the one in charge of water flow.

"I'm sorry, Capt. Nate got intercepted by one of the teenagers in the Explorer program, so I jumped on the hoses. I didn't mean to step on any toes."

"Okay, I can respect that. Just make sure you let others handle their own responsibilities."

We sat in silence for a few minutes, him watching TV, me whittling away.

"Glad to see you getting your shit together," he said. "Just remember, if you need anything, let me know. You don't have to do everything alone." He paused for a beat. "What are you making?" Effectively dropping the heavy conversation.

I ran a thumb over the wood. "This piece is a replica of one my granddad made for me and my brother, a matching set. Mine went missing right after I left for college. I never carried it because it meant so much to me. Granddad had died the year before, and I didn't want to take a chance on losing it. Somehow, it still went missing during my first semester away at school."

I knew my brother had taken it, claiming it was his. Hell, he'd probably lost his own, or given it to a random girl.

My knife made a deeper gouge than I intended. "Fuck."

"Twins? Really? All this time I didn't know you had a brother. You went to different schools?"

I set the blade back to the messed-up part, trying to smooth out the nick. "Yeah, we're twins. He didn't go to college. He wanted to do the fire service."

I focused on the indentation. It wasn't terribly deep, but I knew it was there and had to fix it. I took a breath and relaxed my shoulders and hands, carefully scraping the sharp blade across the gouge until the surface was almost smooth. The act seemed to calm the immediate flash of irritation that came with mention of my brother. The piece was nowhere near perfect, and the tiny, marred spot would bug the shit out of me. Much like mentioning Loren did.

"He's actually the reason I'm a firefighter. Way back, we went to the fire academy together."

"What department does he work for?"

I held the knife still to keep from creating another gouge and tamped down the decade of guilt that threatened. "He doesn't. He never passed the academy."

"Damn, that's too bad."

If it could just be as simple as that, life would've been a whole lot easier.

"Yeah, it was his dream. Me living it caused a whole lot of family drama." That was putting it mildly. "My mother had begged me to teach Loren. To help him pass. And I'd tried, but when he couldn't pass after the third go round, I gave up. He'd do okay until it came to practicals."

I chanced a glance at Capt, stretched out in his recliner,

remote in hand and focused on the TV. It was easier to talk if I didn't have to meet his gaze. He always seemed to know too much.

I drew in a breath and focused on my whittling. "You can't teach someone to not be afraid of being in the middle of a fully involved container, no matter if it was a control burn or not."

He nodded. He'd been there, he'd know.

"Loren never learned to conquer his fear, to control it and use it to his advantage. He washed out of the program." He and Mom both blamed me. As if his failure was somehow my fault.

"You see them much now?" The weight of his attention shifted to me. I leaned forward in my chair, relocating the newspaper to the floor, more to avoid having to meet his gaze than anything else. A twinge of guilt over the calls I hadn't returned to Mom rose. I stuffed it into a box and firmly shoved it away. I'd talk to her, just...later.

"Nah. I got tired of defending myself to my mom. We don't talk much now because of it." A shaving dropped to the floor, and I toed it with my boot before picking it up. "If she only knew all the shit I covered for him, until I finally just couldn't anymore."

Capt didn't get a chance to respond because the tones dropped. Again. Thankful for the respite, I raced to the truck for my gear.

Hours later, we pulled back into the station, every single one of us grim-faced and covered in soot and dirt.

"Get your showers and meet me in the conference room in ten," Capt ordered.

A couple of guys from another shift met us in the hall, offering solemn looks and solid back claps.

I avoided eye contact with everyone and stepped into a

scalding hot shower to try to wash away the horror of the scene we'd just left. Between the conversation about my family and the call...there wasn't water hot enough to relax the tension that held me strung tight. My hands shook as I rubbed my face. I closed my eyes, turning my face into the spray. A flash of the tiny body curled up under the staircase burned through my mind.

I turned away from the spray, bracing a hand against the cold tile of the sterile shower as the tremors shifted and grew and rolled through my body.

Fuck, I hated this part of the job. I didn't have time for a breakdown. I had to get back out there and see what the next steps were.

In the conference room, Captain Collins sat at one end of the long table, elbows braced, and hands clasped before him, with an expression that would scare most people. The room filled as firefighters, not only on my shift, but from two other stations, filtered in.

Capt waited for everyone to settle, then spoke so quietly I had to strain to hear him. "No one should ever have to go through what you men had to go through today."

In the silence that followed, someone sniffled. A throat cleared.

I drug my gaze from my shoes to glance around the room, then stared at the floor again. My eyes lost focus, seeing only what we'd left behind at the scene.

"It's going to take some time to get over a scene like that. And don't think you're man enough to do it alone. In all my years, I've never seen anything that horrific." His voice broke on the last word.

I looked up to see him swiping a hand over his face, fingers digging in at his eyes.

"Those poor kids..." Big Mo whispered, tears streaming

down his face. Big Mo, a giant of a man with a big heart to go with it, cried at the drop of a hat. It was no surprise to see him doing it now. What I didn't expect was the sob that ripped from Nate.

Capt reached over and clapped him on the shoulder, squeezing it. "I know, son."

Silence hung as a room full of grown men grieved. Heads hanging low, tears flowing. All except for me. I was just...hollow. Unfeeling, unseeing.

After a moment, Capt straightened and cleared his throat. "I'll get us all scheduled with the counselor for a debrief. You'll go in solo. And you *will* go. For now, you're going to take the rest of the shift off. Go home. Go be with people who care about you."

My stomach roiled.

I couldn't go home. I couldn't face my empty house. The hollowness in my chest would cave in and consume me.

"I'm good to stay, Capt." I tried to make my voice strong and clear, so he'd have no doubt.

He levelled his no-bullshit, stern look on me. "No, Thoren. We're all released. Word came down from the chief."

Well, just fuck. Another fucking day off. This forced downtime was excruciating.

I stalled until I was the last one to leave, all but begging Capt to let me stay. To let me be active. To let me do something, anything, to keep from going home. Mom's ringtone blasted from my cell phone. I silenced it without answering, adding to the growing tally of missed calls I needed to return.

Agitated with every single part of the day, I stalked to my truck and pitched my bag into the back. Slamming the door didn't help. Neither did punching the steering wheel. With nothing left to do, I cranked my truck and pulled out of the station.

I'd just fucking drive around. Going home wasn't an option. I didn't have any wood to chop for my side business. Nothing to help drive the anger away and keep those four walls from closing in. Nothing to keep me from burying this hollowness in a bottle.

I'd done such a good job of staying away from alcohol. But if I was going to fail, today would be the day.

Like magic, I pulled up in front of Kylie's apartment. Who knew if she'd even be home, but suddenly my problems and fear of being alone were solved.

I braced a hand on the door frame, willing myself not to bring this bullshit on her, but knowing I was going to do it anyway. I was just that much of an asshole.

She'd probably not even see me, but it was worth a shot.

I waited forever, and then looked at my watch. Of course, she wouldn't be here. Given the time, she was probably at the studio teaching a class.

A short drive later, and I was pacing the wide, front porch at Blue Lotus, trying to gather the courage to go in, when the front door opened. The bright, happy tinkle of the bell inside grated on my ears...as loud and out of place as I was.

"I can hear you thinking, T-Bird." Kylie stood with an arm braced on the door, full of sass and attitude. "Why are you out here pacing, looking like you could burn the world down instead of coming inside?"

She had on a beanie with long hair flowing from beneath the ribbed cuff. The sight of the wig pissed me off, and I wanted to drag it off her head. I needed her–the real her.

I didn't know how to even voice the words.

I tried to speak, but no sound came out. Instead, I just stood there like an idiot, searching her eyes, willing her to read me, to get me. To know that I needed her to take the reins and make this better. To find me in this awful maelstrom of emotions whirling inside my chest.

A guttural sound rose from my throat and then she surged toward me, her arms coming around my shoulders.

Burying my face in her neck, I grasped her tightly and willed the pain to stop.

Chapter Eleven

K*ylie*

One minute I was closing the studio for lunch break and noticing a shadow passing in front of the window. The next I had a shaken Thoren in my arms.

Smoothing a hand over his hair, I whispered against his ear, "What happened, honey?"

He made no sound, just squeezed me harder, his face buried in my neck. His tremors shook us both.

For long minutes we stood on the porch, a telltale dampness chilling my neck. The only thing I could do was hold him.

Eventually his chest expanded against mine on a huge inhale, and then he pulled away.

I cupped his cheek, searching his eyes and finding a hurt so deep it stole my breath. Whatever had happened had shattered him. I didn't know what to say or do. Didn't know why he'd come to me. Did he just need to cry it out? Or be held? Whatever it was, I wasn't taking any chances that he'd slip off and go all suppressed-emotion on me.

I grabbed his hand and tugged him into the studio behind me, afraid he'd bolt if given the opportunity. "Let me get my coat, and we'll go somewhere."

We ended up at the park on the edge of town. Some of the trees had been replaced after a tornado had ripped through the previous spring, leaving parts of Newman destroyed. But with winter in full swing, holiday decorations had been put away, the grass was dormant, and the beds were stripped of flowers. Come next spring, the town grounds crew would rework the landscape and make it beautiful once more. Until then, the whole place looked sad and forlorn.

We strolled quietly along the paved path, holding hands, until we came upon a bench. I stopped, pulling Thoren down to sit next to me.

He sat, his uniform askew, shirt untucked under his heavy bomber-type jacket. His scuffed, duty boots remained unlaced.

The shaking had stopped, even the lingering tremors in his hands, but maybe that was because he gripped mine so hard.

I'd never seen someone look so devastated. I didn't know what had happened, but whatever it was had been bad.

After a few moments of silence, he sat forward, elbows to his knees, still holding my hand like it was his lifeline.

"Tell me what happened," I prompted, squeezing his fingers.

"We had this call." His throat worked as he tried to find the words, his voice was hushed and full of heartbreak.

"I swear, Kylie, it was the worst thing I've ever seen in my life." I held my breath, waiting for him to continue, and yet, not wanting to hear whatever he was about to say.

His throat worked again, tears glistening in his eyes before he slammed them shut. "There was a structure fire, and part of the family didn't make it out."

"Oh no." My heart broke for this man who hurt so badly, and for the family that had suffered the loss.

I tugged my hand free to run it over his back, needing to touch him, to wrap my arms around him. He was so much a natural hero. It was who he was, knit into the fabric of his being. Of course, losing one of the citizens he served would affect him.

"The screams of that mother...I'll never not hear that. And the bodies...they were so little." His voice cracked under the weight of what he wasn't saying.

"They? As in more than one?" My throat closed, painfully tight.

"Three," he croaked. "We failed today." The last word wobbled as a sob broke free. Thoren buried his face in his hands.

I did the only thing I could do and pulled him into my arms. Once there, with the truth out in the open, he finally let go and crumpled, sobbing into my chest. Giant, wracking, painful sobs.

There was something about seeing a big, strong man break down that pierced my soul. No words would bring back three precious little children. As protective as he was, it made total sense that he would take responsibility for the loss, no matter that he wasn't the cause. Just like he'd done when he'd stepped in to take care of me, Thoren took the reins and handled the problem. Only this time, the problem had been too big.

When he finally quieted, I wiped my own tears, then cupped his cheek again. Maybe it was my need to comfort him. Maybe I was tired of fighting the pull between us. All I knew was this man was hurting. We'd been through some heavy stuff together, and we kept coming back to each other. To provide comfort, to seek comfort. I could lie to myself and say it didn't mean anything.

But it did.

I let go of my stupid rule and leaned in and kissed him.

His soft lips were firm against mine. I'd caught him by surprise.

As I pulled away, he tightened his arms around me again, his eyes searching my face, still tortured, but now questioning.

This time when our lips met, the lingering connection that flowed between us ignited, and the world narrowed to his mouth on mine, our tongues dancing. Maybe it was all the years of denying kissing in my sex life, or maybe it was just that it was Thoren. But as he gripped my head, shifting to deepen the connection, driving us from solace to something more, I sank into the best kiss I'd ever had.

* * *

I hustled to answer a quiet knock at the front door. We'd gone back to Thoren's house, mainly because I sensed he needed to be in his own space but didn't want to be alone. He was back to acting mostly normal after his emotional release, but I was still concerned.

After some time outside, he had come in to watch a movie with me and fell asleep on the couch. We didn't speak of the kiss in the park, or what it might mean. Fine by me. Things were heavy enough. And if I could still taste him on my lips, that was just a bonus.

"Hey, Captain." I opened the door to Thoren's boss. I'd met Captain Collins once before at the hospital, when I'd gone with our friend Jordan after her boyfriend, Nate, had been injured in a house fire. Truth be told, I'd been super worried that Thoren had been injured, and had panicked worse than Jordan had.

He stood before me, hands in his jacket pockets, giving me an assessing look before nodding. Apparently, I passed his approval. "Hi, I was just checking in on Thoren."

Protectiveness rolled through me. "Isn't it odd to be checking up in person, instead of just making a phone call?" I couldn't stop the snarky attitude.

He'd been the one responsible for Thoren's suspension. Naturally, I assumed he was really checking in to make sure Thoren was holding it together and not drowning in a bottle.

A ghost of a smile stole across his face, and just that small movement took him from grumpy jerk to amused silver fox.

"I'm checking in on everyone, not just Thoren. Want to look them in the eye and make sure they aren't lying to me."

Oh. Well.

I glanced over my shoulder. Thoren was waking up from his nap, hopefully he wouldn't mind me inviting guests into his house. "He's hanging in there. You want to come in?"

My phone rang from the kitchen, blaring Jordan's ringtone. I opened the door wider for Captain Hottie, calling over my shoulder, "Come on in."

I took Jordan's call, moving to the kitchen so I could keep an eye on the men, and also not disturb them.

"Hey, are you with Thoren?" Her voice was hushed on the line. At my confirmation, she continued, "Oh good. He told you about the shitty day they had?"

Thoren, looking adorably groggy from his nap, and

Captain Hottie chatted in low voices across the room. Despite the nap, Thoren still had those awful shadows under his eyes.

"He did."

"I was thinking maybe we'd all get together and have dinner. Maybe try to take their minds off it."

"Captain Collins just came over. Why don't we send out an invite to the group and have them come to Thoren's," I volunteered. "Can you reach the others from their station?"

Jordan promised she could make it happen, and I decided to make myself useful by prepping the kitchen for company while also letting the men have their privacy.

There was something about Thoren's space that was perfect and cozy, but for whatever reason, it seemed to haunt him almost. I needed to repay the kindness he'd shown me when I'd been sick. Maybe having his friends here would change the energy, and they for sure could use some time together, working through that terrible call. Maybe doing this for him would ease some of my own guilt I'd been carrying at being such a burden to him lately.

A little while later, Jordan and Nate showed up, followed shortly by Mike and Leah bearing steaming hot pizzas.

I didn't know if Mike had been on that horrible scene, but he'd know about it.

The men were outside, sitting around the fire pit, while Jordan, Leah, and I were huddled in Thoren's kitchen. He had a long counter with seating for three. I stood across from them with my back to the stove, so I could look out the window facing the yard where the men chatted. Every so often, my gaze would drift over to make sure Thoren was still doing all right.

"So...you and Thoren?" Jordan asked quietly.

I grabbed a rag and wiped a non-existent spot on the counter. "Nah. Not really."

Why did admitting that make me sad? I'd gotten over being so mad at him after he'd shown up to be my nurse. But I would be lying to myself if I didn't admit I wished things had gotten more physical when we were stuck in his mountain cabin. Maybe if we had gotten it out of our system, I wouldn't be constantly thinking of him now.

"Jordan." Leah's soft voice had me pause my scrubbing and look up. I knew that tone. Judging by the smirk on her face, Leah was up to no good. "I think that, maybe for the first time in a very long time, Kylie is catching feelings."

I tossed the rag at her, horrified. "Shut your mouth. I have done no such thing." I absolutely would not admit that to anyone.

Her eyes closed to slits as she studied me. "I don't know that I believe you."

My best friend knew me too well. She used to, anyway. Now that she was with Mike, I saw her at the studio, but not so much outside of that. And that stung.

"I'm not the one that got a man and forgot she had friends," I blurted. Both of us blinked at the hostility that rang in my out-of-the-blue accusation.

"Um, do you guys need me to leave?" Jordan looked like she wanted to crawl under the counter. I didn't blame her. I wanted to do the same. Of all the people in the world, Leah didn't deserve my temper. Obviously, I was just being sensitive. Over the top.

Wasn't that what everyone thought of me, anyway?

I was too much for most people to handle.

Leah gaped at me, hurt flashing across her face. Ashamed, I ducked my head. "I'm sorry, Leah. I don't know where that came from. I shouldn't be taking my issues out on you." I toyed with the edge of my beanie, the special one that had extensions that matched my former locks, making sure it was still firmly in place.

"Why not? You're allowed to have feelings. And you're allowed to let someone know when they've disappointed you." She leaned forward, reaching out to me. "I'm sorry if I've neglected you. You've obviously been going through some things you needed support with. I just wish you'd spoken up."

But that was my MO, wasn't it? Just keep things surface level.

I'd been going through so much I hadn't told her about.

"I have a lot I need to share," I admitted, smoothing the locks that curled at my shoulder.

"You wanna start with why it looks like you're wearing a wig?" Jordan pitched in.

I arched a brow at her. "And here I thought I'd done such a good job of buying ones that looked natural, like my hair."

For a heartbeat, she looked stunned. Then a gentle, pitying smile graced her perfect face. I detested that look.

"There's nothing wrong with it," she countered. "If anything, I'm jealous, because your hair always looks amazing."

Her words floated over my sensitive self-awareness like sandpaper. It was the exact wrong thing to say. Jordan with the perfect blonde curls, and Leah with her perfectly messy bun. If they weren't so damn sweet, I'd hate them out of spite.

Once upon a time, I'd had fire-red hair with blonde streaks, and I missed it. I'd taken for granted that I'd always have a mass of thick, beautiful hair. Admitting it felt shallow and ridiculous and bougie. I hated every part of this stupid alopecia for making me feel less than myself.

"Not everything is as it seems." I spit the words at Jordan. "Sometime life isn't all peaches and cream there, Granola Girl."

Damn, why was I such a bitch?

Jordan blinked like I'd slapped her. I hated that I put that hurt look on her face, yet unable to stop myself from lashing out. Such a fucking rollercoaster of emotions. I had to end it.

With a huge sigh, I glanced out the window at the guys. They were out there dealing with hard core, real-life things that mattered, and here I was being hateful and mean because... Well, just because it was my default. My self-defense built by years of being put down and made to feel less than.

It took effort, but I forced myself to face Jordan. "That was uncalled for. I don't know what's wrong with me, why I feel like I need to hide behind the attitude. You're so sweet, and you don't deserve my temper tantrum. I'm just being bitchy."

Before I could reconsider, I reached up and snatched the beanie with extensions off my head.

Jordan broke off a small gasp, and I couldn't face Leah. Instead, I played with the extensions, the ones I'd had specially made to look like my original hair, hanging like a red and blonde waterfall from the cap in my hand. "I've had some stuff I've been dealing with."

"Honey, I think you've been keeping a lot bottled up." My best friend's voice sounded as shocked as I'd ever heard.

Leah left her chair and came around the counter, placing a gentle hand on my shoulder. "Kylie, what's going on?"

Tears flooded my eyes as I ran a hand over my patchy, shaved scalp self-consciously.

"I cut my hair right after I got back from my hiking trip because I couldn't stand looking at the reminder of who I used to be. Thoren buzzed it short for me during the week he took care of me."

"Are you sick?" Jordan finally found her voice.

I shook my head, watching my fingers run through the extensions. "I have something called alopecia areata. Basically, my hair is falling out. I noticed it in small spots at first, and I could cover it with strategic hairstyles. Then it just kept getting worse, the patches kept getting bigger, and I couldn't hide it anymore." I ran my hand back over my shaved head.

I couldn't bear to look at them. Somehow, my girlfriends seeing me like this was worse than Thoren seeing me. "It's been hard to teach class, constantly worried about my wig coming off and my secret getting out. My confidence really took a hit. The only thing worse than showing you guys is telling my parents."

Outside, Thoren had stood up and was gesturing to the other guys. Then he was heading into the kitchen through the back door. I struggled to slap the hat back on, but his voice stopped me. "Why are you putting that thing back on? Is your head cold?"

"No."

"Well, leave it off. Looks better without it anyway." He grabbed a bottle of water from the fridge and bustled out the door like he hadn't just rocked my world.

"He's right, you know." Jordan broke the silence. "You don't need the wigs. You're beautiful as you are. I can understand wanting to wear them. But you could also rock the hell out of that buzz you've got going." She floored me with her kind words.

But my friend, who I'd hidden this secret from, watched me with glistening eyes. Had I hurt her to the point she couldn't forgive me?

We'd been so tight, before Mike, before alopecia. Best friends for a decade. She had a giant heart and a sensitive soul. God, I'd missed her so much.

"You've been dealing with this alone?" Her voice was low and concerned, and I felt like an even bigger ass for not reaching out.

"I should've told you. But I could barely face the truth myself," I whispered, remorse coloring my every word.

"Oh, honey." Leah stood and came around the counter wrapping her arms around me in a tight hug. "You don't owe me anything. I'm just sorry I wasn't paying closer attention."

Jordan joined us in a group hug. "I love you guys. Kylie, we're here for you."

We hugged it out until Jordan suggested going out to join the men.

Mike's cell phone rang as we approached, and he paused to press a kiss to Leah's lips before sauntering to the edge of the yard.

Jordan slid under Nate's arm, and Leah went to sit in Mike's chair. I hung back awkwardly, not knowing if I needed to go stand next to Thoren, or to take the empty seat next to Captain Collins.

Thoren held his hand out to me, the simple gesture making something sweet bloom in my chest.

He tucked me into his side with an arm around my shoulders and placed a kiss on my temple. "You okay?"

"I could ask you the same thing," I hedged, poking a finger into his belly.

"You took off the wig in there. How you doing with that?" His eyes searched mine, the depth of understanding in them touching that fragile place inside me. The place I kept so guarded because it had been hurt so many times before.

I checked in with myself. My friends had offered no judgment. They hadn't stared or made me feel anything other than loved and supported. No one else acted like it was a big deal. For the first time in a long time, I felt like I could hold my head up and own my situation.

I slipped my hand into his and gave it a little squeeze. "I'm actually good with it, I think. Right now, anyway."

"Good." He laced our fingers and stunned me again as his lips pressed against my temple once more, leaving me floundering as to what all this meant while he turned his attention back to the rest of the group.

"Captain," Mike called, pocketing his phone as he rejoined the group.

"I told you guys before, call me Mac when we aren't at the station," Captain Collins all but growled. Jeez, he was hot for an older guy.

"Okay...Mac." Mike shifted his stance to what I referred to as Man Pose, legs braced as if he was about to impart some information the group wouldn't like. "Just got a call. They got the results on some evidence from this morning's scene."

Mac stilled. "They find something?"

"Yeah, it's a match to evidence they found last week."

"You think this latest fire was set by the same guy?" Nate asked.

Mac sat back in his chair and took a long swig from his

beer. It was the first time I'd noticed alcohol. I glanced around. Everyone was drinking except Thoren, and I immediately wondered how he was feeling.

I gave his hand at my shoulder a squeeze, drawing his attention. His eyes met mine, and like he could read my mind, his lips tipped up at the corner. He squeezed my hand back. *I'm good*, he seemed to say.

"Yeah, I do," Mike finally said. "And I'll tell you guys, they have a suspect, but they can't seem to find the guy to bring him in."

For years, we'd all had a running bet that Capt had been a cop at one point. In that moment, I was positive. Mike and Captain Collins had the same level, hard-ass look, the cop in them coming out.

He looked at each of us one by one. "This goes nowhere."

We all got real serious, real fast. Once he was satisfied we understood the gravity of the situation, Captain Collins nodded for Mike to continue. Mike had obviously taken his role as new fire marshal very seriously over the last few months. He'd gone from doing building inspections, to scene investigations. But no matter what job he held, I still saw him as the cop he'd been when he'd inspected Blue Lotus.

Before my eyes, he shifted from the laid-back man chilling with his friends into his cop persona, his gaze leveling on Thoren.

"His name is Loren Watkins."

I gasped. Beside me, Thoren froze, and every head turned to look at him.

Chapter Twelve

Thoren

Mike said my brother's name and all the blood rushed from my head. The fire still crackled. Kylie was still tucked under my arm. But all eyes were on me, and rage held me frozen in place.

"That cocksucker." The words came out low. Mean.

My own fucking brother.

This had to be why my mother kept calling me. A whole year of no contact from her, and suddenly, she's blowing my phone up. She knew he was up to something and was looking for me to save his ass. Again.

"Dude, is he related to you?" Nate exclaimed, wide-eyed in shock or anger or disbelief. It was hard to tell.

Leah and Jordan both looked concerned. I couldn't even look at Kylie.

I dropped her hand and paced away, unable to take anymore. These people had become my family over the years, and they were finding out my darkest secret. My brother was a criminal, and my family not only looked the other way, but they also expected me to handle the problems when things went sideways. I didn't want to be associated with that part of my past any longer.

Taking a moment to figure out what to say to the people who meant the most to me in the world, I stood looking over my land and ran through every possible scenario that could make sense. Nothing came to me. No way would Nate and Mike understand why I'd kept this secret from them.

Returning to the circle of chairs around the fire pit, I braced on the back of an Adirondack chair and looked at my best friends. A wild mixture of embarrassment and anger rose hard and hot. My own blood was the cause of the fires.

"Yeah. He's my twin." I dropped that bomb and waited. Mike, as lead investigator, would already know, but the rest of them needed to hear the whole story. "Not identical, but we look enough alike that I often got blamed for shit he did. He's been a criminal for a long time, stupid, low-level stuff. I had no idea he would do something like this." My voice trembled with the force of emotion behind them.

I looked at my captain. "I've spent my nearly my whole life cleaning up his messes, but I promise you, Capt. This is news to me."

Captain Collins peered at me with eyes that somehow saw everything. "I believe you."

Relief shot through me. For once, someone believed me over my smooth-talking loser of a brother without hesitation.

"Just like that?"

"Yes, just like that," he said with a nod. "I trust you with my life, and the lives of the men and women you work with. You say you didn't know. I believe you." Relief coursed through me. His words were a balm I hadn't known I needed.

"And why are we just finding out about your brother

now?" Nate bristled, pinning me with a look. I didn't know if that look said I was an asshole for dropping this bomb on them, or if he was just pissed in general about the whole situation.

Mike just looked pissed off. I felt like the worst friend, keeping secrets from them. But really, I'd just tried to eliminate my toxic family as much as possible.

"It's not that I don't trust you guys. I just don't have anything to do with him, haven't spoken to him in years. Not since I graduated the fire academy after he failed out. He hated me for graduating and living his dream. Every time we talked, we fought, until I just gave up. I got tired of dealing with the constant bullshit from him and my mother, who believes that I should never have continued pursuing a career in the fire service without my twin brother."

"Why did you?"

Why did I? I pushed away from the chair and gripped the back of my neck. A flame danced around a log, mesmerizing in the way it licked along the underside, following up the length of log.

"My brother had been infatuated with the dance of the flame, wanting to harness its beauty, to control it. He became obsessed with it, wanting to pursue a career playing with fire. Turns out, he couldn't handle being in an active fire and would freak out.

"There were so many times my brother fucked something up where I came to his rescue, helping him get out of whatever jam he'd gotten himself in to. Doing his homework so he'd at least graduate high school, giving him alibis with Mom when he'd come home late and stoned.

"When Mom begged me to put a pause on my college classes, and go through the fire academy with him, I'd grudgingly agreed. I hadn't been too fired up on college anyway, but I knew I was going to do something with my life. I'd done all my core work and couldn't decide which direction to finish with. Going to the fire academy gave me a purpose. Made me realize that I wanted to do more than a regular job."

Nate nodded. He was the most agreeable of my crew. Mike, however, kept his expression unreadable.

"I didn't plan on it, but once I got to the academy, I knew the fire service was what I wanted to do. Problem was, it was Loren's thing, and they felt like I was disrespecting him. Like I was somehow doing him a disservice when I continued the coursework. He couldn't pass the control burn portion of it. Kept getting scared when the time came to do practicals. They were both furious that I didn't quit when he failed out."

"It meant something to you," Mac stated.

I nodded. "Yeah. By the time I got through the academy, it wasn't just his thing anymore. It became mine as well."

"What's up with the drinking?" he fired back, taking me by surprise with the change in topic.

Kylie stood and circled the chairs, coming to stand beside me in a silent show of support.

"Honestly, I don't know if I have a problem or not. I just know that it's either all or nothing. I can't seem to stop once I get started. So, I'm just trying to stay away from it."

It was hard facing this truth for myself, much less admitting it to these people who meant the world to me. "The fact that I want a drink more than anything right now, but I wouldn't be able to stop at just one, tells me it might be a problem," I admitted.

Mike stood and crossed over to me. Kylie bumped my shoulder and slid away as he took her place. I watched her retreating back because it was easier than meeting Mike's gaze. I waited for the judgment, for the derision in his voice, the confirmation that I was totally fucking up. Instead, he clapped me on the shoulder in a show of solidarity. "Let me know how I can help. Both with this, and with your brother's situation."

Nate joined our little huddle. "Yeah, Thor. You aren't alone in this. If you need us, you call."

"Thanks," I croaked through a tight throat, amazed by my friends and also ready to be done with this whole conversation. "What do I do about Loren? Do I try to contact him?"

"Let the authorities do their thing. You stay out of it," Mike advised.

"Um, guys?" Kylie called from the fire pit. "So...I think I saw him a while back."

Mike spun at that bombshell. "Where?" Damn, he sounded like a mean bastard sometimes.

"At the hospital when Nate was there a few months ago. I could've sworn it was Thoren passing through the emergency room, in a maintenance uniform, but he had a hat pulled down low. But then, Thoren was there in the lobby in his bunker gear. I thought it was weird at the time, but then I got all wrapped up in worrying about Nate. Honestly, I'd forgotten about it until just now."

She sounded too casual, fiddling with the fire poker, jabbing haphazardly at the already-stoked fire. I knew Kylie well enough by now to know there was more to that statement. For whatever reason, she wasn't giving them everything.

"Where was Loren the last you heard?" Mike asked me.

"Last I knew he was down near Savannah."

"Why would he be here, now?"

"To make my life a living hell? I don't know. I haven't seen him since I moved here."

"There any reason to think he might be targeting you?"

Was that what Loren was doing? Deliberately starting fires that I would respond to?

"Not other than what I've already told you. But who knows with Loren? He's always been the baby and blamed me for everything that went wrong in his life. I moved hours away, so I could make a fresh start."

Mike's stern expression had the hair standing on the back of my neck. "You're a long way from any neighbors out here. Keep an eye out just in case he decides this is some personal vendetta."

The conversation turned, and I tuned it out, playing Mike's warning over in my head. Another round of beers went by, and this time, they didn't even bother to offer. A gesture I appreciated.

That my brother could be the one causing the destruction, hurting people, made me sick to my stomach. What could take him so low? Why was he doing this? It had to be related to me. Otherwise, why would he be targeting my community?

Though I remained distracted, it felt good to be with my friends, even amid chaos. I appreciated that they were all with me and gave the guys—even Captain Collins—a hard hug and back slap as they left.

Kylie found me at the fire pit, dousing the dregs of embers, after she'd walked everyone out. "Are you okay?"

I set the water pail by the back door and met her in the doorway. She'd finally ditched that ugly-ass hat and stood with a shoulder leaned against the door frame, bald-ish head gleaming in the light, concern written all over her face. She was so beautiful. Not just on the outside.

"Hey sunshine, what was up with your comment about seeing Loren at the hospital?"

Color rose high on her cheeks. "What about my comment?"

She turned away, avoiding me, and I knew for sure that she was hiding something then.

"Come on, I know you well enough to know you didn't tell them everything. What'd you leave out?" She fussed with the seat cushions on the outdoor furniture, plumping pillows that didn't need plumping.

I stepped into her space and took her hand, turning her to face me. "Come on, tell me."

She heaved a huge sigh. "I don't want to. It'll just go to your head."

"You said you thought you saw me. Were you there looking for me?" A smile tugged at the corner of my mouth.

That adorable blush grew higher, and she wouldn't meet my eyes. A blushing Kylie Monroe was a beautiful sight, and I liked this version more than I liked the sassy smartass side of her. She was proving to be more than I'd ever expected. Kind, sweet, nurturing, and still could be a total ball-buster.

"It's okay." I couldn't stop the grin from spreading across my face. "You don't have to say it."

She tugged her hand, but instead of letting her go, I pulled her closer.

I dropped the teasing and caught her chin, forcing her to meet my eyes. "I didn't know what I needed earlier. I just knew that I needed you." I trailed the back of my finger across her hairline. "Today was one of the hardest days I've ever experienced on the job." I swallowed thickly. "I'm not sure I'll ever be able to forget that scene."

Kylie slid her hands around my waist and leaned into

me, allowing me to hold her. All teasing from the moment before was gone.

"I'm so sorry. I don't know what to say or do to make it better."

"You being here helps." I kissed her forehead. "Will you stay?"

"Of course."

"Thank you. For being here. For supporting me." I wanted to tip her face to mine and lose myself in her lips like I had in the park earlier. But I didn't know if her position on that intimacy had changed, and I'd respect her wishes, no matter how bad I wanted to bash the rule. I'd take what little comfort I could in this moment. Even if I wanted more.

"Come on in, it's cold out here," she said, pulling away from me. I missed her immediately.

After following her inside, we took turns getting ready for bed, and met at the hallway to my bedroom, her arms full of pillows.

"What are you doing?"

She shrugged. "We're having a sleepover, I thought I'd make a pallet. A reminder of the cabin."

The cabin, where she thought I'd rejected her because I didn't want her, when in fact it was just me fucking everything up again.

"I've got a better idea. There's a perfectly good bed in here, and I promise to be on my best behavior." I tugged a pillow from her and lowered my voice. "I just don't want to sleep alone."

She grabbed my hand. "You're not alone. I'm here. We'll get through this night and any other nights." The truth of her words shone in her eyes. She'd be here if I needed her.

As I rolled into the bed and lay there, trying not to

touch her, replaying the events of the day. My mind kept returning to the moment that stood out above all. That kiss. The way she felt in my arms. Even now, my body responded to the memory of her mouth on mine.

She turned towards me. "Thoren?"

"Yes?"

"Did you notice what happened earlier?"

"You mean when you laid one on me? Yeah, it was the best part of my day."

Her fingers played with the hem of my t-shirt. "You're the first guy I've kissed in a really long time. It meant something."

I turned to face her, trying to get a look at her face, to make sure I was hearing her say what I thought she was trying to tell me.

Taking a chance, I rose on an elbow, leaning over her, but giving her space to pull away if she wanted to.

With movements slow and sure, she reached up and cupped my face, urging me closer, until our lips met in a soft caress.

And I was in heaven.

Cupping her jaw, I cherished this offering. It was more than a kiss. This was Kylie letting me know that I meant something to her. That whatever this was between us meant something.

I broke the kiss, my breath coming harsh as my blood raged through me. "I'm not fool enough to take this for granted. This means something. Doesn't it, sweetheart?"

She leaned up, nipping my bottom lip in answer and I lunged, pressing her to the bed, drinking from her lips as if she alone could give me life.

At her push on my shoulder, I rolled to my back, absorbing her weight as she rose over me. I smoothed a hand down her back, wrapping my arms around her, inhaling her scent, and getting lost in the silk of her mouth.

Our breaths came hard as our tongues tangled. I didn't know where I stopped and she began. All I could think of was *more*.

"Now is the time to stop if you don't want this to go further," I whispered against her lips, not trusting my voice.

"Just promise me you won't change your mind halfway through this time," she panted.

"Baby, wild horses couldn't drag me away."

Chapter Thirteen

Kylie

If anyone had told me that I would be the one to initiate sex with Thoren, especially after feeling like he rejected me, I would've called them a damn liar.

But one taste of his lips, and that simmering tension between us exploded. I knew his body. Every part of me wanted to feel him inside of me again. But this act, this intimate mouth-on-mouth action, was new for me, and it was beautiful.

I kissed him like I'd never get enough of his pillow-soft lips, and that magic suction thing he did. I wanted him to kiss me everywhere. But more than that, I wanted him naked. Now.

Struggling with his shirt, I tried to strip him without breaking the connection. "I need your skin on mine," I commanded against his lips.

Chuckling, he wiggled his body, doing his best to accommodate me, while also trying to get me out of my clothes. We became a desperate flurry of tangled clothes and thrashing arms.

With a gasp of accomplishment, I wrangled free and sank against him, relishing the warmth of his body, the way his sparse chest hair tickled my sensitive nipples. Losing myself against the feel of his skin on mine.

Eventually I broke away and sat back, running my hands down the wide expanse of his chest, enjoying the way his muscles rippled under my fingertips.

He flexed his hips, pressing his hard length against me, his heated gaze setting me on fire.

"I need you," I gasped. Wrapping a hand around his length, I knelt and grinned up at him. Slowly, I licked him from base to crown, trailing my tongue over the veins on the underside, and swirling around the engorged head.

His lips fell open on a groan. Reveling in the pleasure that surged through me knowing that I could make this man putty in my hands, I made sure his eyes were trained on me as I took the tip of him in my mouth.

"Ah God. Fucking A, Kylie," he said, his chest heaving.

I sucked him to the back of my throat, letting my teeth barely skim the ridge of his crown as I withdrew.

Two strokes later and he flipped me over, spreading my legs. "Gotta say, I'm glad we're done with the no-kissing rule." He looked down on me like he wanted to devour me. "Sorry, sweetheart. I gotta taste you."

The cool air hit my wetness, a delicious contrast to my heated skin as he fell between my parted thighs. He lifted a leg over his shoulder, tugging me where he wanted me. Then, his mouth was on me.

"That no kissing thing was stupid anyway," I gasped as he licked my clit with enough suction to make my toes curl.

What a fool I'd been to miss out on this pleasure for so long.

He paused. "So, you've had that rule for a while, and not just with me?" he asked, nipping the sensitive skin of my inner thigh.

Embarrassed heat flashed over me, and I couldn't answer.

"So, it's been a while since anyone has done this?" He slipped a finger inside me.

My breath hitched and my body clenched around him. "I haven't been with anyone since that night that you and I..." I gasped, robbed of the ability to speak as he slid his finger out, spreading my wetness through my folds, and back up to circle my clit again. My hips canted in search of more.

"Hmmm. So responsive," he murmured with appreciation. "I wonder if..."

He didn't finish his sentence, and I didn't care. His tongue traced my folds, and then he sucked my clit.

An orgasm bloomed low, building heat at my core in a way I'd never experienced. I cried out, fisting the sheets, needing more of the pleasure he was unleashing in my body.

"Come for me, Kylie."

I liked that he used my name. That he validated me being there with him. As if he saw me for me and didn't offer any shiny platitudes.

He shifted his fingers, and I was lost, exploding under him in a wave of pleasure.

I floated down, trying to catch my breath as he withdrew his hand, sliding it up, leaving a glistening trail of my wetness on my thigh. "I'm not done with you yet. Condoms're in the drawer. Put one on me," he demanded.

I fumbled as I unwrapped and slid the condom on, his shaft throbbing against my hand. He notched the crown at my entrance, eyes glued to where we joined, and slid deep inside, stretching me in one smooth move.

His eyes rolled back as his eyelids fluttered close. "Fuck, you're so wet."

I thrust my hips seeking more. "I need you to move."

"Just hold on, give me a second." He hovered over me, head hung, eyes closed.

When they opened, his gaze locked with mine, the intensity so heady, it felt like a physical touch.

Then he began a slow glide out, then slammed back into me.

"You feel amazing," I gasped. "Do that again."

He withdrew slowly and drove into me again, causing us both to groan.

"I can't do controlled this time, Kylie."

This time.

"Oh yes," he growled. "We will definitely be doing this again. But this time? I'm taking what I want from you. You're mine."

He rolled his hips, shifting so that he hit that magical spot deep inside. His hand at my leg slid down to my belly, creating pressure on my pelvis. Then his fingers grazed my clit. And between the pressure of his palm on my pubic bone, his fingers on my clit, and his dick thrusting inside me, I exploded in the most intense orgasm I'd ever had.

"Beautiful," he whispered. "Watch me."

I opened my eyes to see him throw his head back as he ground into me. Deep inside, his cock pulsed as he released his pleasure.

He was the one who was beautiful. Strong and graceful,

tender but erotic. I could spend a lifetime watching him come.

I moved my leg off his shoulder, suddenly feeling vulnerable, wanting to hide under him.

As he collapsed over me, he cupped my face in his palm, capturing my lips in a kiss. He tasted of me.

His arms slipped under my shoulders, and he rolled us over, never breaking the kiss.

I felt him slide from my body, still semi-hard.

"Let me take care of this condom, and then we are doing that exact thing again."

"We are?"

He kissed the tip of my nose. "I'll be fucking you all night long." Another nose kiss "Get ready, Kylie. Now that I've had a taste of you, once won't be enough. Not this time."

* * *

Waking up next to Thoren had become my favorite thing to do, even if I didn't want to admit it. Technically, we'd slept together for the better part of two weeks. But waking up to him wrapped around me, spooning me after a night of epic love making, was a whole different experience altogether.

I turned in his arms, sliding a leg between his, enjoying the skin-on-skin contact.

He shifted, allowing me to burrow into him. I pressed my face into the curve of his neck and felt his hand cup my head, as if he liked that. Then he ran his hand over my hair, his fingers stroking me in a gentle caress.

The sweet action made my heart hurt. What I wouldn't give to have my long hair back, so I could feel him running his fingers through it.

Fighting off the feeling that I wasn't enough for him, I slid from the bed. Thoren seemed to like this new me. As much as he did before. In fact, it almost seemed as though he liked me more now than before I'd started losing my hair.

The thought was sobering.

In the bathroom, I stood in front of the mirror, trying to gather the courage to make myself really study my own reflection rather than just gloss over the image before me.

My hair had grown out a little and looked like a patchy buzz cut.

Thoren came up behind me, wrapping his arm around my middle, encircling me in a hug.

"What are you doing?" His voice sounded low and intimate in my ear and my body responded by relaxing against his.

"Trying to come to terms with my reality," I admitted through a tight throat.

He dipped his head, finding that sensitive spot behind my ear, where he nipped, sending shivers skittering cross my skin. "What? That you're drop-dead gorgeous?"

I rolled my eyes. "That is so far from the truth."

His head popped up, his eyes meeting mine.

"That's the truth, Kylie. You are a beautiful woman."

His words touched a sore piece of my heart. A hollow emptiness where my self-worth used to live.

"You don't believe me." His tone held some surprise. Then he turned me around, looking directly into my eyes. "Why don't you believe me?"

I didn't answer. Couldn't.

My mother's voice echoed in my mind, reminding me to always make sure I looked my best. To make sure I wore the right clothes, fixed my hair, never left the house without makeup.

"It's just hair, Kylie." His words drew me out of my head when I remained silent for too long.

"I know." Logically. But I didn't really believe that. I couldn't. So much of my upbringing had centered on outward appearance, mine and others'. And how shallow did that make me?

"No, I don't think you do. Let me explain it a better way." He spun me around to face the mirror again.

"Watch," he demanded.

Trailing a finger over my bare hip, he said, "Your beauty isn't because of the skin that holds your bones." His finger skimmed up my belly, circling my navel. "Your beauty is because of your heart that feels so strongly for others." His hand traveled the valley between my breasts. "The way you take care of the people in your life." He traced the ridge of my collarbone. "The way you nurture your clients to be the best version of themselves." His palm lay flat at the base of my neck, cradling me. "It's your honesty."

His hand caressed up my neck, his thumb tipping my chin up until I was forced to face my reflection in the mirror.

"Your beauty is in the twinkle in your eye, the smile you give to others, and those come from your generous heart."

He kissed my cheek and rested his against my temple. "It doesn't matter if you have a head full of hair or if you're bald or if you have warts on the end of your nose. That doesn't change who you are on the inside. Only you can let this determine how it affects you."

He kissed my cheek again and left me to stare at myself in the mirror.

I couldn't hold my own gaze for more than a minute, though I tried. It was hard to see myself the way he saw me. Frustrated, I flipped the light off, leaving the room. Maybe someday I'd see myself through his eyes. But today wasn't the day.

I found Thoren in the kitchen glaring down at his phone. Images of that feral look in his eyes, the deep V between his brows as he pumped into me, his dirty talk...all had heat pooling low in my belly.

"What's wrong?" I asked, my voice coming out more husky than I intended.

Thoren heaved a huge sigh, obviously immune to the hormonal challenge he was putting me through. I filled a glass of water and met him at the counter.

The sun streamed in through the front windows, highlighting his handsome bedhead. The open floor plan allowed the light to fill the space, washing it in a soft glow. I loved the openness of his house. He needed a few plants, maybe some throw pillows. Definitely some art on the walls.

Like a record scratch, I halted those thoughts. What was I doing? Redecorating his space after sleeping with him?

"Just another missed call from my mom," he grumbled, "followed by yet another text. It's to the point now that she knows I'm avoiding her, but I can't call. I don't know what to say." I left my water on the counter and wrapped my arms around him. "I can't imagine what you're going through right now, T-bird. It's a lot, but you're not going through it alone. I'm here for you if you need to talk about it."

Chapter Fourteen

*K*ylie

Walking into the Blue Lotus studio felt like coming home. After being away for so long, first with the trip and then being sick, I had a newfound appreciation for the simple aesthetic we'd created. It felt good being back into a routine, and walking on a cloud of post-orgasmic endorphins didn't hurt either.

Thoren had shown exactly how much he appreciated me being available to him, by bending me across the counter.

The front lobby was welcoming, set up with benches and cubbies for our students to store their items while they practiced. A restroom and smaller private session room, where we hosted women's circles, lined one side of the building. On the other side of the hall, the main, large group room even held tracks for aerial yoga.

When Leah and I had designed the concept for our studio, we'd envisioned every detail. We collaborated on the program designs, but she maintained the aesthetics and did most of the marketing while I handled most of the book-keeping. We made a great team, even if our numbers were a little low.

Leah entered the office and lit a candle, one of her many rituals. "How's it looking?"

"Doing financial statements is not one of my favorite things," I grumbled.

She plopped into the plush beanbag chair on the floor, sitting cross-legged, one of her favorite poses. "Necessary evil. Is it any better? It seems like it's better. Our classes are filling again."

I reviewed the bottom line again and shook my head. "It's better, but we are going to have to get some more diversity in our structure if we are going to stay open."

Leah's brow drew in confusion, then she smiled. "We could brainstorm activities in the community to bring awareness."

Anxiety at hosting a class outside of our normal space speared through me. Not because I didn't want to host. But our studio was a safe space. My clients knew me, knew us. I'd quit wearing my wigs and had been accepted by the clients I saw regularly. It was another thing entirely to put myself out there with potential new students.

But could I step outside of my comfort zone if it meant growing our business?

"We could host some sessions in the park," Leah began, "maybe offer some free or donation-based sessions, to bring in new people. Maybe pick charity a month to give the donations to?"

I nodded, liking the idea. I looked over the numbers again. "I don't think that's going to be enough. We need to branch out. Maybe look into a contracted type of work."

Leah looked adorably confused. She was one hell of a yoga teacher and designer. She was not the best businesswoman. That fell to me. "Like if we teamed up with a local business for some corporate-type sessions?"

"Yes, exactly like that."

She snapped her fingers, her eyes lit, and energy radiated off of her. "Karen mentioned last week that she went to a beer yoga thing at Lone Creek Brewery. What if we try to get in on that?"

"I mean, that's the idea, but they already have a program." I didn't want to shoot her down, but I was skeptical.

"Okay, so let's make a list of all the places we can think of that might be interested in a partnership. How about that community up north? They have that goat farm. We could do goat yoga on their market day."

Her enthusiasm was contagious, and it took me right back to when we'd first had the idea to start our studio. She might not be a savvy businesswoman, but she had creative ideas in spades.

She continued, "Or maybe the Humane Society would be interested in bringing some puppies. Plus, you could still call the brewery and let them know we are interested if they want to add additional classes or need a fill-in teacher."

Her expression was so earnest it made me want to try all of her ideas.

"Okay, I'll make some calls."

An hour later, I walked out on a high of energy to find Leah cleaning the teapot station.

She faced me, hope written all over her face. "So? How'd it go?"

I gripped her hands, and the bags of tea she'd been holding scattered.

"Leah! Oh my gosh, it worked. I called the brewery. Their regular teacher is moving, and they need someone new. I guess one of our clients goes there and was bragging on us! The manager recognized our studio by name and wants us to come do a working interview!"

A line formed at her brow. "How will that work? Do we both teach? Because I already have full classes on Saturdays."

I gulped down the fear, knowing that she wouldn't want to change the schedule on her current clients.

"I know." I swallowed thickly. "I would do it." The thought was both exciting and terrifying.

Leah squeezed my hand, her gaze searching mine. Her expression shifted from concern to confidence. "Yes, and you would be amazing at it."

"But—"

She squeezed my fingers again. "No buts. I know this is a scary step for you. You are the best teacher I know. And you have a way of making people feel calm and comfortable." My best friend watched me so earnestly, I began to believe her. "You can do this, Kylie. When is the class?"

"Tomorrow."

The front door of the studio opened, and Jordan's voice rang down the hall. "Hey, ladies! What's going on?"

Leah dropped my hands and spun. "Kylie is going to audition for a teaching position at a beer place!"

I cracked up at both Leah's choice of words.

Jordan's face screwed up in confusion. "Ohhh-kay?"

"What she means is, there is an opening at a brewery to teach a yoga class for their beer yoga series. I'm doing a trial run as the instructor."

"Oh, how fun! I bet the guys would go with us for that."

Jordan's whole face shone with excitement. "We could go be your pep squad."

And this was why I loved my friends.

"That would actually be awesome. I'm kind of nervous about it."

Her hand landed on my arm, giving me a reassuring squeeze. "Don't worry. We've got you."

* * *

The next day, I looked out from the small temporary stage at the students holding their star pose and felt pride swell within me. The brewery was wall-to-wall yoga mats and sweating patrons. All the tables and chairs had been removed, and the entire room was filled with rows of beer-drinking yogis. It was an amazing sight.

Some people were flush-faced, some had shaking arms. But they'd all done everything I'd asked of them. Even chuckling at themselves when they couldn't hold a pose. A group of ladies in the front row were all breathing heavy but looked so peaceful with their eyes closed. In the back row, Jordan, Nate, and Thoren were doing their best to keep up.

The positive energy in the room flowed through me in the best way.

I'd kicked ass teaching this session, and it showed on the faces of my students.

After I offered the group peace and light and released them, one of the ladies from the front approached. I stood and swallowed the instant nerves at talking to a stranger. I'd chosen to represent the real me and had gone sans hat. It was time to embrace the new me. I couldn't very well preach self-love and not love my own body the just way it was. Hiding behind my wigs felt fraudulent.

The woman offered me a shy smile. She'd been looking at me most of the time. I was definitely wary of what she'd say, feeling super self-conscious about my bald head.

"I just wanted to say thank you so much. That class was amazing."

I smiled at her genuinely. "Thank you, I was really nervous coming into an established class. I'm so glad you enjoyed it."

Her friends gathered around and began discussing how amazed they were at how good they felt after the session.

As they gushed and complimented me, I looked over their heads to find Thoren watching me. Pride shone in his eyes. Pride for me. He gave me a thumbs up and pointed at the bar, asking if I wanted something. That he'd come to this place, when drinking was a concern for him, meant something. I watched as the bartender filled a glass of water and a seltzer. Being here wasn't testing his resolve. He could handle the challenges that came his way.

And as the ladies left and I cleaned up my mats, I realized that I could handle it, too.

I looked out over the room again. No one paid attention to me. They were all smiling and relaxed. I'd done that. I'd helped them find that happy glow. Years of helping clients find their yoga practice proved beneficial. I didn't have to be some super zen yogi, or some rockstar instructor. I just needed to be myself.

My strength came from my abilities, my knowledge. I was more than this exterior. I could face these trials and make them wins. Even if we didn't get this contract, we could do something else. Expand our business in other ways and continue to grow.

The manager of the brewery approached me, a wide

smile on his face. "That was amazing, Kylie. I'll be in touch next week."

I beamed at him. "Thanks, David. I appreciate the opportunity."

As I finished my clean up, several students inquired about where they might take another class. Thoren waited patiently until I'd finished with them, then offered me a seltzer. "Reward for a job well done."

"Thanks." I accepted the glass with a wide, goofy smile on my face. "That was pretty nerve-racking."

"Really?" Jordan peered out from behind Thoren. "We couldn't tell. You did amazing! A real pro up there. And the people loved the class. Everyone is talking about it."

"I can't believe I'm even here, but the pre-yoga beer was worth it," Nate said, wincing at Thoren. "Sorry, didn't mean to be insensitive."

Thoren waved him off. "Dude, it's fine. I'm good with it. I've just decided that I do better when I don't have anything. I don't even have a craving for a drink."

"No shit?" Nate's eyebrows shot up his forehead. "That's great. But let me know if it makes you uncomfortable."

Jordan grabbed Nate by the arm. "Come on, let's go get in line for the food truck. I hear those empanadas are amazing. Kylie, y'all grab a table, we'll be right back."

Thoren pulled out a tall chair for me and stood with his arm across the back, his side pressed close to mine. "You did great up there." The approval in his rumbly voice spread through me, warming me from the inside out.

I peered up at him. "Really?

He brushed the back of a finger across my cheek. "Yeah. That guy's a fool if he doesn't hire you."

"Well, I don't know—"

"Trust me," he said, leaning close enough that I was the only one who could possibly hear him. "Look around this room. Look how happy you made all these people. You have a talent, Kylie. I'm glad you took a chance on yourself."

That pride I'd had right at the end of class swelled again, making my throat tight. I leaned into Thoren. "I'm so glad you were here. It helped having you out there to focus on when I got nervous."

He pressed a kiss to my temple. "You didn't need me, babe. You had this in the bag. But I'm glad to be your support crew. Anytime."

I closed my eyes as the sweetness of his words washed over me. What would it be like if I could always count on him to be there for me? I had no doubt that Thoren was loyal, and if he said he'd do something, he'd do everything in his power to make it so.

Nate and Jordan came back with our food, and the four of us sat enjoying our downtime while a steady stream of yoga participants walked by and thanked me for the session.

As we packed the car to head home, I smiled to myself. If I landed this contract, it would go a long way toward expanding our cash flow. And for the first time in a long time, the thought of teaching new people didn't fill me with dread.

Chapter Fifteen

K*ylie*

After beer yoga, we dropped Jordan and Nate off at their house, grabbed some steaks, and went back to Thoren's. The evening was cool but nice enough that we planned to grill.

"Have I told you how grateful I am that you aren't as picky an eater as Leah is?" Thoren asked as he prepped the steaks.

I sat across from him at the long counter, assembling a salad, still riding the high of a successful day. "She's not picky, T-Bird. She's vegan."

"I don't even know what that means other than she doesn't eat meat."

We were still in our workout clothes, and I took a moment to appreciate the way his sweats draped over his body. The way they framed his efficient movements. I'd borrowed his hoodie at the brewery and now I snuggled into it, loving being surrounded by the scent of him while doing this simple chore of cooking a meal we would share.

Letting my guard down with him had been the best

decision I'd ever made. I slid off the stool to give him a hug. Who knew that badass Kylie liked to cuddle so much? I shook my head at the thought. Being with Thoren was opening my eyes to so much about myself.

Like how I enjoyed being held as I fell asleep.

Or how I liked knowing he'd have dinner ready for me when I got out of class.

"Did you have fun today?" I asked, planting my chin on his chest to look up at him.

His arm snaked around my waist. "Of course, you're dead hot in those leggings. I was looking at your ass the whole time."

I swatted his chest. "No you weren't, I was facing you the whole time."

"Well, I was at least imagining how many of those poses we could do together."

"Were you now?" I smiled slyly and rubbed our hips together, enjoying the feel of him growing hard between us. "You know, there's this thing called Tantric yoga I've been wanting to try."

"If it involves more of watching you, I'm game." He waggled his eyebrows, earning a laugh and a swat from me. "You were beautiful up there today. You looked so happy."

I flushed at his compliment. "I don't know about beauti—"

A finger landed on my lips, shushing me.

"I'm serious, Kylie. You looked so happy and confident. You paid attention to every person and made them each feel seen, and they ate up every minute of it. The whole thing was beautiful to witness."

He stunned me. Touched me somewhere deep in my heart of hearts. Without knowing it, he'd just given me the greatest compliment I'd ever received. He'd seen people touched by something I offered. Something other than phys-ical beauty, something that went straight to my heart and bloomed.

My practice was about empowering my students and helping them find their inner peace, the same way I was learning to find mine. "Thanks for being there today."

Thoren kissed my nose and released me, grabbing the steaks on his way out to the grill.

After dinner, we were cleaning the last of the dishes when his phone rang in his pocket, and he let out a groan.

"What's wrong?" I asked.

With a low rumble of exasperation, he silenced his phone without answering. "My mother keeps texting me and calling me. I've got half a dozen missed calls from her."

"What do you think she wants?"

He paced the length of the small kitchen. "She probably wants me to step in and help my brother out." His hand flew out towards his phone. "I haven't talked to her in over a year. I imagine she's only calling now because Loren is in trouble."

I leaned back against the counter to stay out of his way. Considering I hadn't even known he'd had a twin until recently, I had to assume they didn't have a close relation-ship. People didn't hide their family or go without commu-nication for just any reason. And Thoren was such a good soul, I couldn't imagine him cutting someone out of his life unless the reason was extreme.

"Are you going to?"

He spun, giving me a disbelieving look. "Hell no."

His terse words hung in the air. I shoved my hands in the hoodie pocket to have something to do with them. The room grew chilly with his sudden change in mood.

"Are you going to call her?" I asked.

He looked torn. "Part of me wants to, just to confirm my suspicions."

That made sense. I nodded. "But do you think it's a good idea to talk to her, especially knowing your brother is a suspect?"

I poured a glass of water to have something to do while he pondered my question. Once I turned back, he mumbled, "Probably not."

I set the glass of water on the counter and went to him, wrapping him in a hug.

"What's that for?" He stood stiffly against me.

"You just looked like you needed it."

His body softened, then his arms closed around me. "See? Beautiful," he whispered, and placed a kiss near my ear.

I pulled away, leaning up to press my mouth to his.

"Why don't you think about whether you want to talk to her, and if maybe you need someone of the law enforcement variety to be with you when you do? In the meantime, I'll try to take your mind off this situation."

"What'd you have in mind?"

With a sly smile, I backed away, tugging him toward the bedroom. "We'll think of something to pass the time."

It was late when a knock sounded at the door. Thoren pressed a kiss to my hip, then rolled out of bed. Moments later, I slipped into one of his flannel shirts, tugged on my leggings, and went to see who kept him from coming back to me.

He stood in the open doorway, one hand on the door, his muscular shoulders filling the space, blocking whoever was outside.

"I'll ask you again, what the fuck are you doing here?"

Intrigued and alarmed by a tone I'd never heard from

him, I tried to peer beyond to see who'd brought out this side of him.

"Just wanted to drop by and see my brother. Can't I do that?"

Oh my God, Loren was here. I grabbed my phone, ready to call 9-1-1. I didn't know if they had enough evidence to bring him in for questioning, or if that had already happened.

"No," Thoren barked. Startled, I dropped the phone. "I thought I made myself clear last time I saw you. I'm done bailing you out, letting you take from me. You need to get the fuck out of here."

His voice vibrated with anger.

"Oh, now," Loren taunted. His voice was nearly identical to Thoren's, but creepier. "You don't mean that."

"I damn sure do. I've got nothing to say to you."

I snuck to the kitchen, trying to get a good look at the man terrorizing my town. Through a crack in the doorway, I caught a glimpse of him. His hair was a bit longer than Thoren's, and he didn't seem to be nearly as filled out. But otherwise, from what I could tell, if they'd both been wearing a hat and the same shirt, I wouldn't have been able to tell them apart.

"Who's that pretty little thing hiding in the kitchen?" Loren's tone changed, and all the hair on the back of my neck stood on end.

Shit.

Thoren's free hand shot out, blocking Loren. "None of your fucking business, Loren," Thoren barked. Geez, it was hard saying their names together, what had their mom been thinking?

Loren spoke again, his voice quiet, and Thoren's entire

body went rigid. And then he lunged. Loren chuckled a low, sinister laugh. "You always were so easy to provoke."

"Okay, brother. I guess I'll see you around."

Thoren stepped back without a word, slamming the door.

He whipped his phone out of his pocket, jabbing at the screen. "Mike. Loren was here."

I crossed my arms over my chest, not entirely sure if I should say something, or if I should go back into the bedroom. It seemed that I'd done enough by getting Loren's attention.

"I didn't let him in, didn't try to apprehend him. I just wanted you to know he made contact. I'm trying to keep my ass out of trouble here."

I stood, rooted in place, helpless to ease the agitation rolling off of him.

He gripped the back of his neck so hard the muscles in his forearms stood out. "Of course I'm upset. I don't want anyone thinking that I'm helping him, especially if he's guilty of what they think he is."

A pause followed as he listened.

"I don't know where he's staying. I didn't get much info from him. Mostly, I just told him to get the fuck out of my sight. But Mike. He saw Kylie."

My heart skipped a beat with his pause. Why hadn't I just left well enough alone?

"Yeah. I'll keep you posted if he makes contact again."

He hung up, returning the phone to his pocket. Blowing out a frustrated sigh, he spiked his fingers through his hair.

It had to be hard, knowing that someone you were supposed to love was being accused of such terrible crimes, especially when you'd always been the one to look out for that person. Disappointment rolled from him in waves. He looked so beat down and forlorn.

I crossed to him and ran a hand up his arm. "So, that was kinda fucked up. Are you okay?" I wanted to take away this trouble for him. Bring back my happier Thoren.

"Not really, but I will be."

He'd come a long way from the guy in the cabin, the one who believed he needed a stiff drink to make it through a tough situation.

"How can I help?" I asked, pressing a kiss to his bare chest.

"You being here is what I need." He gave my waist a squeeze. "But I'm concerned that he saw you. I wish he hadn't. There's no telling what he'd do."

In this moment, my issues about losing my hair seemed vain and superficial. I was ashamed of how much I'd let it affect me. His brother, who he'd felt responsible for his whole life, was possibly an arsonist.

"We'll make it through this," I promised, pressing my lips to his.

I'd do everything I could to help. Thoren didn't deserve this heartache and drama. He deserved all the happiness. I'd just have to find a way to make each moment have a little sparkle of joy until we could get through this.

Picnics always seemed to make everything better, so I texted Thoren to meet me at the park.

It was empty, because we were the only people crazy enough to have a picnic in winter. But the day was fairly warm. It was winter in the South, after all, and we were having a glorious fake spring day.

I laid out containers of soup, some sandwiches, and a small cheese board on the metal fixed table and watched as Thoren's truck pulled in behind my Jeep. He slid out of the seat, slipping on a ball cap, then glanced up and caught me watching him. An adorable grin spread across his face.

He was fucking sexy in a ball cap.

No matter how much I chided myself, I couldn't drag my eyes away from the sight of his long legs, eating the distance between us. He had on baggy sweatpants, well-worn and amazing in their ability to clearly outline his dick as he strode towards me. It was very distracting.

"What's that look for?" He tipped the brim of his cap as he kissed me then took the seat next to me, crowding into my space like he couldn't stand to be away from me a moment longer.

All I could think about was the fact that he was obviously going commando, in sweatpants. And any woman alive would be tuned in to that fact. The thought of another woman getting even half the show I was had me seeing red. "What in the hell are you doing?"

He drew back at my sharp words, confusion written all over his handsome face. "I'm meeting you."

"Where are your normal clothes?" The words were shrill, almost hostile, and it was his fault for making himself so, so...available for everyone to see.

"What? I just came from the gym."

Jesus Christ. He'd been free-balling at the gym? With scads of underdressed, super-toned ladies?

"What's wrong with what I'm wearing?"

Bless him, he looked so innocent. Did he not know that loose-fitting sweats were most women's catnip?

"You're telling me, you went to the gym wearing that?" I flicked my hand indicating his choice of outfit.

"No, I put this on post workout. After my shower." He looked down at himself. "I forgot to bring my normal clothes. I had these in my truck..." He seemed to realize what my issue was as he glanced down at the half-hard state he seemed to stay in whenever I was around. His gaze darted to mine, a sly grin lifting on one side of his handsome face.

"Is that why you were checking me out so...hard when I walked up?"

Cheeky bastard with his emphasis on hard.

"I wasn't checking you out. And also, you can't just walk around in public like that," I ground out. My libido was perking up. I did not want my libido to perk up.

"Why? No one is looking at me except you."

"You couldn't know that when you pulled up. There could've been a park full of unsuspecting females, just waiting to get an eyeful of Tiny Thor."

"Did you just call my dick Tiny Thor?" His eyes lit with amusement. He sidled closer. "I don't know if I like the sound of that. I think you mean Mega-Thor."

"Quit being ridiculous. The point is, you need to at least wear underwear if you are wearing those sweatpants."

"Why, Kylie...," he said as one stupidly perfect brow rose, "are you jealous?"

My cheeks burned. I was ridiculous. I knew I was ridiculous. But still. He was walking around with his obvious well-endowedness on display, and I did not like it. Not one bit.

He braced an elbow on the table—the very small table—leaning in close, surrounding me, every cell in my body completely and incessantly aware of his. "I think you are." He scooched closer, trailing his nose over the sensitive shell of my ear. "I think you like the thought of having my body all to yourself."

My breath hitched, all the blood in my body racing to one very specific spot between my legs. I squirmed in my seat, which only made him chuckle.

"So I'm not the only one affected here," he murmured. "Good to know. Besides, the state of Tiny Thor would be your fault."

He licked a line up the column of my throat, eliciting a whimper from me. I was freaking powerless against this tiny spot, and he fucking well knew it.

He knew all my secret spots.

Snaking an arm behind my back, he leaned closer, his body warm and hard pressed next to mine. "What'd you bring for lunch, Kylie?" God, his voice. Throaty and low. Promising.

He picked up one of the crackers I'd laid out for our lunch and flicked it into my lap. "Oops, I dropped one."

His big hand found my thigh, long fingers sliding up and up, stealing my ability to focus on anything other than what he might do next.

"Remember that time you grabbed my junk at the bar?"

I opened my mouth to answer but was robbed of breath as the sneaky bastard slipped his fingers between my legs, pressing the tight bundle of nerves over my leggings. I writhed in my seat, wanting more.

A little panicked and a lot turned on, I glanced around the park. There were a couple of runners stretching at one corner, but I didn't see anyone else.

"I was helping you out. Your fly was unzipped." I clenched my thighs together against the onslaught of his fingers. The pressure was exquisite.

"Yeah, and payback is hell. Isn't it, beautiful?" He made another circle with his thumb.

A little moan escaped the back of my throat. "What are you doing?"

"I'm just getting that cracker I dropped. I wouldn't want to make a mess." It sounded like that's exactly what he wanted.

"Other than that, I'm meeting my girl for lunch." He was all innocence as his thumb hit the exact right spot.

My body shivered in response.

He chuckled. "She seems a little tense," he said, like it was totally natural for him to grope me in public. "Maybe she thinks some other woman caught my eye."

His tongue traced my ear, before gliding back over that sweet sensitive spot.

Desire shot through my system.

My fingers itched to turn the tables and give Tiny Thor a good long stroke. It'd been a solid week since we'd been together. He'd been called in for overtime at the station, and I'd had a girls' night out with Leah and Jordan.

I'd finally made it a point to invite him to lunch because it seemed like the only time we could spend a moment together.

"You're coming back to my place after your classes today," he said, his voice a low sexy rumble.

"Yeah, and we're going to talk about your choice of words a minute ago. Your girl?" I clipped, squirming in my seat, thankful for the metal table and food laid out that might block the view of any passersby.

"Yeah." He slipped his hand inside my pants, spreading my legs, granting him access. "Mine."

God help me, I liked the idea of belonging to this man. I

gripped his wrist, letting out a soft moan as he slid a finger along my crease.

"We'll have to be quiet. As much as I love your sounds when you come, I don't want to share them with anyone else. Can you be a good girl and be quiet while I finger you in this park?"

I blinked, trying to get my eyes to focus again. More runners were gathering in the corner. Damn, it must be a running club. Oh my God and they were all older ladies, who would surely be scandalized to witness Thoren getting me off in broad daylight. And maybe a little jealous.

"You can't do this, Thoren. We can't do this."

"Sure we can. Besides," he slid a finger inside me, causing my breath to hitch, "I can tell you like the thought of getting caught."

I let out a slow breath, trying not to pant, because damn him. He was right. The thrill of possibly getting caught sparked a fire in me and had me clenching harder around his finger. I was so close.

"God, I can feel you how much you want this." His throaty groan only heightened my arousal. Our eyes met and held. "I've got you Kylie. Trust me."

With his smooth moves and the delicious thought of doing something illicit in public, I tucked my face into his neck, as an orgasm barreled through me.

Thoren's cheek rested against mine as we caught our breath. Too soon he leaned over me, placing a kiss under my ear as he settled my shirt back. "Beautiful."

He slipped his arm around my back, gathering me close. I leaned into him, floating on a post-orgasm high, noting that the running group had grown.

"I can't believe you just did that," I whispered.

"You like it, though. And it was fucking hot." He kissed my cheek. I loved these little displays of affection.

The ladies were done with their stretching and were beginning to power walk towards us. Heat spread across my cheeks. We'd been so close to being busted.

"Looks like we were right on time." Thoren chuckled.

"No kidding."

I recognized a flash of white hair bustling amongst the group. Mrs. Francis O'Malley, Leah's neighbor, a cantankerously fun elderly woman. I wanted to be just like her when I reached my golden years. She waved at me and gave me a giant wink.

"Hi there, Kylie. Is this your fella?" she called, batting her eyelashes at Thoren. Never let it be said that Mrs. Francis wasted an opportunity to flirt.

"Mr. March from last year, right?" She sidled up to him, running a wrinkled hand over his shoulder.

"Francis, behave!" another white-haired lady yelled.

"Oh, stuff it, Eunice," Francis muttered. To me she whispered, "She's just jealous." Francis eyed Thoren again. "Are you in the calendar again this year?"

"Yes, ma'am."

Her mouth turned down in a pout. "They messed up my pre-order and then sold out before I got my copy. They said they were doing another print run, but it's been forever that I've waited, and I'm starting to lose my patience." Her gaze traveled the length of his torso.

Thoren blushed adorably under the old woman's scrutiny, immediately earning more rubbing and flirting from Francis.

"I'm certainly excited to see it, even if it'll be two months old by the time I get my copy. I can't wait to see you and that handsome Mike be shirtless!"

"Come on, Francis! Leave those love birds alone," someone from the group yelled from down the path.

"Um, Mrs. O'Malley, your group is leaving you," I said.

"It's alright, honey. Eunice will need a pee break when we get to that bar at the block. I'll catch them there."

Needing a break right at the bar seemed like excellent timing. They'd definitely get refreshments while they were there. With a wink in my direction, Francis spun and hustled to meet her friends.

"She's so awesome. I want to be her when I grow up." I chuckled. Francis rejoined the group, and they rounded the corner, every elbow swing and brisk step in sync. Like a flock of exotic birds, all dressed in their flashiest gear.

A tiny thread of unease trickled along my senses as they passed out of sight. Maybe I was hypersensitive because of that excellent orgasm Thoren had given me. It wasn't like I'd screamed out loud, but I couldn't shake the feeling that we were being watched. I scanned the park, trying to find the source of my unease. Lord help me if some mother and child had been witness.

Movement at the corner of the woods, on the back edge of the park, caught my attention. All the fine hairs on my arm stood on end. A man emerged from the tree line, too far away to see the details of his face, but I could feel his stare. I froze.

"What's wrong?" Thoren asked, tensing beside me, like he felt the threat too.

"There's a guy over there, watching us. It's giving me the creeps."

Thoren's entire body went rigid as he spotted the guy.

"Do you recognize him?" I asked.

"Too far away to be certain." Thoren unfolded and stood, facing the direction of the lurker. He took a step forward, blocking my view. I shifted in time to see the guy turn, skirting over the hill and out of sight.

"Fuck," Thoren growled and spun, gathering our things.

Now it was my turn to ask what was wrong.

"It's time to go."

In a flash, Thoren had our things loaded up and was ushering me by an arm to my car.

"T-bird, chill," I demanded. "What the hell is going on?"

"I hate that he got a glimpse of you when he came to the house. Now to see him out here..."

Thoren picked up the pace, his long legs eating the distance, and I had to practically run to keep up. "Please tell me what's going on. You're scaring the shit out of me."

"I'm almost positive that was my brother. I haven't seen him in years, and now I've seen him twice? Something's not right."

I thought of the women's group. Dear God, he couldn't hurt those sweet old ladies.

My mind flashed to the fun Thoren and I had been having moments before, and my face heated. What if Loren had witnessed that?

We reached the cars, Thoren let go of me long enough to toss the remains of our picnic in the backseat, and then he herded me into his truck.

"Thoren, what about my car?"

"Mike and I can come get it later. I don't want him having any more information about you. He's seen you. That's too much as it is." The agitation in his voice did little to calm my nerves.

Like a total psycho, he locked me in and bolted around the front of the truck, missing my epic eyeroll. Thoren jumped in the front seat and I unloaded. "Over-protective much? He's not going to snatch me while you're running around like a weirdo."

"Kylie," he barked, then paused as if he were trying to calm down. "I'm trying to keep you safe." He shut down the rest of the conversation by cranking his truck, slamming it into gear, and peeling out of the parking space.

I bit my tongue. Grumpy Thoren was fun to tease. Mad Thoren I didn't like so much. He made stupid decisions, like tossing me into his truck without discussing the situation with me. We drove around, making ridiculous loops and backtracking until Thoren felt it safe enough to head to the yoga studio. He parked in the back parking lot, and hurried us to the back door.

I stalked to the office with Thoren hot on my heels, dropped my bag into the desk drawer, and spun on him. "Are you done acting like a neanderthal?"

His fists clenched in response.

Guess I was still dealing with Mad Thoren.

We had a stare off until Thoren visibly relaxed his shoulders. He closed the distance between us, raising a hand as if to cup my jaw. The daggers I shot with my eyes stopped him.

He let his hand drop and stepped away. "He's a suspect in at least one of those fires, Kylie. The evidence is light, but they're still investigating. Protecting people and property is my job. Don't get mad at me for trying to protect you."

I relented a little, trying to imagine how I'd feel if my twin brother was an arson suspect. *Pretty shitty.*

The muscle in his jaw ticked as I waited him out. "When I opened that door to him, I didn't recognize the man looking back at me. His eyes had this crazed light. It worries me."

In two steps I was pressing my palm to his chest. The

angry glint in his eye quelled a little with my touch. I rose on tiptoe and kissed him. "Okay."

His brow furrowed. "Okay?"

I kissed him again because he was there, and I wanted to make the bad feelings go away. "Yeah, okay. Just talk to me. You're not in this alone."

His hand came up, his fingers brushing across my hairline, making me regret that I didn't have a curl for him to wind his finger around, or a lock that he could tuck behind my ear. "He's already suspected of arson. The evidence we have linked him to empty structures, but what happens if he escalates? It's not coincidence that he was in that park. He's come to my house. He saw you. What if he put his sights on you?" Worry flared in his eyes once more.

This conversation was headed nowhere. Hardheaded Thoren was now in the room, so I did the only thing I could do, and hugged him tight. "We'll figure it out. Okay?" I said against his chest.

He never answered.

Chapter Sixteen

Kylie

K I don't know what I expected to happen, but it certainly wasn't the radio silence I got after Thoren left the morning after we'd seen his brother. I'd laid my heart out to him, vowed that we'd make it through his trials together, shared my darkest secrets with him, and done things with him I'd never done before. We'd been through enough to at least warrant a return call of one of the seventy million messages I left.

The first day, I'd taught my classes and though I checked my messages, I received nothing from him. By that evening I called, figuring it wouldn't hurt to just let him know I was thinking about him. Straight to voicemail.

The second day, when I'd received no response again, I realized he'd been on duty, and even though it was unusual, I let that one slide too.

The third day, I'd gone to my doctor and gotten a good report, and wanting to share it with Thoren, sent out yet another text, this time keeping it light. No reply after this, either.

After a week of nothing, I was well into the hell-no-with-this-asshole phase and ready to punch him in the junk the next time we crossed paths. How dare he just fucking ghost me? After all the emotional moments, the fabulous sex... I'd even broken my own rules and kissed the guy, for fuck's sake.

What a fool I'd been. The radio-silence sent me straight into a neurotic crisis. Why wasn't he calling? Was he done? What did I do or not do that made him decide I wasn't worth his time? And why wouldn't the ache in my chest go away?

Had I really let my guard down so much that I'd fallen for the guy? I glanced at the sad-looking woman staring back at me in the mirror, not quite able to meet her eyes. It hurt not being enough for someone. I swallowed back the tears and forced myself to take stock again, like I'd done in that blasted mountain cabin.

My hair was growing back and should continue according to the doctor.

My complexion was a tad sallow from not getting enough fresh air. It definitely had nothing to do with a freaking no-show firefighter.

"No more," I told my reflection. "You are a badass even if you don't feel like one right now. Get back on the horse girl. Don't waste another moment on Grumpy-ass Thoren Watkins."

I dug out my best outfit and best wig. Now more than ever before, I needed to arm myself with the things that used to make me feel like a million bucks.

I did my makeup in full on drama-mode, then I strapped on my highest heels.

One last glance in the mirror and I decided I'd have to fake it until I made it, to mask my broken heart.

My phone rang as I locked up my apartment. "Hey Leah."

"Can you please, please go and check on Mrs. Francis?"

The panic in Leah's voice had me hustling to my car. "Yeah, sure. What's wrong?"

"She was all in a tizzy, and I guess she dropped her phone or something. I couldn't get her to answer me, but I could hear her yelling at someone."

I agreed to check on her, halfway intimidated at what I might find when I got there. Knowing Mrs. O, it could be anything. She had a penchant for finding the best gossip and also skirting the edge of trouble.

As I pulled up to the quaint little row of bungalow houses, Mrs. O'Malley stood at the top of her steps. The porch stretched across the front of the house, with rockers to one side of the door and a cozy porch swing on the other.

"Oh, good. It's a party night," she squealed as I rounded the front of my Jeep.

"Hi, Mrs. O. What's happening? Leah wanted me to come by and check in. Are you okay?"

"I'm just fine, but that joker down the street better not come rolling by my house with that racket thumping from his vehicle again."

I wasn't exactly sure what she was talking about, but it was unusual to see her so riled up.

"Why don't we have a seat, and you tell me what happened?"

She teetered over to her rocker, using the porch rail to brace herself. Once seated, she took a hefty pull from her tea mug.

"Whatcha got in that mug, Mrs. O?"

"The tea wasn't cutting it. I had no choice."

I lowered to the chair next to her, a half empty bottle of

bourbon sat on the porch. Her eyes were wild, her cheeks flushed. She really was upset.

"What happened? You look frazzled as all hell."

"Well, you would be too if some jackass came by, blaring his music loud enough to rattle your dentures. I was enjoying my perfect evening, and then boom boom boom, thump thump thump. I couldn't hear myself think, Kylie. It's like he deliberately drove slower and slower, so that he could harass everyone in the neighborhood." She flailed her arms in a wide circle on that last bit, the contents of her mug splashing over the top.

"My phone was ringing off the hook. Gladys down the street was worried to death. You know she wears hearing aids and is sensitive to sounds. Leah called right after I got off the phone with Gladys. I reckon I was a little riled up. Then I did what the rest of these fools were too chicken to do, and I handled the problem." She finished with an affirmative nod.

Oh no, this didn't sound good.

"Mrs. O, did you call Mike?" I had a feeling she hadn't. "He could've called in some of the guys from the department."

"Well hell no," she cried. "I didn't have time to waste for the boys in blue to show up. Plus, I had to be strategic with my timing and hide so he wouldn't see me coming."

"I'm almost afraid to ask," I muttered. Dread pooled in my belly as I spied what sat beyond the empty bourbon bottle. "Why is there an empty egg carton on your front porch?"

She sniffed loudly and drained her mug, downing what was probably straight alcohol in a single gulp. "Like I said, I handled the problem."

An older-model, neon green Geo pulled to a stop in

front of Mrs. O'Malley's house, dripping in busted-up eggshells. The trunk of the car rattled with every beat of the bass.

"There's that little shit again. He lives in the neighborhood, down in the cul-de-sac, and is always driving by with that rattle mobile." To the young man she called, "Came back for more?"

A red-faced teen, looking barely old enough to drive, crawled out of the driver's seat and stood in the middle of the road. "You're gonna get it, you old biddy. You trashed my car, and you're gonna clean it up."

Mrs. Francis wobbled to her porch rail, half hiding behind the column. "I told you to turn that racket down!"

His arms flew wide as he yelled, "You can't just throw things at people, lady."

"I can do whatever the heck I want. You've lived in this neighborhood long enough to know how to act."

It was definitely time to defuse the situation.

I straightened my shoulders and arched my back, making sure I caught his attention. Using my best slow, sexy walk down the sidewalk to his car, I stopped on the opposite side of the nauseating car. When his eyes latched onto my hips and breasts, I clasped my hands in front of me, making sure to push my breasts high. Teenage boys were so easily distracted. At least I still had sex-appeal to someone.

I channeled Marilyn Monroe. "Hey there. What's your name?"

He licked his lips and squeaked, "Jeremy."

I offered him my most seductive smile. "Well, hi, Jeremy." I breathed his name, watching his pupils dilate. "Did you just get a new sound system in this sweet ride?"

It was fucking hard to keep a straight face, but I had to,

lest Francis get it in her head to perform her version of justice again.

His lanky arm reached out to lovingly wipe away an eggshell.

"Yeah, I just got it this weekend. I was just cruising around, and that old biddy came out of nowhere, pounding my new baby with raw eggs. Now I gotta go wash her again."

There was absolutely nothing new about this vehicle. Except maybe the sound system, which probably cost more than the car.

"Well, Jeremy," I lowered my voice conspiratorially, "she gets cranky, because your sweet ride here interrupted her evening." I gave him a wink. "Why'd you come back?"

He shrugged, looking sheepish.

"Were you going to give an old lady a hard time?"

Color bloomed on his acne-scarred cheeks.

I tsked then added, "You know, if you want to cruise, rather than driving through a neighborhood, you could hit the parking lot at Mickey D's. That's probably where all the cool girls are anyway."

His eyes lit. "Hey, you're a girl." It was incredibly hard to keep my eyeroll in check. "You think I'll get noticed in this beauty?"

Oh, he would definitely get noticed. Probably not in the way he wanted. "No doubt about it," I lied, fishing around in my purse. "Here." I offered him a five. "Swing by and get a car wash on your way. And maybe turn your radio down when you go through the neighborhood."

"Okay. Thanks, lady." His beaming smile turned quickly to a frown. He climbed into the car, muttering about finding a touchless carwash, then pulled away.

I walked back up the sidewalk to find Mrs. Francis leaning against the door.

"Thanks, dear. Now, come inside and tell me where you're going dolled up. Are you meeting Thoren? Honey, he's a looker."

An hour later, I parked my car at my apartment and walked the two blocks to my favorite bar, ready to put Thoren behind me.

The Alamo was housed in a hundred-year-old building. Once upon a time, it had been a theater, and the owners had embraced the historical vibe. Arched windows, antique-looking lighting fixtures, a red-velvet stage curtain. The old theater marquee still lit the sidewalk, announcing special events. I marched under the lights, fueled by female empowerment, ready to take on the world.

Mrs. O's version of a pep talk had started with her inquiring where she could get a pair of red stilettos "just like those" and ended with me pouring my heart out to her, admitting that Thoren had ghosted me for a week, and now I didn't know if I wanted to see him or not.

She'd pursed her lips after pulling out her annual calendar and finding a picture of Thoren. "Sounds like you were in deep. Best way to get over that kind of loss, is to get back on the horse. But I'll tell you this. No matter how good he looks or how special you think he is, if he can't treat you like the queen you are, he's not worth your mascara."

Only when I walked into the bar and saw him sitting there, elbows on the bar-top, shot glass in front of him, my anger did a one-eighty.

He looked dejected, his hands cupped around that

stupid glass like he was breathing it in, savoring it before tossing it back.

Recalling Mrs. O's "queen" talk, I stomped down the steps and let righteous indignation take full reign of my emotions.

By the time I got to him, every hurt feeling, every bit of anger, all the self-conscious berating, everything I'd pushed down for a week, came roaring to the surface.

"You son of a bitch." I was yelling before I even reached him.

Heads turned at my outburst. Every one except Thoren's. Did he turn around and face the music like a grown ass man? No. No, he did not. His eyes closed as he hung his head. Like just hearing my voice exhausted him.

Well. Fuck him.

Marching up to his side, I unleashed a barrage of every curse word I could think of, so much that the bouncer threatened to haul me out if I didn't settle down.

Finally, I got control of myself, glaring down anyone that made eye contact with me. "What are you looking at? You've never seen a woman lose her shit? You wanna be next?"

Only after all of that did the jackass move, lifting only his head to look at me. "Are you done?"

This motherfucker. "As a matter of fact—"

"Good, because I have something to say. You're gonna listen, and I'm not going to yell over you, or repeat myself." His eyes flashed.

Inhaling sharply, I crossed my arms over my chest, hitching my hip to the side in what I hoped was the perfect body language for, "You can't hurt me anymore." Though, now that I'd unleashed my angry rant, the only thing left to feel was exactly that. Hurt.

Why hadn't he called?

Why hadn't he messaged?

Was I so insignificant to him?

Every soft word about how beautiful, how desirable I was, every soft look he gave, every tender caress. All of it was a lie.

I gestured for him to continue, hoping that I still wore the mask of anger. I couldn't bear the thought of letting him see how he'd hurt me.

Guarded eyes assessed me.

Finally, he turned to fully face me, one arm on the bar, one on the back of the chair, thighs spread wide. Completely open to me and looking at me with...longing in his eyes?

"I didn't mean to be an asshole." His words were spoken so softly, I took a step closer, lowering my head so I could hear him. "I didn't mean to hurt you." He swallowed, his gaze roaming my face like he was memorizing me. "If there was anyone in this world that I could be happy with, that I'd even consider spending my life with, it would be you. I meant every single word I said to you, Kylie. You are beautiful. Intelligent. Strong. I'd love to spend my life making up for the past week and how I hurt you."

His eyes misted as he stared at me. "I'm a fool for you. I'm a fool because of you. But we can't go any further than what we had."

The words drove the knife deeper into my heart. Sitting drooped at the bar like he carried the weight of the world on his shoulders, he looked as if it hurt him as much to say the words as it hurt me to hear them.

"I don't understand," I whispered like a pathetic, lovesick fool.

The corner of his mouth lifted in a sad smile. "I know, sweetheart. I'm so sorry."

An eternity passed as I studied the resolve in his eyes. Something was wrong in this situation. I was missing something. Why would he do this? I broke the intense stare off between us, my gaze landing on the still-full shot glass.

Steeling my voice and nodding at the glass, I asked, "What's that about?"

"That's me, trying to find answers at the bottom of a bottle," he admitted on a sigh.

Disappointment warred with my other emotions. "Is it working?"

With a slight jerk of his head he said, "I've been staring for hours every night. Nothing's helped so far."

He didn't exactly say it, but I chose to believe that he meant he'd not had a drink, since the glass was still full. Plus, it also sounded like he'd been pining for me too. My pitiful heart cracked, splintering the haze of anger that lingered.

"Thoren," I whispered. "Just tell me what happened. I'm so confused."

The noise level in the bar had returned to normal levels. In the far corner, over by the digital jukebox, a couple of girls stood making music choices. In another corner, a group of men in golf wear downed beers. Along the bar, people chatted. In our space though, the air was charged with things left unsaid.

His eyes swam with sadness. "It has to be over, Kylie. I'm sorry."

Why? I wanted to ask. We'd skirted around each other for so long, finally coming to a place and time where it worked. We fit so well together. Almost as if we'd been meant for each other. My mind couldn't make sense of the words.

"Is there a reason? Did I do something?" I was sure my heart was in my eyes, and this was so unlike me to almost beg him to take it back. To take me back. To vow that I'd change or that we'd fix whatever was wrong.

I didn't recognize myself as I stood before him with my heart bleeding.

He stood, stepping into my space and tucking hair behind my ear while his eyes roamed my features like it was the last time he'd see me. He pressed a kiss to my forehead, before dipping to mutter in my ear, "Take care of yourself, Kylie."

With a brush of his sleeve against my arm as a parting touch, he walked away, taking my heart with him. Leaving me standing alone.

I gathered myself with as much dignity as a jilted lover can and stumbled my way out the door. Numbly, I walked to my apartment in my wasted heels and let myself into the dark room. After I'd locked the doors, stripped out of the ridiculous dress and shoes, and drug the wig off my head, I sank into a hot bubble bath. Only then, did I let the tears fall.

Chapter Seventeen

Thoren

I waited down the block, hiding in the shadows of a storefront doorway, watching for Kylie to exit The Alamo. Keeping my distance, I followed her, making sure she got inside her apartment safely. Despite my vow to stay away from her, I couldn't make myself let go. It fucking killed me to see her, and not be able to touch her and tell her the truth. But my brother had done enough damage, and I wouldn't put her at risk. It was safest for her if I stayed away.

I hung out in the shadows of her courtyard, watching to see if she'd been followed by anyone other than me.

In the dim light of the streetlamp, I saw a man approach the gate and spend a minute studying the keypad entry. He glanced up toward the second floor before walking away, his gait familiar.

I'd followed that gait for most of my life, on ballfields, in the schoolyard.

Loren.

That glance up made my stomach churn. Kylie was the

only one on the second floor. That he knew who she was, and where she lived, sent terror flooding my system.

The last words he'd spoken when he'd visited rang in my head. "*I will take it all away from you, brother,*" he'd hissed, and then with his next breath his expression had morphed into a crazed smile. "*She sure is pretty.*"

All it took was a split second to know that he'd make good on that threat. Whatever his despicable reasons were, he'd find any way he could to hurt me.

I fucking hated that he'd seen Kylie and knew where she lived. Knew that she meant something to me. Removing her from my life was the only thing that would remove his cross hairs from her.

Or so I'd thought. Yet here he was. Standing outside her apartment, peering at it like he was studying it for his next job.

My plan to stay away from her for her own protection had failed. Spectacularly.

I could no more stay away from the woman than I could quit breathing. And seeing the pain I'd caused her absolutely gutted me.

I wanted to crawl on my knees to her and beg her to forgive me for being such an utter dumbass. I was a total fool thinking I could ever stay away from her. Somehow, she'd become as essential to me as the air I breathed.

And now this motherfucker was lurking, threatening my woman.

Staying in the shadows, I eased up to the gate to see where he'd gone. Only after I noted the empty courtyard did I slink up to her apartment and let myself in with Leah's key.

Her apartment was trashed, like she'd spent days inside. The scene reminded me of the cabin when I'd rescued her off the mountain. Except this time, it was tissues, rather than liquor bottles littering the tabletops.

A trail of clothing and the wig she'd been wearing led to the bathroom. Sobs echoed through the closed door, and guilt slammed through me.

That was my fault.

My actions, the words I'd said, had reduced Kylie Monroe to sobs. I'd never felt like a bigger bastard.

The look in her eyes when she'd confronted me at the bar, the way it shifted from anger to hurt, had twisted my stomach. I wanted to bust through that bathroom door and sweep her into my arms. Promise her I'd never hurt her again.

But I didn't deserve to be her hero.

Instead, I sank to the couch, and let her have her privacy. Allowing her space, and soaking up the anguish she released, as if I could take it away from her. Trying to come up with excuses for the way I'd treated her, even for my actions less than an hour ago. Maybe if we could just keep up the appearance that I was no longer in her life, I could still protect her.

Once she got out of the tub, I'd have a chance to beg her forgiveness and hopefully convince her to give us another shot. Or at least convince her that she was in danger, and to let me stay to protect her.

The overhead light blinded me a millisecond before Kylie let out a terrified scream.

"Thoren, what in the actual fuck!" She picked up a throw pillow off the couch, pinging me in the head with it.

"Ow!"

I ducked too late as another pillow bounced off my shoulder. I threw my arms over my head to block the next blow.

"Stop, Kylie! Let me explain!"

From the kitchen, the sound of pots clanging had me looking up. I jumped from the couch, backing away from her, hands stretched out, as if I could stop her if she really wanted to hit me. She stood in the kitchen, with one hand securing a towel, and the other brandishing a large cast-iron skillet.

"Good God, that thing is huge. Put the pan down, Kylie. I'm not here to hurt you."

"No, you son of a bitch! You already did that, didn't you? When you used me, then ghosted me."

Behind the shrieks, and the wide eyes, and the high color in her cheeks, lurked something more. A deep, hurt-filled chasm that, if the sobs hadn't earlier, showed me exactly how big of an asshole I was.

She'd cared for me. Really cared. Maybe more than she wanted to admit...or even realized.

I lowered my hands and voice as if approaching a wild animal. "Kylie, we need to talk. Just...come over here so we can sit and maybe have this out. Without you bashing me in the head."

She stared at me, fuming, chest rising and falling with every breath. Finally, her shoulders lifted with her inhale, and she closed her eyes before letting the breath go. Apparently back under control, she set the pan on the counter and straightened her spine as if readying for battle.

She was stunning. All passionate fiery attitude. I wanted to strip that towel off, sink into her, and have that passion unleashed on me.

She sat stiffly on the edge of the couch, legs pressed tightly together, fidgeting with the edge of the towel before laying her hand primly on her knees. "Okay, Thoren. You've broken into my apartment. Tell me exactly why I shouldn't call the cops and have you arrested."

I scraped a hand through my hair. Where to start?

"Why not from the beginning?" she replied when I obviously spoke that thought out loud.

"Okay, here's the deal. You know my brother is suspected of starting the fires. And you know that he came to my house the other night when you were there."

At her nod, I continued, "What you don't know, is that when he was there, he threatened me."

Her body went rigid. "He what?"

"He threatened to ruin me."

I could see the questions she wanted to ask running through her mind. "But there's more. He also threatened you."

She visibly swallowed, staring at me wide-eyed. "Why?"

I lifted a shoulder. "He hates me, he has ever since I didn't quit the fire academy after he failed out."

"But that's ridiculous. You had nothing to do with him failing." God love her for her fiery eyes, for her coming to my defense even when she was mad at me.

"I didn't say it made sense. It just is what it is." How could I expect her to understand what I couldn't comprehend myself?

Her gaze ran over my face. "So, what did he threaten about me?"

I didn't want to tell her, because I didn't want to scare her, but she deserved to know. "Nothing specific. He just said in this creepy, menacing voice, 'she sure is pretty.'"

"Why would he say that?"

I let my gaze take in her beautiful face. She had no idea. "Because it's true. And he knows I care about you." The truth of my words echoed between us.

She played with edge of the towel, watching me with a narrowed gaze. "If you care about me, why the radio silence for the last week?"

The truth clogged my throat. "Because I'd do anything to keep you safe. I've followed you for the last week. Making sure you got home every night. I stupidly thought that if I stayed away from you, if he didn't see us together, he'd leave you alone. Then tonight, I noticed that I wasn't the only one following you, and it became crystal clear that he would make trouble."

I wanted to cross this space between us, wrap my arms around her. Protect her from the world.

"He's not going to touch you. I promise you on my life. He's not going to hurt you." My voice was low and guttural, the words coming from my soul.

She scoffed at that. "So...what? You're going to follow me around every day?"

"If that's what it takes." I'd do anything to keep her safe.

"Don't be ridiculous." Her eye roll was epic. "You can't be with me twenty-four seven." She stood and for a half a heartbeat the towel looked like it might come loose. She secured the top edge and eyed me. "I don't even know if I believe any of what you're saying. I mean...can I trust you at all now?"

Towel secured, she began pacing. "And why do you think you're the one that needs to handle this? Why wouldn't you just call in the cops and let them do their job? I'm sure Mike has friends he could call to push the issue."

She was right. I could have called in a favor from anyone at the PD.

"I didn't want to take a chance of losing you."

She stared blankly at me. "That's the stupidest thing I've ever heard. You didn't want to lose me, so you didn't call, didn't text. Basically, you just ditched me after the best sex I'd ever had?"

Her voice grew louder with every word, eyes flashing, color rising above that damn towel. "I even broke my own rule and freaking kissed you. That should've been your clue that this was more than a one-night stand, temporary relationship for me." She flung her hands, palms up, toward me. "Why didn't you just talk to me?"

My heart pounded at the realization that I'd made one too many mistakes. She'd never forgive me, and I'd lost her. All the frustration I'd felt unloaded in a shout. "I fucked up, okay?" The words felt like they'd been ripped from my soul.

Seconds that felt like hours passed as I waited for her to respond.

"So make it right." She delivered her ultimatum.

"What?"

"Make it right. Prove to me that you trust your friends, that you trust me."

"How?"

I was dumbfounded. How could I fix this between us? How could I keep her safe, knowing that Loren was out there watching her, just waiting to do God-knew-what?

"Call Mike. Right now."

"It's after midnight."

"So? Call him. Ask for his help. Tell him what's going on and ask for help."

Denial ran through me hot and fast. I immediately shook my head, but caught myself because she was speaking again, a look of disgust on her face.

"See? This is what I'm talking about. You have a known problem. And people to reach out to, to ask for help. Yet, you sit here thinking that you can do a better job yourself. That you can handle it yourself."

She shook her head and glared at me. "You think you're so much better than everyone else."

"No! That's not it at all!"

"So, what is it then?"

I pushed up from the couch, needing to pace, the four walls of her apartment confining me. I wanted to bust through the door, chase Loren down and beat his ass, and have everything go back to normal.

Instead, here I was, getting reamed for doing what came natural for me. Taking care of things, trying to fix the problems that Loren created. Even when I didn't want to, I was doing it.

"All my life, I've been running behind Loren, fixing things. When we were kids, Mom made us both do tutoring, and I'd get blamed if he didn't learn it. When we were in high school, he'd go get high, and it'd be my fault for not keeping him out of trouble.

"We both had jobs at this mom-and-pop farm, and if the jobs didn't get done, we didn't get paid. He'd slack off, and I'd end up doing everything, because I knew we needed the money.

"One time, he was supposed to take the electric payment down, because they were threatening to cut off our power. He decided to go party with the money instead. We spent a week with no power. Eventually, I just became my brother's keeper."

I paced across the room, needing to get away, and also to get closer. Wanting to reach for her because if she could forgive me, everything would be alright. "I guess it's just what I'm used to. If I want to make sure something gets done right, I just do it myself."

By the time I finished confessing my soul and turned to face her, she'd leaned back against the back of the couch, arms folded across her chest, towel sliding deliciously up her leg.

"Poor Thoren." She shot me a look of mock sincerity. "That still doesn't explain why you didn't trust your supposed best friend with this."

"My grandpa died because the power was cut off!" I roared. "That loser got high, and my grandpa died because of it. If I'd taken care of things that day, my grandpa might not have died the way he did. The power wouldn't have been out, with the gas running so that when he lit a candle the entire house blew up.

"So no. I don't trust anyone. I handle the shit that needs to get done, because I can only count on one person, and that's me." My chest heaved with every harsh breath that sawed in and out. "You can sit there, staring at me like I'm crazy, but no. I don't trust anyone except myself to keep that bastard away from you."

We stared at each other while I acted like a dragon, breathing fire from my nose.

Finally, she straightened and closed the distance between us. Close enough to touch and looking at me with crystal clear understanding in her gaze. "I don't want to be some obligation to you." Her voice was soft but her tone certain. "If you keep having to save the day for me, at some point you're going to resent having to, and where will that leave me? And you didn't have to walk away from me. We could've handled it together if you'd just trusted me enough to help. Trust your friends enough to help."

"Will you let me stay if I do?" I countered, because suddenly, I needed to be near her more than I needed air to breathe.

She paused for a long moment, considering. "Yeah. You can stay. But *only* if you call Mike, and clue him in." She tugged the towel tighter. "And you're sleeping on the couch."

A half-hour later—after I'd gotten off the phone with Mike, after Kylie had sat with me, giving me silent support —she flipped the lamp off and stood in her doorway, wishing me good night.

I thought for a half a moment that she might reconsider. Instead, the bedroom door snicked shut behind her. Probably for the best. I'd just stay here on the couch where I could intercept anyone trying to come in. And since I wouldn't be sleeping anyway, I'd lay there all night, knowing exactly what I was missing.

Chapter Eighteen

Kylie

K"Hands to heart center...and Namaste." I performed a bow to the full class of yogis in my beginner class, my hands pressed together in prayer, thumbs pointed at my heart.

The candles I'd placed in a patterned formation on the studio floor flickered in the draft. Soft meditative music floated from the hidden speakers, and darkness fell outside the Blue Lotus, wrapping the space in a peaceful serenity.

I quietly held my seat as my students began clearing their mats away. This was my last class of the day, and I was tired. Thoren had been at my house for almost a week. And subsequently, I'd not slept in nearly a week.

It was hard to fall asleep knowing he was just outside my bedroom door, especially since every night I'd woken to erotic dreams of him. The memory of his body, and how good we'd been together, threatened my resolve that we not sleep together again.

Every time my thoughts would stray to Thoren in the shower, or rising over me in the bed, or lifting me up on the kitchen counter, I'd deliberately remember that week he'd ghosted me and how badly it had hurt.

So, I ignored the way he slept shirtless. And the way the muscles in his back rippled when he stretched. And the way he shifted his cock when he stood first thing in the morning.

If things were different, I'd offer to ease the erection that tented his sweatpants when he first woke, and we'd start our mornings in a more satisfying way.

But things weren't different and wouldn't be, no matter how horny I was. It had been a long, sexually frustrating week.

I blew out a breath as I stood to stretch.

Wintertime in Georgia meant shorter days and longer nights, and I was ready for the reprieve of spring. It didn't help that we offered late classes several times a week. Those days seemed endless because the sun set so early.

Sheer curtains covered the floor-to-ceiling windows, gathered in the center with colorful ropes. Outside, in the world, cars passed the studio in a steady stream of headlights. Movement on the far street corner drew my attention.

It wasn't normal for people to loiter in this area. That's why the man caught my attention. I'd seen him before class, in the same spot outside the laundromat. His white short-sleeve t-shirt and jeans weren't unusual for Georgia, but we were having a cold snap, so it'd struck me as odd. As I stared, the end of a cigarette glowed, then the orange tip dropped to the ground and extinguished, as if he'd stubbed it out with his foot.

Freaking litterer.

I ushered the last of the students out of the studio and did my nightly cleaning. Leah was off, having a date night with Mike, and Thoren would be by any minute to escort me home.

As I shut down the computer system, a firetruck raced by. And I was right back to thinking of Thoren.

It was natural of me to notice the engines and sirens more now, especially since I had a better relationship with his crew, I reasoned. And if I worried about them being on call, it was just because Thoren and I had been through some pretty intense stuff. I cared about him. I still wanted him. I just didn't want him to break my heart again.

As the sirens diminished, I lifted a small prayer of safety for the responders.

Going to the back of the studio, I paused at the bathroom, my reflection catching my eye. I'd quit wearing the wigs so much, though I still covered my head. I tugged the hat off and took a good long look at my reflection. My eyes looked tired. My patchy hair was growing back. But other than that, I looked healthy. Not broken like I'd been just months ago.

Thoren had helped with that. Whether he knew it or not, he'd helped me find myself again. And the truth was...I missed us.

I came out of the bathroom to find the object of my obsession hovering at the front door. I wanted to believe that he kept coming around because he truly cared for me. But I sensed it was more that he just felt like protecting me. I mean, his brother was after me.

But I didn't want a relationship based off of duty and responsibility. A wave of sadness washed over me as I opened the door, making my eyes brim with tears.

"Hey," he said, shutting the door and locking it. He turned to face me and then his long legs ate the space between us. He didn't hesitate, just wrapped me in a bear hug. I closed my eyes, soaking in the connection. It would suck to lose this because he felt so good.

He crowded close to me, his mouth dangerously close to mine. "What's this sad look for?"

All it would take was the slightest effort on my part and those lips I wanted so badly to kiss would be on mine.

"What's wrong, sweetheart?"

"What are we doing, Thoren?

He slid an arm around my waist, my hips brushing against his. It felt so right to be near him, surrounded by him. I was tired of the games. Tired of the distance between us.

"I miss this," I whispered. "I've missed you."

His other hand snaked up, gripping the back of my neck, holding me close to his hard body. "I've missed you too, baby."

And then he kissed me, his tongue invaded my mouth in that perfect way he had of driving me wild. I whimpered against his lips, my arms wrapped around his neck, and every inch of my body strained to be closer to his. I shifted on a foot, lifting my leg to wrap around his waist. His hand gripped my thigh, fingers digging in and shifting me to press the rigid length of him into my already wet center.

He broke the kiss and stooped to lift my other leg around him, then carried me down the hall toward my yoga room.

My yoga mat and blanket were still on the floor, my mood candles still lit, soft music still played over the speakers. The melody low, hypnotic. Erotic.

"This will do nicely." He grabbed my bolster—a long firm pillow—from a basket inside the doorway and flipped it onto my mat. In one swift move, he released my legs and removed my shirt and bra. Then he knelt on my folded blanket, dragging my tight pants down my legs, leaving me bare to him.

"Fuck, I love it that you don't wear underwear under these leggings."

"More comfortable that way," I mumbled stupidly, unsure of how we went from saying hello in the doorway to me naked in my yoga room. Then I lost the ability to think because he lifted my leg over his shoulder. Starting from my knee, his hot mouth devoured a line up my inner thigh, nipping and sucking. Driving me crazy with desire.

The moan that ripped from my throat as he found my clit echoed off the bare walls, followed closely by his growl of approval.

He continued his assault, adding his fingers until my knees grew weak, and I leaned on him for support.

His arms caressed up my back, shifting both legs over his shoulders, and then I was being lifted, and lowered to the floor, my butt propped on the bolster.

I watched as he undid the buckle of jeans, palming his rock-hard dick. Whimpering as he gave it a long stroke.

"You want this?" he purred.

I nodded, unable to drag my eyes away from him. His powerful thighs, his trim waist, the ab muscles that rippled under his own touch. A feral look graced his face as he gazed down at me.

How oddly erotic it felt to be naked, laid out for his pleasure, while he loomed over me, still mostly dressed.

"Arms over your head, baby," he demanded, ripping his shirt off one handed and barely shoving his jeans down before positioning himself at my entrance. On a long slow glide, he entered me, driving all the way in while my inner muscles tightened around him like a fist.

"Oh god, you feel so good," I breathed. "So full. So right."

He grunted and began thrusting. Gripping my hips, pounding into me like he couldn't make it hard enough. Deep enough. The wet slap of our bodies filled the empty room, the sound bouncing off the walls, and intensifying the experience.

"Look at me when you come, Kylie," he demanded, lowering himself so that his chest hovered over mine. He slid his palms over mine, linking our fingers, the act intimate and claiming all at once. I arched my back, needing to feel the weight of him on me. My nipples brushed his chest, barely touching, but so sensitive that the slightest friction had me crying out for more.

He rolled his hips in that magical way of his, his masculine grunts matching the sounds rising from my throat. I clutched his fingers, my nails biting into the skin of his hand, using my legs to drive my hips up to meet every thrust.

And still I wanted more.

Wrapping one leg high on his back, and one around the flexing muscles of his ass, I used my strength, forcing him to pound into me harder and harder, until my body felt like it would split wide open. Tension grew, and I knew that the orgasm building inside me would wreck me.

He leaned low, taking one nipple in his mouth, his teeth grazing the tip. My orgasm exploded in a blinding flash of color and light that seared its way through my body, tensing every muscle, stealing my ability to breath or even make a sound. His hand traced up to the back of my neck, holding me as he drove harder, extending my pleasure.

On a shout, his body tensed, his mouth clamping down on my neck. Biting me, marking me. Making me his.

We lay there, panting, as the room came back into focus.

He shifted, pulling the bolster from under me, settling back on top of me with his weight braced on his arms.

"Now, let's talk about what made you so upset before we christened this room."

His dick was still hard inside me, and he wanted to talk?

"No better time."

I shoved at him, realizing I'd spoken aloud, but he didn't budge. Instead, he gripped my arms and tugged them over my head, pinning me beneath him, once more.

"I need you to listen." He paused, his throat working. "I care about you, Kylie. So much."

"Don't you say those words to me right now." I glared at him, because if he actually told me he loved me, I might lose my shit. Of course, I wanted to hear them. But not when we'd had the most amazing orgasm ever, and his dick was still inside me.

His eyes cleared as his gaze roamed my face, then he smirked. "Why? You don't believe them?"

"I'll believe them more if they come at a random time rather than as a 'thank you for the amazing sex.'"

"I can't think of a better time. I can feel all of you, every little indrawn breath you make clutching me again and again."

I struggled against him. I didn't want this. The same old, same old, not-special, required words.

"Ah, I get it," he said knowingly. "You want the whole princess treatment."

I quit struggling and glared at him. "I most certainly do not."

He grinned. "Of course you do. That's what you were saying before. You don't want to be a responsibility. You want more." His grin grew into a full-blown smile. "You want to be treated like a princess. Wooed."

"No. I just want someone to see me. The real me. And give a damn about her," I spat back, knowing full well that I was making a colossal mistake, but I couldn't make my mouth quit running.

He pulled out, releasing me like I'd slapped him. He stood, glaring back at me like I'd just said the most offensive thing he'd ever heard.

"And you don't think I see the real you?" His voice was rough with anger.

"No. I think you see me as someone who has to be saved. This thing between us isn't real, Thoren. It's built on a fucked-up situation and your overdeveloped sense of ego. You think you've got to save everyone, especially me. Well. I don't need saving." My heart thumped in my chest.

I didn't want to be just his responsibility. I wanted him to love me just because he loved me.

"Wow. That's...pretty harsh." He retreated, yanking on his clothes. "And all this time, I thought we were being open and honest with each other."

He slipped on his shoes and continued, his voice growing louder with anger. "I thought we were in this together. That I was taking care of you, and you were taking care of me. That we were building something together. Good to know it was just a servicing for you."

I found my leggings and yanked them on. "It's not like that."

"Oh no!" he yelled, anger boiling over. "All my life, I've taken care of everyone else. Looked out for my brother when my mother wouldn't. Bailed him out with not so much as a thank you. Sacrificed myself so that they wouldn't have to endure whatever the fuck punishment they earned. And now you tell me that everything I am, is not what you want?"

"I didn't say that," I said from behind my top as I slipped into it.

"Yes, you did. You said exactly that."

I stared at him, his words replaying through my head, and bringing a terrible realization. He showed he cared by acts of service. And I'd just told him that I didn't want him to take care of me.

I watched in horror as he stalked out of the room, suddenly aware that I was the asshole.

I bolted after him. "Wait, Thoren..."

He froze with his back to me. "Why do you do this to me, Kylie?"

"What?" I forced through a too tight throat.

"Why do you pick fights?"

"I'm scared," I blurted. A twinge of relief trickled through me as he slowly turned to face me. "I'm scared that I'm not enough."

The truth popped out and hung like a giant disco ball, highlighting all the unattractive messy emotions swirling between us.

"I was never good enough or pretty enough for my family. They always wanted to change me to make me better. That's why I'm so afraid that once the obligation is over, you'll be done with me. I'm afraid that you'll leave me if I don't need you enough."

He eyed me, hands fisting at his side. His throat bobbed on a swallow like he was trying to find words to respond. "I'm terrified that I can't protect you. That my brother is going to take away the most important person in my life."

I eased forward and took his hand, choking on an apology. "I'm sorry. This is all so much. I just want you to be with me because you care about me."

He tugged me forward into his chest and wrapped his arms around me. "Kylie, I do." His lips pressed against my forehead, his voice a low rumble in my ear. "It's because I care about you that I want to protect you. I want you safe. Not out of obligation, but because I couldn't stand it if something happened to you."

I held onto him tightly, letting his words sink in. "I'm so ready for this to be over so we can go back to a normal life," I admitted against his chest.

His arms tightened around me, and I felt him kiss the top of my head. My eyes stung with relief. "We wouldn't know what to do if we had normal. You'd get bored and go look for an adventure somewhere."

The knot of tension in my chest released. "Maybe, but at least I'd have you with me."

"I promise you, we'll get there."

Every part of me wanted to believe him, but I couldn't shake the feeling that things would get worse before we got our normal.

Chapter Nineteen

Kylie

After our argument, we'd gone to Thoren's house, where we'd made love until we'd both passed out.

I'd woken first and watched him sleep for a bit before taking advantage of the short time we had together before he was due on shift. Leah was on the early schedule at the studio, and I would be closing again.

With things still feeling tender between us, I figured it'd be a nice gesture to bring Thoren lunch. I unloaded bags full of sub sandwiches, struggled my way into the small lobby at the front of the station, and hit the call box with my pinkie finger.

"Can I help you?" A deep male voice came across the speaker. Mo maybe?

"Hey, it's Kylie, I brought y'all some lunch." I waited, shifting the bags to not drop them.

The door opened. "Kylie-girl. What's happening?" Mo flashed me his perfect teeth.

"Hey, big guy. Just trying to treat my favorite fire-fighters."

Mo relieved me of the bags, and held the door for me, then ushered me down the hall to a large open room where the rest of the crew was gathered at the round kitchen table. All of them wore an expression of Grave Man-face, except for Thoren, who looked like he wanted to blow a gasket.

"Is this a bad time?" I asked, coming to a halt inside the door.

Mo placed the bags on the table in front of the crew. "No, just hashing out some info we just got."

Thoren stared at his Captain, a question in his eyes. Mac, obviously a mind-reader, simply nodded.

"Come here," Thoren ordered, holding a hand out to me. I got close, and he pulled me to his lap, sliding his palm around my hip.

"What's going on? You guys all look wired."

Thoren opened his mouth and tried to speak, then closed it again, swallowing hard. His entire body vibrated beneath me. My gaze shot to Mac, who cleared his throat and said, "Harrison just called with an update on the child-fatality case."

My stomach plummeted like I'd gone over the top of a huge rollercoaster. With the thunderous looks surrounding me, I was pretty sure what that update entailed.

"Oh God," I whispered, turning to Thoren. "Your brother?"

A single nod was all he could muster through his tightly-controlled rage. I slipped an arm around his neck and pulled him closer.

"He's gonna fuck up, guys. It's just a matter of time until we catch him." Mike's disembodied voice came through a phone at the center of the table. I hadn't even noticed it was there.

"Kylie needs a detail," Thoren croaked. "Can you make that happen?"

"Yeah, I'll talk to squad and get her on rotation. Sorry for not being there in person to deliver this news. I'm on my way back from GBI headquarters now and didn't want to wait to share."

Mac picked up the phone and took it off speaker. "Thanks for the update." More was said, but my attention had shifted to Thoren.

Nate stood, coming around the table to grip Thoren's shoulder. He gave it a squeeze and met my eyes, like he was silently conveying a message to me. These men and their inability to express themselves. But even as I had the thought, I understood what Nate seemed to be saying. *Take care of our guy. Don't let him fall down the rabbit hole again. He's gonna need us.* Or maybe that's what I wanted him to say.

Mo stood from the table and offered, "Kylie-girl, you ever sprayed a firehose?"

No, and I didn't want to then. But one look at Mo, and his concerned glance at Thoren, and I agreed. Maybe together, we could distract him and get him out of his head.

"As a matter of fact, I haven't, big guy."

"Come on then, little one. Today's your lucky day, we've got some that need testing."

* * *

Hours later, multiple passing sirens interrupted my final savasana of the day at the yoga studio. My mind whirled, and I sent up protective vibes for whoever was involved. As the last of the students left, I stepped on the porch outside the studio. The smoker was outside the laundromat again. A police cruiser—the detail Mike had assigned for me—sat in the parking lot at the ice cream shop. I waved in acknowledgement and hurried to gather my things.

The acrid smell of smoke tinted the air and a haze hung over downtown. This was no false alarm. Thoren and his crew had a real fire. A large one from the looks of it. My heart raced, and I sent up another prayer of protection for them as I walked to my car.

The Blue Lotus was several blocks away from my apartment in the heart of town. Close enough for a good walk on a nice day but requiring a car in the winter when it was cold and wet. I crested the hill, coming into downtown, when traffic came to a dead stop.

Alarm bells rang in my head. The fire trucks were near my apartment. And the huge plume of black smoke rose from my block.

Dread rolled through me.

I parked in front of The Alamo and ran the remaining two blocks toward my home. Two big fire engines blocked the street. One with a raised ladder blasted water from the bucket. Hoses snaked across the sidewalk. An ambulance blocked another corner. People in fire gear worked, running from the trucks to disappear around the corner.

A uniformed officer met me at the perimeter of the trucks, holding his arms out to prevent me from running past him. "I'm sorry, ma'am, you can't go any farther."

"I think my apartment is on fire," I cried, heart thumping in my chest.

His expression remained stoic, but he instantly radioed to someone named command. I recognized the gravelly voice that responded.

"That's Mac Collins!" I cried. "Tell him it's Kylie Monroe, Thoren's friend. Tell him it's my apartment building."

The guy relayed the message while I paced, wringing my hands. Looking for any sign of someone I knew.

"Kylie." Captain Collins appeared from behind the first truck, motioning me to meet him on the sidewalk.

From the closer vantage point, I could see that the whole building wasn't on fire. Only my apartment.

"Do you have someone to call?" Captain asked. "Maybe Mike or Leah? Mike should be on his way here soon."

I nodded numbly.

"Best get on that then. You can stay with me until they get here." He shifted closer to me, staring up at the activity. Big hoses ran from the trucks up the stairs, and men were grouped outside. A riot of emotions coursed through me. Fear for the ones in the fire. Panic, followed closely by sadness, that I'd lost everything that I owned.

"Go on and make that call now," he said, his voice almost gentle, in direct contrast to the badass vibe he gave off.

I clung to his solid strength and managed to drag my attention away from the activity to call Leah. She and Mike showed minutes later, Jordan right on their heels. The women sandwiched me between them, and Mike talked with the officers on duty.

"Hey, Captain, you need to see this," a voice yelled. A firefighter approached, holding out a plastic bag.

"What the hell is that?" Mac's gruff voice was scary as hell.

"Looks like a keychain," the firefighter said, turning the bag over in his hands, studying the contents.

"Where was it?"

"Tacked to the front door."

"Fucker's ballsy," Captain muttered.

"Uh, Captain, what's going on?" I interrupted.

"Kylie!" A voice bellowed across the courtyard, and then a large body wearing an air tank and helmet came loping at me. As he neared, he stripped off the helmet and mask.

Thoren looked at me with anguish in his eyes and I knew I'd lost everything. He didn't stop coming at me, even as my vision grew watery and he wavered before me.

My knees went weak, the world tilting as all the energy drained from me. Strong arms caught me, clutching me to a broad chest.

"I'm so fucking sorry, baby. We did the best we could, but it was gone before we even got here." Thoren's voice was a tortured whisper in my ear.

"Way to go, asshole. We hadn't confirmed that it was her apartment," someone behind Thoren griped.

"It's okay. I'd find out sooner or later," I mumbled.

"You recognize this?" Captain Collins held the bag out to Thoren, who blanched.

"Yeah, I know it. That's the keychain my grandpa taught me to make."

"That's what I thought," Mac said, frowning at the contents of the bag. "Looks just like the one you were carving at the station the other day."

He dropped the bag to a clipboard he held and met Thoren's eyes. "It's taken some digging, but we finally realized that one of these has been found at every structure fire. Left like a calling card."

"That confirms that it's Loren doing this then, doesn't it?" Thoren closed his eyes, chin dropping like he'd taken a physical blow. Like he'd been expecting this news, but the reality of having the knowledge was still hard to bear.

"Or someone's setting you and him up. But seeing as how I was with you all day and all evening, you're not the fucker setting shit on fire." As if remembering us, Mac turned to me and my friends. "Pardon me."

Thoren looked at Mike. "I need a favor, man."

"Anything," Mike responded.

"Let Kylie stay with you tonight until I can get off duty and take her to my place."

"Uh, Thoren, I'm standing right here."

"I know. But I need you to listen to me right now." The underlying plea in the sharply spoken words quelled the urge to clap back at him again. "I'm asking Mike to help me keep you safe. I'm asking you to go with him."

"Asking or telling?"

"Asking in a telly way." He almost smirked. It wasn't much, but enough for the moment. "Please, just go with them. I'll get what I can out of your apartment. But this was intentional. And it was intentional because of me. So please, just go where I know you are safe."

He leaned down and laid a hot, heavy kiss on me. The world tunneled in that desperate moment. Like he put all his hopes and dreams and everything important to him into that singular kiss.

Thoren released me, cupping my cheek, gazing into my eyes, before looking at Leah and Jordan. "Take care of my girl."

"I guess I'm going home with you guys," I said meekly to Leah, watching Thoren's retreating back. I hated this. Hated feeling knocked down and fragile.

"We'll take good care of you," Leah said.

"We can make it like a slumber party," Jordan piped in.

Mike joined our girl huddle with a soft look at Leah, and then escorted us to our cars. I was to follow them, and Jordan was to follow me. Like a little caravan of protection.

The drive to Mike and Leah's took us back by way of the yoga studio. Tears pooled in my eyes as we passed the building. Aside from my apartment, the Blue Lotus was the thing I'd been most proud of, starting it from the ground up with Leah.

Almost literally. When we'd bought the old house, we'd stripped it bare and refinished all the floors ourselves, painted every single thing inside. Built our clientele from nothing. What little money I'd had left from my pageant wins had gone into the startup of the business.

At least I still had the studio.

The image of that guy smoking outside the laundromat flashed in my mind. He'd been staring at the studio.

I pulled into Mike and Leah's drive and bolted from the car.

"Mike!" I cried, running to meet him at the driver's door.

He exited the car, eyes darting around, scanning the area like usual. "What's wrong?"

"Earlier, the fire trucks passed by the studio. They had to have been going to my apartment, given the time. But right after they passed, I noticed a guy standing on the corner. Maybe I'm imagining it, but it felt like he was staring at the studio."

Mike's gaze darted back to mine, his body going rigid. Leah rounded the rear of the car, joining us.

I didn't want to scare her, but he needed to know where my head had gone. "What if it was him, and he hits the studio next?"

Without a word, Mike stalked away, already on his

phone. Leah strung her arm through mine, gently guiding me inside where we sank into the loveseat together, Jordan coming to sit in the chair next to us.

"What if we lose the studio, too?" I whispered, squeezing her hand, trying hard to hold myself together.

"Then we rebuild." Leah's voice was strong. Sure.

Oh, how I wanted to believe that. But I just couldn't seem to grasp it. Panic rose in my chest. I wanted to run out the door, run away from this drama.

"Kylie, look at me." Jordan eased from her chair to come to her knees before me. Gripping my hands in hers, she met my eyes. "If that happens, you will rebuild. You will find a way to move forward, and you will be okay."

This was more than lip service. Jordan had survived a tornado destroying her home and everything she owned. She spoke this truth from her heart.

I pushed away from the seat, needing to pace before I bolted.

"You know, losing my apartment isn't nearly as terrifying as even the thought of losing the studio. You'd think it would be the other way around."

"That makes sense because the studio is a part of your soul. You've built a beautiful space that you share with others."

Jordan was right, of course, but...

"It's more than that though," I whispered, searching their faces, willing them to see what I couldn't seem to find the words to say.

Finally, the words came to me. "It's like, that yoga studio is my proof to the world that I have more value than just what my parents made me believe," I whispered.

"How so?" Leah's voice was as gentle as her gaze.

"Can you explain that?" Jordan asked. Their calm

demeanor settled over my frayed nerves, allowing me the space to think and feel and process.

My cheeks heated at a secret I'd never shared. "Growing up, my parents, my mom mostly, made me enter all these beauty pageants. She drug me around the entire southeast, stuffing me into frilly dresses that itched. Making me learn corny dances and primping me to within an inch of my life."

"Aw, I bet you were cute," Jordan said with a smile.

I shook my head. "I was miserable. I hated every minute of it. My mom's whole world seemed to revolve around me being crowned the next beauty queen of whatever pageant we were competing in.

"When I was sixteen, I rebelled. I just wanted a normal childhood. I wanted to play and go to movies with my friends. Instead, I was dieting and doing facials. I could never cut my hair the way I wanted or wear the clothes I wanted. She controlled every aspect of my life. Holding my winnings over my head. Mom promised that once I won a pageant, I could do whatever I wanted with the money."

I paused a beat. My sweet friends just sat quietly, waiting, listening, offering me their support.

"When I turned eighteen, I finally won a pageant. I don't even remember the name of it. I vowed that it was my last. I took my prize money and left for college. Honestly, I was sick of their suggestions on how I could 'enhance my looks.' I felt...worthless, soiled.

"In college I found my yoga practice and that helped me find my strength and heal. That's where I found Leah." I smiled at my best friend. "Then, after college, Leah found this town, and we started the Blue Lotus."

Leah nodded. "We did create something beautiful."

"That's just the thing. In those walls, our clients find

their strength, they heal. They realize that their health is as much mental and spiritual as it is physical. They become more than the vessel that covers their bones. That place has more value than what it looks like on the outside. And people love it for what it has to offer."

I quieted, finally admitting to them as much as to myself, "All my life I felt like I'd never be good enough. If I didn't have the perfect hair or wasn't the prettiest in the pageant, I was made to feel...unloved, unworthy. All I ever really wanted was to be loved for myself."

"What did your dad think about how your mom acted?" Jordan asked.

I huffed a sardonic laugh. "My dad was too busy running his plastic surgery center and sleeping with his nurses to care. If we weren't underfoot and all he had to do was pay the bills, he was happy."

Never had my dad looked at me and told me he was proud of me. "He was happy that I won a scholarship, but even then, all he did was tell me I owed it to him for all the pageant fees he'd paid."

"Wow, he sounds like a real ass."

I nodded.

"I'd tell you to try to mend that relationship if I thought it would do you any good," Leah started. "But you are so much better now than when we first met. You are happier and healthier. And I think it's good that you removed that toxicity from your life." She wrapped an arm around my shoulder. "I just wish that you could see in yourself all the wonderful things that others see in you."

A lump formed in my throat, making it almost impossible to speak. "The yoga studio is my place. It shows the world that I am capable. I can't lose it," I croaked.

My friends wrapped me in a hug, murmuring words of

encouragement. Assuring me that everything would be okay, even if something did happen.

Mike bustled through the room, breaking the emotional moment.

"Sorry, ladies," he said as he perched on the loveseat behind Leah. "Got some good news and some bad."

He rubbed a hand sweetly down Leah's back. "We'd already gotten a tip that someone was hanging around the studio, and officers had already checked it out."

My emotions immediately flipped from despair and worry, to pissed off righteousness.

"And?"

"That's the bad news. He was gone before they could get him and bring him in for questioning."

"Damn." When would we catch a break?

"Don't worry, we'll catch him. Sooner or later, he's going to fuck up. In the meantime, I think it's a good idea if you stick together. Don't take any chances. We don't know what this guy's motive is."

I watched him run his hand down Leah's back lovingly. Their love was deep and true. And I was only slightly jealous.

In a flash, my mind shot to Thoren.

I wished that he was here with me. Comforting me. Assuring me he would protect all that I loved. And that was a problem, because I was on the verge of losing everything because of him and his brother.

How could we ever make it, if all he ever saw in me was duty and responsibility? How could I move forward with him, knowing that our relationship threatened the only thing that I held dear?

Chapter Twenty

horen

Three a.m. was an eerie time.

The streets were quiet, in stark contrast to the hustle and bustle during daylight hours. The only people milling about might be a random worker leaving a bar, a few cars on the road.

And usually, we had at least one call where someone who'd had a headache for days suddenly found themselves needing a ride to the emergency room.

This night or morning or whatever you called the time of day, I was doing a secondary walk-through of Kylie's apartment, checking for hotspots.

Because my fucking brother had burned her place down.

Luckily, whoever had renovated this old building had put in a sprinkler system that had helped control the burn until we could get on scene and put a stop to it. But she'd still lost more than half her belongings, and what remained would need a thorough cleaning to remove the smoke smell.

Rage boiled under my skin as I took a second look

around the room. I should've punched him in the face when I had the chance instead of taking the high road. I pulled my phone out and hit my contacts list, not even giving a shit that it was three in the morning.

"If I ever get my hands on that fucker, he's done," I growled into the phone when my mother answered. "I'm telling you right now, Mom. Loren has gone too far. If you know where he is, now is the time to tell me."

"What? Thoren?" My mom sounded disoriented.

Good, I'd woken her up. She didn't deserve a peaceful sleep if the rest of us couldn't have it. Neither did Loren, that fucker. I doubted that Kylie was resting at all.

"What are you talking about?" Mom mumbled, drawing my attention back.

"I'm talking about how my brother is in *my* town, burning things up, Mom. Tonight, he torched the apartment of a woman who means something to me. If you know where he is, now is the time to come clean. Or else you're going to find yourself being charged as an accomplice." I had no idea if that was the truth or not, but the threat sounded good at the time.

"Now wait a minute, young man. You don't know that he did that."

"Yes, I do. He left a fucking calling card."

She huffed into the phone. "I don't believe that for a minute." Taking up for him just like she always did. "Why would he leave a business card if he was breaking the law?"

That was as close as she'd ever come to admitting that he was a troublemaker.

"He didn't leave a business card. He left a message...to me. He's lost it, Mom. Gone too far and done too much. He's not a reasonable person making rational decisions. He's fucking crazy. And if I—"

"Don't speak of your brother that way," she hissed.

I clenched my fist to keep from throwing my phone. This had always been and would always be her way. Sweet little Loren never did anything wrong. I'd always been expected to clean up after him, to make things right, always would be in her eyes.

"We might be twins, but he's not my brother," I vowed. "I'm done protecting him and looking out for him, finding ways to get him out of trouble. He's gone too far."

"Thoren, you don't mean that."

"I absolutely do," I gritted through clenched teeth. "I was the one putting the bodies of the children into bags from where he burned their house down, with them inside." My voice shook with emotion. She gasped on the other end of the line. "I'll have that nightmare in my head for the rest of my life. Every time I close my eyes, I see them. Now you will too."

"I know your brother has had some...issues... in the past. But why do you think he's responsible for these horrible things? He would never do such a thing."

Her perfect innocent little baby could do no wrong. I was about to rock her world.

I changed my tone to conversational. Relaxed. A total lie. "You remember when Grandpa taught me how to whittle?" At her affirmative sound, I continued, "Well, we keep finding versions of that keychain I loved so much, the one grandpa taught me to make, on every scene." I waited, letting that sink in.

"That doesn't mean anything. It could've been anyone putting them there," she argued.

"Loren never could stand that I was so close to Grandpa." I scoffed at the memories floating through my head. "He chose to get high and fuck around instead of spending time with Grandpa, and he's jealous as hell that I have those memories, had that time. That Grandpa left him out of his will. I guess he blames me for everything that ever went wrong in his life."

I paused to take a breath. "He's just not a good person, Mom. And he's letting me know it's by leaving a mock of that keychain at every fire he's set. Letting me know he's one step ahead of me. Taunting me."

I glanced around Kylie's destroyed apartment once more. Rage fired through my veins. He'd hurt my woman. What if she'd been home and had gotten trapped?

"You mark my words. We will find him, and he better hope the cops get him before I do. If you know where he is, if you're still making excuses for him, knowing what he's capable of...you're just as guilty as he is." I ground my teeth together, clutching the phone like I wanted to squeeze my brother's neck. "I'm asking you one more time. Do you know where Loren is?"

"Thoren, I'm not telling."

I ended the call before she could sugarcoat the situation.

Nate came up to me, his face drawn in concern. "You okay?"

"Yeah, just letting my mom know that I'm done with my brother's bullshit, so she can pass it along to him. I'm fucking over them."

"You think he did this?"

"There's not a doubt in my mind."

Nate's eyebrows lifted high on his forehead, and his cheeks puffed out as he blew out a breath. "That's intense, man."

"It is what it is. He's a piece of shit, always has been. Mom just didn't want to see it."

I surveyed the room again. "How can I ever make this up to Kylie?"

"This is not on you. Remember what Capt always tells us. You are the solution, not the cause." Nate clapped me on the shoulder, turning me toward the door, pushing me out into the early dawn.

The solution. I was always the solution for my brother.

"I'm done being the solution for him, Nate. I cut them out for a reason a long time ago."

We met up with the rest of the crew at the truck and headed back to the station to clean up and debrief.

My unfinished project sat in the box that I carried my whittling tools in. Mocking me. Nate noticed me glaring at it.

"Thoren, dude. You get any madder, that vein is going to pop in your forehead."

I pushed the box away and sank back in my chair. "I can't help it. My own fucking brother is responsible for all of this. Those kids and now Kylie's apartment, and who knows what else before that."

"Be grateful—" Nate started.

"No. Fuck that." I cut him off. "Whatever you were about to say, just stop. Fact is, my fucked-up family hurt people. I'm not grateful for anything."

"I was going to say be grateful that Kylie wasn't in the apartment."

He had a point, but I was beyond being rational.

"Watkins!" Capt barked. "Knock it off."

My eyes shot to his. I crossed my arms over my chest.

"Calm your ass down. This is not your fault. You're sitting there, acting mad at your brother, and you should be because he's a piece of shit if he's responsible for this. But you're still taking responsibility for shit that doesn't belong to you, whether you realize it or not."

Capt braced his arms on the table, leaning toward me, his piercing grey gaze seeing more than I wanted to admit. "I've told you before, but maybe you didn't get it, so I'll put it to you a different way. You're not the cause of bad things that happen. You can't take personal responsibility for the calls we run. This career will eat you up if you do that."

He paused, searching my face. "You do your job the best you can. Sometimes it means we give everything we've got, and it's still not enough. We lose the battle to the fire, or the patient or victim dies. But every single time, trust that you did everything that you could. You can only control your response. Let the rest go."

I swallowed thickly, feeling called out like a kid caught red-handed. "But Capt, how can I face Kylie, knowing that my brother did this?"

He studied my face for a long minute. "You care about her. You tell her that. But maybe don't assume that she blames you. Give her a little more credit than that."

He leaned back in his chair, leaving me hanging on his next words.

"And maybe quit being so arrogant as to assume that everything is your responsibility to fix or handle. Sometimes, you might just need to let someone else handle their shit, and you just be on the support team. You don't have to be the hero for everyone, all the time."

"I called my mom and told her I was done with him, and with her, if she's harboring him." I hadn't exactly said those words, but I felt them.

"Can you walk away from family like that?"

I thought about his question. There was a big difference between avoiding calls and willingly cutting someone out of your life. "I think I have to. I tried to back off from them after the academy. But now..." I shook my head in disgust.

Nate shoulder-bumped me. I'd forgotten he was even there, focused as I was on what Capt was saying. "If you're looking for family, you know you have a brotherhood with us. And friends are the family we choose. We're not going to let you down. You need anything, call on us. Mike and I, hell, any of these guys, would do anything for you."

The table grew silent after all the truth bombs landed.

I felt...humbled. My anger calmed as friendship and belonging seeped in. Nate was right. I had a family in these men, and in Mike and Leah, and Kylie. I could trust them with anything.

Capt pushed away from the table. "I've got reports to write. Y'all make sure this kitchen gets cleaned up before you get out of here this morning." He grabbed a bottle of water from the fridge and stalked down the hall toward his office.

Big Mo, who'd remained quiet the entire time, stood as well. He stretched his arms overhead before coming around behind me, his big beefy hand landing on my shoulder. I looked up into his expressive eyes. For such giant of a man, he was a big softie.

Let me know how I can help, his look seemed to say. Or maybe he was threatening me. Hard to be sure. With a hard squeeze, he turned and lumbered down the hall, his wide frame nearly taking up the entire opening.

I sat in the day room, with nothing but the light over the sink pushing back the dark, replaying the entire night in my head. How my crew had done their duty, going the extra mile once I'd told them it was Kylie's place that we responded to.

Then, Mike had come and taken her home, where I'd

know she was safe. Their actions proving that I could count on them. The realization struck deep and true. I wasn't in this alone.

There was no doubt in my mind that Loren had done this on purpose. I just didn't know why he'd sunk so low. Why he was hurting people. I let the anger loose, not even trying to control my rage at the thought of what he'd done. Those children...the loss so great, my mind couldn't even wrap around it.

With a ragged sigh, I pushed out of the recliner and went to pack my bags for end-of-shift. We'd need to make one more check on Kylie's apartment before end-of-duty, and I wanted to be ready to go to her the minute my relief arrived.

With her in my head, I pushed all the other mess aside.

Back at her place though, sifting through the remains, doubt crept in. What was I doing, staying in her life? If I cared for her, why would I put her in danger by hanging around? It was clear that Loren had some kind of vendetta against me, and he was using her to get to me.

I was nothing but trouble for her. I couldn't protect her. I rubbed the heel of my hand against the instant burn in my chest. It was time to admit that I was in deep with Kylie. And even if it scared the shit out of me, this time, we'd make it work.

Chapter Twenty-One

K*ylie*

"Thanks, Jordan," I said, hanging up the phone. Standing in Thoren's kitchen surrounded by a mound of paperwork from my insurance company, the weight of the world hung heavy on my shoulders.

It had been a week since my apartment fire. I'd spent every possible minute either with Thoren, or one of my friends when he had to work. My nerves were frayed, even though he'd valiantly tried to distract me with epic sex.

I wanted more than anything to get my stuff back and maybe have a moment of solitude. Not to mention I was tired of living in mostly the same clothes because all my other stuff was being treated as evidence.

"She have any advice?" Thoren's deep voice behind me cut through the haze of my overwhelm.

"Not really. Our situations are so different."

His hands landed on the tops of my shoulders and began massaging. I closed my eyes, sinking into the near-painful relief of the stress caused by days of trying to get my life in order.

All my talk about not being wanted or feeling cherished had been utter bullshit. I'd been so selfish and blind not to see that Thoren had given me all that and more.

"Thanks for doing what you did," I said, emotion clogging my throat.

His arms slid from my shoulders, around my belly, pulling my back to his front. "What'd I do, baby?"

"You acted all heroic before because that's who you are. You live it. It's not something you just turn off. Also, your crazy girlfriend is a selfish asshole."

He spun me in his arms, tipping my chin up to face him. "What's this about?"

"I'm just realizing how wrong I was, and how much I appreciate all that you do. All the ways you take care of me. I don't think I could go through this without you."

"It's about time you realize how awesome I am," he said, the corner of his lips quirking up in a ridiculous grin.

I swatted at his chest, loving the twinkle in his eye.

"Just wait, sweetheart. When all of this is over, you're gonna get full on princess woo-ing." He kissed the tip of my nose. "For now, how about we take a break and head over to Mike and Leah's?"

I frowned. "You think it's safe? I mean, I hear there's still a bad guy on the loose."

"Or we could climb back in bed and have sex again."

I rolled my eyes. "As good as that sounds, my poor vagina needs a break."

His chest puffed up, a lecherous grin spreading across his stupidly handsome face. "Come on, grab your shoes. What better place to be than at a former cop's house, right?" He kissed me again. "Plus, I can tell you're getting a little stir crazy, and a little cranky. We'll grab some take out and go hang for a while. Nothing will go wrong. Trust me."

"Oh my God, how could you forget your wallet? You literally had three things to get. Keys. Phone. Wallet." I ticked the items off my fingers as Thoren pulled into Mike and Leah's drive. "Now the food is gonna be cold by the time you get there."

"Settle down, little vixen," Thoren said, with all the patience in the world. "You're just hangry."

"Trust me," I mocked in my best impression of his stupid voice. My head swiveled towards him. "I did trust you," I argued, "and now I'm gonna starve to death because you freaking insisted on dropping me off before going back to get your wallet!"

That stupidly calm voice replied, "Mike's is closer. You go hang with your chill yogi friend. Maybe she'll rub off on you."

"You just wanna get rid of me," I grumbled.

Thoren took my hand and kissed my knuckles. "Never. Now get out."

With a blown kiss and a wink, he waited until I'd entered their house, safely under Mike's watch, before driving away. I couldn't very well blame him if he did need a moment's peace. I was an emotional basket case, and he'd been catering to me ever since the fire. Even now, he might've sounded brusque or rude to anyone else, but he was giving me what I needed, payback snark, and time with my friend.

Leah was on the phone in the kitchen when I walked in. She took one look at me, poured me a glass of wine, and led me to the couch.

"Tell me what that look is for."

Was she crazy? "My life is nuts right now. You know this."

"Aside from the fire, it is?"

Bless her sweet soul. But even as I had the thought, I realized that maybe she had a point. "Well, there are some good parts in all of this. Thoren and I are stronger than ever."

"That's good," Mike offered. "It took you two long enough to get your shit sorted."

"Gee, thanks."

He shrugged. "Here's what I know. He cares about you. You care about him. You both acted like you couldn't stand each other, until that fateful mountain trip. It's time to get past all the bullshit and just be happy."

Maybe he was right. Maybe it was as simple as that. Apartments and things could be replaced. If the authorities could just catch Loren, life could get back to normal. And we could just...be happy.

"Hey, look. We need to run across the street and check on Mrs. O'Malley. She'd asked us to come over before you guys called, but we were busy." An adorable blush tinted Leah's cheeks.

Mike grinned like a Cheshire cat.

Leah continued, "She's got an issue with her water heater. You want to come with?"

I didn't know if I could handle dealing with Mrs. O without sustenance.

"Nah, I'm going to hang here and wait for Thoren. We'll come over when he gets back," I assured them.

Mike glowered. "I don't like this."

I rolled my eyes, but Leah hit him with a soft love sick

look. "Honey, she'll be fine here. It'll just take a minute. Plus, we'll be right back."

Bless her soul for giving me a moment alone in a safe place, even if I was counting the minutes until Thoren got back.

The muscle in Mike's jaw ticked as he watched me. Finally, he relented. "Lock the door behind us."

I did as he requested and flopped back on the couch. The house grew silent without the two of them in it. I shifted, stretching out. Maybe I could catch a quick nap while I waited.

Somewhere in the old house a floor creaked. My heart rate shot straight into overdrive.

This was the first time I'd been alone since the fire. What had been a welcome reprieve became unsettling. Loren was still on the loose. What if he'd seen Thoren drop me off and Mike leave?

I dialed Thoren's phone but got no answer. After several tries, I texted.

Surely, he'd had time to get home by now. Unease rolled through me.

My phone rang, the sound loud in the quiet house, startling me. I blew out a breath as I lifted it, trying to get control of my ridiculous skittish nerves.

The name of the alarm company that covered the studio scrolled across the display.

"Hi, this is Adept Security Services, calling to let you know an alarm has been activated."

"An alarm? What kind?" A tremor of fear flashed through me. What if Loren had decided the studio was his next target?

"It looks like a smoke alarm. We'll need a key holder to meet the fire department at the location."

I agreed to meet them and hung up. Hesitating for a split second, thinking maybe I should call Mike and let him know, I snatched Leah's keys from the counter and jogged out the door. I'd call Mike on the way.

With my heart in my throat, I raced toward the studio.

My phone rang, startling me. Thoren calling. I fumbled to answer. His voice came across clipped, before I could even say hello.

"Kylie, Loren's gonna hit the studio. I called Mike, but he didn't answer. I'm headed that way. Let Mike know." The call ended before I could get a word in edgewise.

Sudden, choking fear coursed through me. That idiot. No doubt he was going to try to take Loren down on his own. I doubled down, racing through a four-way stop. I had to get there before he did something dangerous. Or worse, before Loren did.

Chapter Twenty-Two

Thoren

I entered through the back door of the yoga studio, crouching low. Smoke tendrils curled toward the ceiling in the front room. My adrenaline had been in overdrive since I'd set foot in my house and flipped on the lights to find a perfectly carved wooden replica of Kylie's yoga studio on the counter. Somehow, my brother had gotten into my house, and left me his calling card and a note.

Will the Blue Lotus bloom again?

There was no way in hell I was going to let him take this away from her. The fire extinguisher was attached to the wall just beyond the bathroom. First step, put out the fucking fire. Second step, beat Loren's ass. I knew that son of a bitch was close by, watching. He'd want to see this, take credit for creating chaos.

I bolted for the extinguisher, wrenching it from the wall, and took two steps toward the fire.

The back door slammed shut.

I spun to the terrifying sound of the lock clicking. Pain slammed into me as a body crashed into mine, tackling me from the side. The blow knocking me forward, sending the extinguisher flying.

"Finally got you where I want you, brother." Loren loomed over me.

He jerked me onto my back, then his fist plowed into my cheek. Pain burst in my face as my head snapped from the force of the impact. Hot rage flowed like lava in my veins.

I was going to kill this motherfucker.

I struck out blindly, wrestling to get my legs situated where I could push Loren off me.

With all the power I could muster, I shoved my foot into his chest and sent him flying. The back of his head hit the wall with a loud crack, his body sliding down the wall.

I was on my feet before he fully hit the floor.

"You son of a bitch." Grabbing him by the throat, I unleashed my fury on the features that mirrored mine. One blow glanced off his cheek. The next connected with a solid thwack. His nose burst in a spray of blood as the cartilage caved under my knuckles.

I couldn't stop.

I allowed the red haze of rage to take over. Blow after blow, one for every building that he'd destroyed, for the lives he'd taken. For the lives he continued to threaten.

I paused to catch my breath, pushing off him, allowing my tunnel vision to recede. Loren rolled over on all fours, head hung low, his body bowing as he coughed and spat.

A curtain of smoke had formed while I'd been beating the hell out of my brother. The sprinkler system and small extinguisher were little defense against the fire at this point.

I prayed that the department had been notified and would arrive any minute, but I'd try in the meantime.

I lunged for the extinguisher, just as Loren swiped my leg out from under me. I hit the floor on one knee, searing white-hot pain blasting up my leg.

He came up with the extinguisher.

"Oh, no you don't." Loren loomed over me. His face bore the marks of my fists, but the crazed glint in his eye made me freeze. He swung the large canister, connecting with the knee I'd just shattered.

I fell face down to the floor, howling in pain.

He laughed, the sound skittering over my spine. "We're going to see just how good you are." The extinguisher hit the floor and rolled further away as he landed on my back.

He was stronger than I remembered. Bigger. I glanced over my shoulder to find his whole face bloody, eyes starting to swell, but no sign of defeat in sight.

"What are you talking about?" I wheezed, struggling against his hold.

A crash of the glass pitcher from the tea stand doused me in water. I rolled under him to deflect another hit. He landed a couple of solid blows to my kidneys, shifting the pain from my leg to my back.

"I'm talking about you always being the perfect brother. The perfect student, the perfect athlete. The perfect grandson. Then the perfect firefighter. You just had to take that away from me too, didn't you?" He pushed off me and stumbled back, wiping his face against his shirt sleeve, leaving a trail of blood behind.

"Loren, that's a damn lie and you know it. I tried to help you." All the times I'd tried to do right by him, and he was blaming me?

"Fighting fires was my dream!" he yelled, unhinged.

Around us, the smoke curtain crept lower. As much as it killed me to admit, I'd lost my shot to do any good. It was time to bail and wait for the big hoses to come in. There was no way I could walk. I'd have to crawl out.

I rolled to my belly, pulling myself by my arms in what I hoped was the direction of the back door.

"Where the fuck you think you are going?" Loren rasped, grabbing my ankle, and dragging me farther into the hall, closer to the blaze.

I clawed at the wood floor, scrambling for purchase. Finding none, I rolled, kicking at his hand, taking perverse pleasure in the grunts I caused.

"Did you think you'd get out of this?" He growled.

I no longer recognized the voice that used to be so similar to mine. His was cold, harsh, angry. Hell, I no longer recognized the man.

My life was in his hands, and instead of saving me, my brother was going to watch me die. Maybe die alongside me. I kicked at him with my good leg. He caught it, wrapping something tight around the ankle.

"Are you trying to kill us both?" I yelled over the roar of the flames.

He kicked me in the ribs so hard a telltale crack ricocheted through my body. I wailed in pain. He finished binding my ankles and moved to my arms, giving me another solid kick as he passed my ribs.

I struggled to breathe as he bound my wrists together. "Look, brother, I finally figured out how to tie all those fancy knots that you said I'd never learn."

Satisfied with his work, he picked up the knotted rope around my ankles and started down the hall. "All those times you told me I was afraid of the fire," he continued conversationally, like we both weren't about to die. "Well, I'm not afraid of her now. Come closer so we can watch how she dances."

He drug me farther into the building, closer to the fire, dropping to his knees in a fit of coughing as the smoke grew thicker. It was pitch black now, and I knew that if I didn't get away from him soon, the smoke would overtake both of us.

"See how beautiful she is?" His voice changed, awe and fascination lacing his tone. "Her flames just roll. Look at all those colors." His unhinged monologue was interrupted by another fit of coughs.

"Loren, you can't see the flames." I wheezed, still struggling to get away from him. "It's in your head. You can't even see your hand in front of your face, you fucking idiot."

"This building was the perfect age," he continued, voice sounding ragged and nothing like the man I once knew. "The wood burns fast and hot. Hear those pops? Pop. Pop." I could've sworn he was smiling.

He sank to the floor beside me, turning my face toward the glow. "Lisss-teeennn to the dragon breathing," he said, drawing out the word. "You remember when we were little kids and Grandpa took us camping? We made that campfire and learned how to make s'mores."

The unhinged tone in his voice scared the shit out of me. It was almost as if he'd rather sit here, watching the fire, than try to get out.

Somehow over the years, his fear of fire had morphed into this horrible fascination. If I couldn't get out of here, get away from Loren, he was going to kill us both.

My mind jumped to Kylie.

My God. What if I never saw her again? Never held

her. Never kissed her. Never made love to her. Never got to tell her how much she meant to me. How much I loved her.

"Loren, please." My voice broke. "Don't do this."

"Grandpa taught us to fish and whittle on that trip," he continued like I hadn't spoken. "I wanted to keep fishing, but you got that stomach bug, and kept puking over the side of the boat. We had to sit on the porch and just make those stupid wooden figures." He broke off in a fit of coughs.

The smoke curtain lowered. I tugged the neck of my shirt over my nose, coughing through the shards of glass in my throat. I really needed a wet towel for filter breathing, but the wet shirt would have to do.

"Loren, we have to get out of here," I wheezed.

"No. This time, you aren't getting your way. This time, we're doing what I want to do."

He'd lost his damn mind.

Kylie's face as we'd made love flashed in my head. I squeezed my eyes shut against hot tears. All the hurt I'd caused her. All the useless bullshit we'd put each other through. I wasn't going to cause her any more pain.

It was a straight shot out the back door. I just had to get there.

I rolled my head to look at Loren. His hold on me had grown lax, and he lay with his eyes closed. I inched away from him slowly, not knowing if he had smoke inhalation and had passed out, or if he was dead. The little kid in me that recognized him as my brother howled in pain. I curled into a ball and untied my ankles. I used my teeth on the poor knot he'd made at my wrists and flung the rope away.

"Dammit, let's go," I cried, knowing that if he didn't move, there was no way I could save both of us.

But I had to try.

I gripped him under the arm, trying to pull him with

me. He didn't budge. Dragging him was not an option. The building groaned under me, as the fire grew hotter. If I didn't go now, while I still could, we'd both die.

Leaving a part of me behind, I army crawled blindly to where I thought the back door might be, praying I'd left the door open and would be able to get through.

I inched forward, feeling my way. Until I hit a wall.

Fuck, where was I?

They'd had no furniture in the hallway. Was I in a corner? Was I even in the hall still? I had no idea if I'd made a wrong turn. I touched along the wall, never finding the door I expected.

I roared in frustration, the sound searing through my charred vocal cords. But I had to hang on, the crew would be here any minute.

I imagined the layout of the room.

If I'd crawled into the studio room from the hall, there should be a long window directly ahead of the door. Running a hand up the wall, I felt nothing.

But what if my trajectory had been off?

I shifted to explore to the left and hit another wall. I was in a corner. But which corner?

I tried to imagine Kylie sitting in this room, stretching her beautiful body. She'd be heartbroken at the loss of her studio. I'd help her rebuild, if it meant I had to drive every nail myself. But to do that, I had to live.

"Fuck!" I screamed into the void of pitch-black smoke, pouring every ounce of rage and fear coursing through my body into that one word.

Muffled shouts came from behind me. It sounded like men yelling through masks. It sounded like rescue.

Thank God, they'd gotten here.

"Here!" I tried to yell, but it came out weak. Fuck, this was no good. They'd never hear me.

I banged my fist against the wall, hoping they'd recognize the pattern.

I continued banging a pattern, even as I shifted over, feeling for the window. I was getting the fuck out of this fire.

Capt had been riding my ass to not take on everyone else's responsibility. And this time, I hadn't. I'd known my crew was on their way. But I'd truly fucked up by trying to handle this fire on my own, and not waiting for the rest of my shift to back me up. I hadn't wanted to let Kylie down, but if I died in this fire...

I pushed the thought aside and replaced it with visions of her laughing, and loving, and just being her beautiful self. I had to live for us, for her.

I yelled again and pounded harder.

* * *

Kylie

I was going to kick Thoren's stubborn ass. Then, I was going to kiss him until he begged me to stop. Then I was going to kick his ass again.

I didn't know what I expected to see when I arrived at the studio, but it definitely wasn't an empty drive. No engine in site, and smoke rolling out of the front of the studio.

I called 9-1-1, and they confirmed that the fire department was on the way. All I could do was stand outside and watch my dreams burn.

The back door was closed. Thoren's truck was parked in the back lot, the driver's door hanging open, like he'd come racing in and jumped out of the truck.

That dumbass probably charged full bore into that burning building without waiting on backup.

With a shift and groan, the fire grew larger, and my ire shifted to bone-deep fear.

Maybe he wasn't in there.

I pushed that ridiculous notion aside. Of course he was. But what if his crazy-ass brother had lured him, and hurt him, and now he was trapped inside?

The fire seemed to be in the front, so I ran for the back door. No, that was a stupid idea. What was I going to do? Charge in there like a damn fool?

I sprinted around the side of the building to check the windows. See if I could see anything.

The roar of the siren blasted through the night.

I raced to meet the truck, yelling, as the crew jumped down. "I think Thoren is in there!"

Big Mo spun on his heel. "What'd you just say?"

"Thoren got here first. I think he's still in there." I repeated frantically.

Big Mo yelled at the rest of the crew, and they sprang into action. I backed up, staying out of their way, hating the helpless feeling coursing through me.

Fuck that.

I was Kylie Fucking Monroe. I didn't take shit lying down. Ignoring the shouts coming from behind me, I sprinted up the sidewalk.

The crew busted into the back door as I passed the corner of the house.

The nearest window faced the street, the closest room to the back door, and my favorite room to teach from. The room that Thoren and I had made love in.

The cold night air was freezing my head, making me wish I'd grabbed a beanie. This was a fool's errand, and here

I was, tromping around in the cold, freezing my ass off, because Thoren's dumbass brother set my damn yoga studio on fire. They probably weren't even in there.

"Thoren Watkins, I am going to kick your brother's ass, and then I'm going to kick yours for going after him."

Glass shattered at the front of the house and I flinched, ducking, diving closer to the bushes that lined the side of the house.

A rhythmic thumping sound came from the closest window.

"Thoren!"

I ran to the window, trying to shove it open from the outside. The fire licked out the front of the building. I pushed harder. The banging continued but grew weaker.

"Thoren! Hold on!"

I sprinted back to the truck, yelling at Captain Collins, who stood near the back of the engine.

"He's here! I found him, but I can't get the window open!"

Mac sprang into action, grabbing a tool from the truck while he yelled into the radio, telling the guys to retreat.

I sprinted back to the window, Mac hot on my heels.

"Thoren! We're here!" I screamed, praying I'd hear a responding thump against the wall.

No sound answered.

The crew rushed around the corner of the building, dragging hoses, while Mac went to work at the window. Big Mo, standing almost a foot taller than the others, grabbed a long tool and shattered the glass in two swings. Then Mac and Big Mo lifted Nate through the window.

With my heart in my throat and my arms laced tightly around my waist, I stood just outside their huddle, waiting to see if my man was still alive.

If he lived through this, I was never letting him leave my side.

I'd spend every minute of every day letting him know how much I needed him, how much I loved him. He was the very best part of me, even when he was being the most infuriating man in the world.

The scene before me blurred, and I began to pray.

Finally, Nate appeared again, hoisting a limp body through the window. The ground crew caught the lifeless form. Huddled together as they were, they blocked my view. Finally, Big Mo hoisted the person over his shoulder and hustled to the ambulance I hadn't even noticed.

As he passed into the light, I recognized Thoren's favorite hoodie and sank to my knees.

Mac turned and saw me. "Fuck."

Reaching out, he offered a hand. When I ignored it, he lowered to squat next to me.

"Come on, don't go soft on him now." His deep rumbling words spoke to that place in me, wrapping around the panic that threatened and tamping it down, while also shoring me up. Like his words alone gave me strength.

I wouldn't quit now.

I had to be strong and see this through. Had to be there when he woke up. Had to help him find a way to process this horrible night and the knowledge of what his brother had done.

Gripping my elbow, he half-drug me to the passenger seat of a waiting police car and barked orders to the officer. "Take her wherever that ambulance goes."

To me he added gently, "He's tough. You know that. We'll meet you there." With a shoulder squeeze, he left me.

The officer was silent on the drive, the mood in the car somber. And through it all my mind blasted through all sorts of scenarios. Was he injured? Of course he was. How bad was it? Was it a simple injury? Or something life threatening?

I choked on the thought.

How could I live in a world without Thoren?

Through an excruciating hour in the emergency room waiting area, I sat numbly, waiting on word, while my friends piled in around me.

Eventually, the rest of the fire crew came in, led by Nate. "What's the word?"

"They're doing some scans now," Jordan answered, reaching up to give him a kiss on the cheek.

Big Mo sidled up and plopped down in the chair next to me. "You did good."

Where everyone else had been offering me sympathetic looks that grated on my every nerve, Mo didn't offer that same sentiment. He just settled in like he had nowhere else to be, prepared to wait however long. The silent show of support broke through the numbness and adrenaline drop and touched my heart.

"You don't go around that house, we would've never found him in time. Fire was too hot." He shifted his beefy arms over his chest, shoulder bumping me. "He's gonna be fine. He's too fucking stubborn to be hurt real bad."

"Thanks, Mo," I said quietly, wanting desperately to believe him.

"Anytime. I like you." He flashed me a bright grin.

"You do?"

"Yeah, takes a real bad-ass chick to rock the bald look. Not only are you fearless, but you've got it going on with that killer look."

I ran a hand over my head and offered him a weak smile.

The corner of his mouth tipped up. "Come on, you can do better than that. Show me that smile Thoren always goes on about."

My smile faltered. "Does he?"

Mo nodded, shifting in his seat to wrap an arm along the chair behind me, the change in positions oddly comforting. "That man loves you. Good thing you love him too, what with you saving his ass like you did."

I shook my head. "I didn't do anything."

"You gave him something to live for. Your name was the only thing he muttered while I toted him back to the bus."

"Really?"

His arm dropped to my shoulder, tugging me in for a hug. "Yes, ma'am. I can't wait to give him shit about it." The grin popped back out.

"Kylie," Mac's deep voice resonated across the emergency department waiting room. The little greeting lady behind the desk glowered at him, which he ignored.

I stood, flashing a weak grin to Mo. "Thanks for the pep talk, Mo."

"Go get your man, girlfriend."

I followed Mac through the emergency department, reminded of another time we'd been in a similar situation when Nate had gotten injured on a call.

"I'm fucking tired of leading girlfriends through the ED," Mac grumbled.

I didn't know how to respond, if that comment even required a response. Instead, I took the opportunity to study him. He was a total silver fox, with his perfect ass filling out his uniform pants. The thought was ridiculous given the circumstances, but ogling his ass was better than thinking about what I was about to face.

He paused by a door, allowing me to enter first.

I met his gaze as I passed, muttering, "Thank you." On impulse I went up on tiptoe to kiss his cheek.

"How come he gets a kiss, and I don't?" The hoarse words came from inside.

I turned to find Thoren propped up in bed, and a barrage of images from the past few hours hit me. From the moment I'd realized where he was going, to finding my studio on fire—I was still avoiding thinking about that part of the night—all of it came back in a split-second replay of the scariest night of my life.

"Because he didn't get himself trapped in a fire tonight like you did." I narrowed my eyes at Thoren as I approached the bed, a torrent of emotion running through me. Gratitude that he was alive, residual fear that I could've lost him. Anger that he'd put himself in danger. All of it rolled around inside me. I didn't know if I needed a good cry, or to punch something.

Thoren watched me, one eye swollen nearly shut. The edges of his face covered in blood and soot, like they'd wiped away the worst of it. Wires led to all kinds of beeping machines, and he had an oxygen mask covering most of his face. He was a mess. Yet under all the contraptions he was still the most handsome man I'd ever seen.

And I wanted to throttle him.

Leaning over his bed, I pulled the mask away and pressed my lips to his, then met his eyes. "Thank you for trying to save my studio." My heart pounded at just the mention of the terror of the past few hours, and my crazy fool of a man had gone in there solo. "You ever pull a stunt like that again, I'll kick your ass."

"Wait, you're mad at me?" he wheezed.

I studied his searching gaze, his dirty face etched in

pain. Looking at me like I was the very air he needed to breathe.

I almost believed that the tightness in my chest was something other than indigestion. That the swell of tenderness and longing I saw in his eyes was a mirror to my own feelings.

I pushed that emotion down, choosing to embrace the other things I was feeling.

"Yeah. I'm a little pissed off right now." I leaned closer, letting the anger swell. "What in the hell were you thinking, running into a building like that? Without gear? Without backup?"

"Kylie, I—"

"No, you're gonna listen right now. Yes, the studio meant the world to me. But it's not worth losing you over. But did you stop to think about that? No. You just charged full-bore ahead." I dropped a hand to rest on the blanket covering him. "I'd rather have you than some stupid building. That can be replaced. You can't. "

"Baby, I'm sorry."

"I know." A tear trickled down my cheek. I swiped at it angrily. "But you've got to start trusting people."

"I did. I trusted that the guys would be there. And they were." He looked at me with pleading eyes.

"But not before you landed in the hospital. If I hadn't heard you..." My throat closed as the panic rose anew.

"Okay, guys. That's enough." I jumped at the sound of Mac's voice. I'd forgotten he was there.

"Kylie, Thoren needs to stop talking. Now isn't the time for a heartfelt conversation."

He was right, and I was an asshole. A confused, grateful, scared half-to-death asshole.

I swiped a hand across my cheek, and sucked in a huge

breath, shooting a half-hearted smile at Mac. "You're right." I turned back to Thoren and reached out to squeeze his hand. "Just rest now. We'll argue about it later."

I gave his hand a last squeeze and leaned to press a kiss to his forehead.

Turning away, I paused by Mac and muttered a soft, "thank you" to him, both for being there, and for stopping me from making a huge mistake.

Chapter Twenty-Three

K*ylie*
I stumbled down the hall, back out to the waiting room, and found Thoren's entire crew waiting. I'd been a part of the vigil team for Jordan when Nate had gotten hurt. I knew these guys were tight and nothing would keep them away. I'd been one of those comforting her, helping her be strong when her man was injured.

I blew past all of them, through the exit, and out into the cold night air.

"Hey, girl." A deep velvety voice drew my attention.

I looked over to find Big Mo leaning against the brick wall outside of the emergency department, one foot kicked up against the wall.

"What are you doing out here? How's your man?"

I shook my head and glanced around the courtyard, trying to ground myself and contain the overwhelming mix of feels. This was the most scared I'd ever been in my life. And I didn't know what to do. "I don't know what I'm doing, Mo. I just had to get out of there."

He nodded sagely, like he'd expected my answer.

"You're running scared, aren't you?"

Was I?

Mo dropped his foot and stood tall. He was a giant of a man, but his warm eyes and quick smile softened him.

I sidled closer to him, wrapping my arms around my middle. "I don't know. I guess I am. It's been a crazy night. Instead of telling Thoren how I felt, I yelled at him like a ninny."

"You need a hug?" he asked, opening his arms wide, flashing me a grin.

I was moving toward him before I knew it. "Actually…"

I hit his big chest, his beefy arms enclosing me lightly. And the tears came. From the depths of my soul, I cried.

"Ah, poor thing. It's going to be okay."

He held me for a long moment while I emptied my tears on his chest. When I finally could speak, I asked his shirt, "Big, you're married right?"

"I sure am, little. Fifteen years next month."

"And does your wife lose her shit on you occasionally?"

His chest rumbled under my cheek. "At least once a week."

I pulled away from him, wiping my eyes with the back of my hand. My face would be raw after this night. "And it all works out? You don't get tired of it?"

"The key to it is having that mutual respect. Eventually I figured out that sometimes, it wasn't about me, it was more about her. And my job is to stick around and man up when she has hard times. To be her support. Mostly, we trust each other, respect each other. Trust in the love we have for each other. And talk out the real issues. Sometimes, it takes a little time to process everything. So don't give up."

Solid advice coming from a man who'd been married a

long time. Maybe I needed to take a breath. Maybe this anger I felt over Thoren risking everything would make sense in the morning.

"You're a real catch, Big."

"I know, Little. It took a lot of patience on her part, but the missus finally taught me that it was worth the work. Everything I am, I owe to her. But that still doesn't explain why you are out here."

Why was I outside with Mo instead of being inside where I could at least know that Thoren wasn't taking a turn for the worse?

"Because I'm a fool."

He planted his big hand on my head, passing me the keys to my Jeep. "Capt insisted we bring your ride for you. Whatever happened with Thoren, you can make it right. Go do what you've gotta do to get your head right. I'll look out for him until you get back."

He gave me another pat and went back inside.

I walked to my Jeep, breathing in the night air. Under the glow of the parking lot lights, all that had happened hit me with a force. I slumped into my Jeep, resting my forehead on the steering wheel.

My studio was gone. But now that all the emotion had bled away, the studio being gone didn't matter.

Thoren could've died.

I could have lost him forever.

And I'd wasted my time with him, being angry about it.

I'd have to make it up to him and hope he could forgive me.

* * *

Thoren

I stared at the door after it closed behind Kylie. The constant beeping of the machines was a low background to the raging war in my head.

"She'll be fine," Mac stated from his seat beside the supply counter.

I scrubbed a hand down my face, the pull of the IV tube giving me a bite. "I don't know, Captain. She was pretty pissed."

He nodded. "That's just because she was scared." He crossed an ankle over his knee. "Give her some time. She's a strong woman. You've got to be man enough to take what she has to offer."

He was right. I knew Kylie enough to know she was lashing out. But I still couldn't help questioning the events of the night.

"Do you think I was stupid?" I asked after a minute.

"Better question is, do you think you were stupid?"

"In hindsight, yes. But running into a burning building is what we do on a regular basis. I knew the guys would be there. If my fucking brother hadn't attacked me, things would've been different."

Mac's brows furrowed. "He was there?"

My eyes popped up. "Yeah, he's the reason I'm so busted up. I didn't get this banged up from the structure fire. We beat the shit out of each other before the smoke got to us."

I didn't want to ask the question that hovered in the back of my mind.

Did they find Loren in time?

Mac must've read my mind because he pushed to stand and walked out the door, pulling his phone out of his pocket.

My guys entered one by one, looking tired after a long

night of work, their eyes holding concern for me. And maybe some sympathy.

By the time Mac came back, I expected him to tell me they'd found Loren's body. On the one hand, I was angry and wanted the son of a bitch to die in that fire. On the other, he was my brother, and I didn't want to lose him.

But truth be told, I'd lost him long ago.

My real brothers were the ones who had saved my life. The ones crowded into the tiny hospital room, offering me their support.

A knot formed in my throat, making it hard to squeeze out the words I didn't want to ask. "What'd you find out?"

"The other crew'd already found him."

"Alive?"

"Yeah. He was flown to another hospital for smoke inhalation." Mac grasped my shoulder. Grief for the young boy I'd grown up with flashed hard and heavy. Mac stayed with me while I cried for the brother I once knew.

"What's going to happen now?" I managed when I was finally able to speak.

"He's under guard. When he leaves the hospital, he'll go straight to jail."

"This might make me a terrible person, but I'm not grieving the man he was if he doesn't make it. I'm ashamed that it was my own blood that caused all that damage. That killed those babies in that fire." I swallowed thickly. "I hope he gets what he deserves."

Mac made a sound of agreement.

"I hope it's over now," I whispered.

Chapter Twenty-Four

K*ylie*

I let myself into Thoren's house with his hide-a-key, feeling like a trespasser. Technically I was, since he didn't know I was at his house. But whatever. My apartment wasn't an option. And I needed to feel close to him.

I dropped my bags on the counter and took stock of his space.

When I'd left the hospital, I'd decided that a surprise attack was my best bet on making things right between us. He'd no doubt run the other way when he saw me, so I needed to make sure I could explain myself before he told me to hit the road.

The only thing was, I still couldn't find the right words. I could think them. And feel them. But I didn't know if I could say them.

Outside, the crunch of gravel alerted me that it was time. I stepped to the door to see Nate's truck, with Thoren tucked into the passenger seat and looking down, gathering his things. He hadn't noticed me, or my car in the drive.

My heart pounded in my chest as I stood there, waiting to see his reaction. This felt big. This...acknowledgement that I was here after all that had happened.

I wiped my palms on my jeans as I stepped off the porch.

Nate rounded the front of the truck, offering me a reassuring smile. "It's good you're here. He's gonna be so glad to see you," he murmured as he passed me.

I stepped out of his way as he swung the door open.

"Fuck, this sucks," Thoren grumbled as he slid out of the truck. Nate caught him, tucking his shoulder under Thoren's arm.

It wasn't until they took a step forward that Thoren looked up. A range of emotions passed over his face. A frown as his gaze passed over my wig. Bewilderment and confusion followed. Ending with what resembled hope.

"Hi," I said quietly.

"Kylie." My name falling from his lips like a soft caress. Like something he cherished.

I offered him a tentative smile. "I hope it's okay that I let myself in. I wanted to make sure you had everything you needed before you got home."

He just stared at me with a stunned expression on his face. My smile faltered.

What if my outburst at the hospital had made him second-guess his feelings? What if I was too late? What if he was done with my drama?

Finally, he shook his head, as if clearing his thoughts. "Yeah, it's fine."

Not exactly the promising response I'd hoped for, but at least he hadn't told me to fuck right off.

"Okay, then. That's good." I nodded awkwardly. "Let's get you inside."

Nate helped him climb the stairs, moving slowly up the porch.

He must've been hurt more than I'd realized if his slow movements and tight breathing were any indication. Nate got him settled on the couch and went back out to the truck, leaving Thoren and me in awkward silence.

"So, can I get you anything? Water? Pain meds? Are you hungry?" I needed to be active, to do something. This palpable tension between us scared the shit out of me.

"Yeah."

"Okay, what'll it be?" I offered an awkward smile.

"Come over here."

Wait. What?

He patted the seat next to him. I inched forward and sat gingerly on the edge of the cushion next to him with my hands clasped at my knees.

He reached over, his big hand covering mine. "Look at me, Kylie."

My gaze met his. I searched his eyes for a long moment, trying to get a read him.

"Okay, guys," Nate said from the doorway. "I'm going to head out. I'll let you two get on with your eyeball study."

"Why are you here?" Thoren asked, as the door clicked shut behind Nate. Finally, we were alone. And my man needed answers.

"Because I couldn't not be here," I admitted, breaking eye contact like a coward, because I couldn't face the hurt I'd obviously caused him.

But being a coward wasn't who I was.

I'd learned to lean on my courage, to face crowds when I was a young girl on stage being judged for my looks. To face my parents when I decided that wasn't going to be my life.

To take all my money and open my own business in a new town.

To face the mirror every day, learning to accept the new me.

I would not wimp out now.

Swiping the wig off my head, I paused for a moment to say goodbye to it and what it represented. To embrace my courage, and let go of the fear. Then I tossed it aside.

I met Thoren's gaze again and swallowed thickly.

"I'm sorry I was an asshole to you at the hospital." Tears pooled in my eyes, but I was done crying. Frustrated, I swiped them away. "I was really scared, and I lashed out in anger. I shouldn't have. I should've said thank you for trying to save my studio. But all I could think of was that you'd gotten hurt, for me. And it scares the crap out of me because this means that I care about you. A lot."

Thoren reached up to cup my face, his eyes tracing the pad of his thumb as he caressed my cheekbone. "I care about you, too."

"You don't think I'm some kind of crazy?"

The corner of his lip tilted up. "Oh, I think you're crazy alright. But that's one of the things I love about you."

My eyes flew to his. Was he telling me...

My eyes narrowed. "Don't you dare steal my thunder right now," I warned. "I'm trying to suck up and tell you that I love you." I poked him in the shoulder. "Don't you beat me to the punch."

A grin stole over his face. "By all means, continue to suck up then."

"Thank you." I cleared my throat and took both of his hands in mine. Fuck, this was harder than I expected.

"Thoren," I started.

"Yes, Kylie?" I heard the grin in his voice even if I couldn't look him in the eye.

"I..."

Dammit, why was this so hard?

Fuck it. I was going for it. I clasped his cheeks. "I know, to the depths of my soul, that no matter how rocky things are, my life is better with you in it. You bring me joy, and frustration, and most of all...love. That's what this intense indigestion is. That's what had me so angry at you for putting yourself in danger. I can't imagine my world without you in it. I need you. I want you." I gazed into his beautiful eyes. "I love you. I'm still a little mad because you got hurt. But only because I love you."

"Yes, I can see that you're still mad."

What?

I pushed off from the couch and spun with my hands on my hips, ready to lay into him. "You—"

He stopped me before I could begin, gripping my hips and pulling me onto his lap.

"Oh good," came his throaty reply. "I was wondering how I was going to get you closer. And look, you fell right into my lap. Does this mean I can kiss you now?"

His hands cupped my face, pulling me closer, and his lips closed on mine, and our tongues clashed in a kiss that rocked my soul.

"I've been wanting to do that forever," he panted before diving back in and sweeping all thoughts from my head again.

He broke the kiss, resting his forehead on mine, brushing his nose softly against mine in the sweetest of ways. "You saved me in that fire."

I pulled away slightly, searching his eyes for the truth.

He nodded once. "I knew I had to live, that I wanted to live for you."

He kissed me again, peppering my face like he couldn't get enough. "I'm sorry about your studio, sweetheart."

I placed a finger to his lips. "It doesn't matter."

He shook his head. "It does. We can rebuild. I'll drive every nail myself if I have to. The point is, I want you to have everything your heart desires, because I love you, too, Kylie." Looking deep into my eyes like he could see my soul he whispered, "All the parts of you. Your funny parts, your brilliant parts, even your crazy parts."

"You do?" I asked because I couldn't believe the words.

"I do. And I'll spend every minute of every day showing you how much I mean it."

Epilogue

*T**horen***

The fire crackled in the pit as Nate tossed another log on top. Mike had Leah on his lap, again, cuddled up, staring at her as if she were the most beautiful woman he'd ever laid eyes on, kissing her cheek every so often.

"Aren't they the sweetest thing?" Jordan said to Kylie as they organized platters of snacks on the outdoor kitchen counter. Gracie, their rescue pup, now fully in her goofy adolescent stage, darted between them. She spotted a squirrel and took off like a shot through the yard.

I looked around the patio, proud of what Kylie and I had built together. Between her ideas and design sense, and my building skills, we'd made a comfortable outdoor living area, big enough to house all our friends.

"This looks amazing, Thoren." Jordan scanned the space before looking back at me with a conspiratorial grin. "It's even better than Nate's back porch." She leaned in. "But don't tell him I said that."

My brows rose high on my face as I looked over her shoulder.

Her eyes closed and she deflated. "He's right behind me, isn't he?"

Nate wrapped his arms around her waist, causing her to squeal as he lifted her in his bear hug. "Challenge accepted."

A peacefulness washed over me, settling in my bones. Most of my friends were here. Mike and Leah, Nate and Jordan. Mac was on his way. Big Mo and his wife had come by. Mike and Leah had even brought her neighbor, Mrs. O'Malley. It felt good having my friends here, surrounding me, especially on this day.

"Oh my God, is that…" Kylie squealed over her phone where the ladies were all huddled. From their stance, I could tell they were up to no good.

"Oh, he's a handsome thing," Mrs. O'Malley tittered.

"People aren't things, Francis," Leah admonished.

"I have no qualms treating him like a sex object. Matter of fact, I think I'd enjoy treating him like a sex object," Mrs. O'Malley declared with a wink to Kylie.

"Uh, Mrs. O. You can't treat this guy like a sex object." Jordan smirked.

"Well, why not, dear? He'd make a fine one."

Mac strolled around the corner and deposited a twelve pack of beer by the cooler.

Kylie spotted him, her eyes flying open wide and the cutest tinge of red tinting her cheeks. "Because we know him. He's a friend."

Mrs. O'Malley eyed Mac like she was inspecting fresh produce, trying to pick the best from the bin. "I think I could manage."

Kylie cracked up laughing as Leah admonished, "Behave, Francis."

"Oh, poo, you're no fun." A balled-up napkin flew through the air.

Leah swatted it away just before it hit her, shaking her head as if she didn't know what to do with the older woman. Mac strolled through the huddled ladies, and I caught Mrs. O'Malley eyeing his ass. Dear God, the woman was incorrigible.

"Hey, Captain," I called, waving him over to the group of guys gathered around my new outdoor bar.

"Is this the finished product?" He eyed my latest accomplishment, running a hand over the smooth top.

"It is." I was proud of the wood cabinet. I'd cut the slab of live edge myself, then sanded and varnished it until it gleamed in the late afternoon sun.

"It's nice. I've been looking at something like this for the lake house."

I nodded. "We can make it happen."

The girls broke into another giggle and then Kylie declared, "Okay, that's enough."

Mrs. O'Malley must've gone too far because every one of the women walked toward us sporting red faces, leaving the older woman tittering. "I'm not lying."

She waved her phone and called, "Yoo hoo, young man. Is this you on this TikTok?"

Every one of the men turned toward her.

Hell, did they all make TikToks now?

Big Mo and his wife were closest to Mrs. O. One look at the screen and his eyes flew wide, his mouth dropping open. "Uh, Captain, I think you need to see this."

Mac leaned over to look at the screen, and Mrs. O'Malley took the opportunity to lay her hand on his arm. I couldn't be sure, but from where I stood, it looked like she gave his bicep a squeeze.

All the color leached from the man's face.

"Way to go, Mrs. O. You've scared him to death," Kylie admonished.

Mac staggered to a nearby chair, clutching the phone in his hand. "Where is this? How'd you find it?"

Kylie sat gingerly in the chair next to his. "We were watching funny TikToks, and it flashed on the screen." She sounded funny. Almost...apologetic.

What in the hell was going on? I stalked over to defend Capt. After all the man had done for me, the look on his face gutted me, and I'd have no part in it.

"Is that..." Kylie started.

Mac just stared at the phone, looking like he'd seen a ghost.

"Kylie, what the hell?"

She took the phone gently from his hand with a "may I?" and turned it toward me. On the screen was a pretty young girl, maybe early teens, standing in front of a screenshot of a photo. Kylie clicked the video, and a young voice blasted out of the speaker.

"Please help me find this man. I don't know his name, but I think it starts with an M. Come on TikTok, help me find my father."

She dropped out of the frame and the couple in the photo came into focus. There, on a tropical-looking beach, young and in love, was a much younger version of the man, but there was no denying it was one Captain Mac Collins.

Holy. Shit.

I handed the phone back to Kylie, closing my mouth.

What the fuck did I say? He looked like he was going to vomit.

"Uh, congratulations?"

Kylie looked at me like I was a dumbass. I responded by raising my shoulders. I was truly at a loss.

She slid forward in her seat, her knees almost touching Mac's. "Do you recognize the woman in the photo? Maybe this is just someone who looks like you."

He stared off, obviously lost in thought. "Yeah, I recognize her."

"Who is she?"

"We met on vacation and spent a week together. I haven't seen or heard from her since."

"Do you want to contact her? I could respond to this video. Find out where she is, and what this means," Kylie offered gently.

Mac scrubbed a hand down his face, then pushed out of his seat. He took two steps, then turned to face Kylie. "Thank you, but no. Let it be."

He looked at me with haunted eyes. "I'm gonna go take a walk."

"Sure, Mac. We'll be here if you need us."

Kylie's arms came around my waist, so I wrapped mine around her, soaking in the moment with this beautiful woman and my friends surrounding me.

"I hope he's okay," she said low against my chest.

I did, too. But I knew that even if he weren't, he had a found family that would stand by him. "He's going to be okay. He's got us to see him through."

She gave me a squeeze and laid her head on my chest. She'd stuck by me, this beautiful woman of mine. Through the good and bad, we had each other. And that's what mattered the most.

"I'm so grateful for you. I hope you know that. I love you, Kylie."

She lifted her head and met my eyes with a smile. "I love you, too."

Not ready to say goodbye to Kylie and Thoren? Go to https://dl.bookfunnel.com/lgi6suy1m9 for a fun bonus!

Want to find out more about me and my books? Join my free Newsletter! https://raefields.com/news/

Author's Note

A while back, I was scrolling social media and ran across a beautiful woman with a shaved head, bringing awareness to a condition called Alopecia Areata. You can follow her on Instagram at @being_mrs_brown.

And for even more information on Kylie's condition visit https://www.naaf.org/alopecia-areata/

Also by Rae Fields

Mike and Leah
Ignition Point

Nate and Jordan
Burn Point

Mac and Liv
Anchor Point

Acknowledgments

As always, thank you to my hubs, for holding the fort while I chase a dream. I couldn't do it without your love and support.

To my family and friends, thank you for cheering me on.

To my 6 a.m. crew and HEA Club friends, your knowledge, encouragement and support are everything. I heart you.

And to Jessica, you're the real MVP- thanks for your wisdom, patience and endless support. Also, thanks for my new chai habit and addiction to Noosa yogurt.

To Marie, Mia, and Julie, thank you for your keen eyes and knowledge of commas. Some day I will figure them out. Maybe.

About the Author

Rae Fields is beginning her publishing adventure and hopes you'll come along for this journey. She feels weird talking about herself in third person and hopes you'll join her newsletter and socials where she can just talk to you, and not feel weird about it.

Find all my links and join my newsletter at

www.raefields.com

Want to stay in the know on all things Rae? Join my newsletter here!

Join Rae's Newsletter

www.ingramcontent.com/pod-product-compliance
Lightning Source LLC
Chambersburg PA
CBHW030129010826
48973CB00002B/480